The Proposal

Katie Ashley

Dedication

For my grandmother, Big Mama—a woman of tiny stature whose courage, faith, and conviction of character earned her status as big. May you always live on not just through the thousands of wonderful memories I possess, but through every woman I write who is strong and deals with the hand life dealt her with courage not complaint, who has an immense love of family and a strong faith, and who is smart, sassy, and sometimes just a little naughty.

Preface

Aidan tried to still the rapid beating of his heart as he raced up the front walkway. Stumbling on the porch steps, he lurched towards the front door. He banged both of his fists against the wood as hard as he could. "Please! Please open up! I have to talk to you!" he shouted. His hand slid down the jamb to the doorbell. His finger punched it relentlessly like a SOS call in Morse Code.

Finally, his desperate ministrations were rewarded by the front door swinging open. At the sight of her tear stained face, his soul twisted in agony. "Please...please just let me talk to you!"

She shook her head. "There's nothing left to say, Aidan. We've been down this road too many times. I've come to the conclusion that your actions will always speak louder than your words."

"No, last night is *not* what I want. It's just I was scared with the baby and everything that's happened between us in the last few weeks."

When she tried sweeping past him out the door, he pushed himself in front of her like a shield. "Aidan, *move*. I have to get to work. Nothing you have to say is going to change the way I feel right now."

"Can't you call in? I love you, and I want to make this right." He raked a shaky hand through his already disheveled hair. He was still in the wrinkled clothes he had worn the day before. He hadn't slept, hadn't eaten—he had spent the night consumed with how to get her back. "No matter what you think, I do love you...and I do want the baby."

She raised her head to glare at him. Aidan took a step back at the unadulterated rage that burned in her eyes. "Don't you dare say that! I know how you really feel about me being pregnant—the burden it is on your life. If anything, it's the reason you were fucking that girl! Because when you're scared, you always manage to screw up!"

Shoving him out of the way, she stomped down the porch steps. He followed close on her heels. "Okay, you're right. It was a burden—maybe it still is. But I realize now I was just being stupid. I love you, and I do want to marry you and raise our child."

She skidded to a stop. Her shoulders sagged before she slowly turned around. "Right now you think that's what you want. But I know you too well. Before we get married or before the baby is born, you'll get scared and cheat again." She shook her head sadly. "I was stupid to think me being pregnant would change you. That somehow it would make you commit. But you can't even be faithful for your baby."

Aidan reached out for her, but she spun away and ran down the sidewalk. When he finally caught up to her, she had locked herself in the car.

He banged his fist against the window. "*Please.* Please don't do this!"

She threw the car in reverse and squealed out of the driveway. The engine roared as she sped down the street. Aidan closed his eyes in defeat. He staggered back, trying desperately to stop himself from hyperventilating.

Then the sound of screeching tires and busting glass caused Aidan's heart to shudder to a stop. He sprinted to the edge of the driveway. His entire world slowed to a crawl at the sight of the mangled heap of twisted metal in the distance.

"AMY!" he screamed.

CHAPTER ONE

Aidan jolted out of his nightmare to find himself facedown on the kitchen table. Sweat trickled down his face. He raised a trembling hand to swipe it away. That was when he realized it was tears, not sweat, soaking his cheeks. He hadn't had a nightmare about Amy's accident in years. It only took a second for him to remember what had brought it on.

Emma.

Everything he thought he had felt for Amy was magnified a million times with Emma. He had only thought he knew what love was. Without even trying, she had managed to illicit feelings in him he never could have imagined. And now she was gone.

A defeated cry of agony slipped from his lips.

"I see we're back to the nightmares, huh?"

Aidan jumped before jerking his gaze over his shoulder. "Hello to you too, Pop. How'd you get in?"

Patrick gave him a tight smile. "I have a key, son."

When he whirled around in his chair, Aidan's head spun, and he had to grip the table to steady himself. "Yeah, well, whatever happened to knocking?"

"I did, but you never came to the door. Now I can see why."

Aidan stared up at the blurry double images of his father's frowning face. One look of absolute and total disgust would have been enough, but damned if in his drunken state, there had to be two.

Patrick leaned back against the counter, crossing his arms over his chest. "Son, I do believe you're shit-faced!"

After snorting contemptuously, Aidan's face smacked hard onto the table. His chest rose and fell in laughter at the fact his father had actually said the word shit-faced. Of course his level of inebriation also made it funnier.

When he finally composed himself, he exclaimed, "Actually, Pop, I was shit-faced five beers and three shots of Patron ago. I think it's safe to say I'm fucking plastered."

"So is this where we are again?" Patrick huffed.

Raising his head, Aidan furrowed his brows. "What do you mean?"

Patrick's face clouded over in anger. "You know exactly what I mean. You're starting the same damn patterns as you did nine years ago, right down to the drinking like a lush."

"I called you because I wanted your help, not a lecture. So if you came over here to yell at me then you can just fuck off!"

The next thing Aidan knew Patrick had yanked him up by his hair and was glaring down at him. "Don't you *ever* speak that way to me again! I'm still your father, and you will show me respect. You got that?"

"Just leave me alone!" Aidan blared, trying to pull himself away.

Patrick tightened his grip on Aidan's hair, causing him to wince in pain. "All right. That's it. I'm going to treat you just like I would a prick of a recruit in The Corp who had screwed up!"

Before Aidan could protest, Patrick dragged him out of the kitchen chair. It clattered noisily to the floor. "Didn't know you still had it in you, *old* man. You're pretty agile for a seventy-two year old," Aidan mused.

"You better shut up if you know what's good for you!" Patrick snarled before shoving Aidan towards the hallway. He might've passed out again if Patrick hadn't kept a firm hold on the scruff of his neck along with his belt buckle.

When they got into the master bedroom, Patrick pushed him in the bathroom. Aidan whirled around to catch Patrick locking the door. Dread washed over him. Nervously he staggered back as

[8]

Patrick stalked over to him. "Shit, Pop, you aren't gonna beat my ass again like the time in high school when you discovered that pot stash under my bed, are you?"

Ignoring him, Patrick went to the shower. After flipping on the water, he grabbed Aidan's arm and jerked him into the stall. Ice cold water rained down on him. Even through his clothes, each droplet felt like a jagged knife piercing his skin. He tried to get out, but Patrick slammed the shower door shut. "You're going to stay in there until you can sober up and discuss what happened like a man!"

Aidan thrashed against the door, but Patrick held firm. "I'm too old for this bullshit, son. I may not be around in nine years when you try to pull another stunt like this again. At least let me die in peace knowing that you've got a wife and child to love!"

Patrick's words froze Aidan more than the cold water pelting him. Just the thought of how he had hurt Emma sent pangs of regret reverberating through him. Instead of protesting any further, he turned and stood under the shower nozzle, letting the icy water sting him like the lashes of the whip. Hanging his head, he wished it was a whip. He deserved to be beaten for everything he had said and done in the last few weeks to Emma and in turn his son. Physical punishment would be a welcome relief to release the emotional torment within him.

"You manning up now?" Patrick asked.

"Yes sir," Aidan murmured under the stream of water.

"Good. I'll go put on a pot of coffee. I'll be waiting for you when you're ready to talk."

Biting his lip, Aidan couldn't stop the tears filling his eyes from spilling over his cheeks. He wanted more than anything for his father to somehow find a way to help him get Emma back. "Thanks, Pop," he said, his voice wavering with emotion.

"You're welcome."

Aidan forced himself to stay under the water until his cloudy senses became clearer. When he could walk without staggering, he got out of the shower. His teeth chattered as he tore off his soaked clothes. After toweling off at record speed, he padded into the bedroom and threw on a pair of pajama pants and a t-shirt.

When he got to the kitchen, Patrick sat at the table. A smile tugged at the corners of his lips. "Sorry I had to go all Marines on you."

Aidan shook his head. "I deserved it. Frankly, you should've kicked my ass."

"Becoming a masochist, are we?"

Shrugging, Aidan poured himself a cup of coffee. "I deserve nothing less. I hurt the ones I care about the most."

Patrick sighed. "I don't know about that. There's a lot of goodness in you, Aidan. I wish you could see that."

"Must not be much goodness in me if I keep fucking up."

"Speaking of that…" Patrick eased back in his chair, resting his arm along the top rung. "Before I offer to help, I have to know one thing."

Aidan arched his brows and took a tentative sip of coffee. The scorching liquid seared his tongue. "What is it?" he croaked.

"Do you honestly want Emma back because you love her, or is it because you feel guilty?"

"This isn't like what happened with Amy," Aidan protested.

"It's just a simple question, son. Do you want to spend the rest of your life with Emma and your son or not? I mean, most men who are truly in love don't go and try to sleep with other women."

Hot, bitter tears stung Aidan's eyes. "I do love her, Pop. That's the God's honest truth." He ground the tears out of his eyes with his fists. Sinking down in a chair across from Patrick, he related all the details of the day on the dock. "Even though I couldn't say it to her then or even tonight when she wanted me to, I do love Emma."

"So the year you tried to get Amy back that was all about—"

[11]

Aidan closed his eyes in pain. "Guilt, not love. She managed to kill the love I had for her by deceiving me. But because of the baby, I was going to stand by her."

"Does Emma know any of this?"

Snapping open his eyelids, Aidan replied, "I only told her about the cheating. I didn't think she could handle the rest."

"I think you need to tell her."

Aidan grimaced. "I will. If she ever speaks to me again."

"I have a feeling she'll come around."

"Don't tell me it's because of your damn Irish intuition," Aidan said, quirking his eyebrows.

"No, it's because Becky got a hold of her leaving here tonight."

Groaning, Aidan rubbed his hands over his face. "Great. I'm sure they'll be leading a charge over here at any moment to roast my manhood over an open flame!"

Patrick chuckled. "Don't sell your sister short. She and the rest of the girls may want to castrate you for your actions, but they do love you and want to see you happy." He leaned forward and patted Aidan's hand. "And they know how you've screwed up in the past and sabotaged your own happiness."

[12]

Aidan's nostrils flared in anger. "They don't know the whole story, Pop. They don't know what Amy did!"

"I know that. It's a secret that stayed firmly between you, Amy, and myself."

Clenching his fists, Aidan said, "Don't you know how many times I wanted to scream at Mom when she was singing Amy's praises, throwing it in my face about how she was married and happy? If she had only known it was Amy who fucked me up in the head for any other woman."

"That was your choice not to tell her, son. I didn't like keeping it from her. Your mother and I had so few secrets, but I kept yours."

Aidan softened his furious expression. "I appreciated it, Pop."

Patrick smiled. "You're welcome." He got up and poured out the remainder of his coffee in the sink. "So, you're going to talk to Emma and tell her the truth about Amy?"

"Yeah. Just as soon as she'll speak to me."

"Good. I'm glad to hear it." Patrick glanced at his watch. "Well, I guess I better be hitting the road."

[13]

Aidan's chest clenched at the prospect of being alone. "It's awfully late for you to be out driving. Maybe you should stay here for the night."

He met his father's gaze. With his eyes, Aidan tried saying what he was too embarrassed to admit: He didn't want to be alone.

Patrick gave a brief nod of his head. "I guess you're right. You don't mind putting your old man up for the night?"

Aidan gave a half smile. "I'd be happy to."

CHAPTER TWO

Three Weeks Later

"N, Thirty-One," the Bingo announcer's voice droned.

"What did he say, dear?" Mrs. Petersen asked Emma, glancing down at her card.

Knowing that Mrs. Peterson was practically stone deaf, even with her hearing aids, Emma drew in a deep breath and shouted, "N, THIRTY-ONE!"

Mrs. Petersen smiled and bobbed her gray head.

When Patrick chuckled beside her, Emma arched her eyebrows. "What?"

"Come on, Emma, you're a beautiful, vibrant young woman. What in the hell are you doing here at the VFW with me and a bunch of other old farts?"

She giggled. "Are you kidding? How could I miss Saturday Bingo? What about all the fabulous prizes I could win? That bulk sized box of Depends is calling my name." When his chest vibrated with amusement, she wagged a finger at him. "Hey, you shouldn't laugh. You've had a pregnant wife and daughters. You know lack of bladder control is serious business."

His eyes widened. "Such a little sass pot, aren't you? What a mouth you've got for such a supposedly sweet girl."

Emma's heart stilled as she heard Aidan's deep voice echo in her ears, *"That mouth of yours is trouble."* A raging ache burned through her chest, and she fought to catch her breath. Trying to push the painful memories away, she shook her head. "Well, you know the real reason I'm here is because you've been having dizzy spells and shouldn't drive."

He scowled. "Becky took *both* sets of my car keys before she and Liz blew town!"

"It's Fall Break for their kids, and they're only going to be in Disney World for four days. It's not their fault they were worried enough about you to take your keys. It's your own fault for allowing that damn Fitzgerald stubbornness to keep you from going to the doctor."

"I have an appointment next week." When Emma raised her eyebrows skeptically, Patrick swiped his finger over his heart and swore, "Scout's Honor."

"If you say so. I should insist on taking you myself to ensure you get there."

Patrick groaned. "Great. Now I have another worrywart daughter on my ass all the time."

[16]

Emma's heart warmed at the notion of being considered as his daughter. Regardless of how she felt about Aidan, she could never, ever distance herself from Patrick and his love.

After a woman with a blue bouffant clapped her hands manically and shouted, "Bingo!" Patrick leaned forward in his chair, a serious expression washing over his face. "So are we not going to talk about the white elephant in the room?"

Emma cut her eyes over to him and grinned. "You mean the fact that one of the prizes is an enema bag?"

Crossing his arms over his chest, Patrick huffed, "That is not what I'm talking about, and you know it."

She ducked her head, staring down at her Bingo card like it was the most fascinating thing she had ever seen. "I'd rather not," she whispered.

"Look, Em, I'm sure you're already experiencing the intense love a parent can have for their child. Aidan is my son, and I love him with all my heart." When she jerked her head up to glare at him, he held up both his hands in surrender. "But that doesn't mean I condone what he did to you. Trust me, I wanted to inflict bodily harm on him." An amused glint twinkled in his dark eyes. "Well, I sort of did."

Emma gasped. "What did you do?"

[17]

He chuckled. "Trust me, it was nothing that he didn't deserve, or that my seventy-two year old ass could actually dish out!"

"You're terrible!" Emma replied, but she couldn't help giggling.

Patrick took his hand in hers. "I just want you to know I'm Switzerland in all this, okay? I love you and my grandchild, just like I do Aidan."

"Thank you. I appreciate that." She squeezed his hand. "And I hope you know I would never ask you to take sides or try to keep you away from the baby because of what happened with Aidan."

"I know that, sweetheart. From the first day I met you, I knew what kind of girl you are, and there isn't a malicious bone in your body." He paused and shook his head. "But if I don't say what's in my heart, I'm going to explode."

Gnawing one of her already frayed fingernails, Emma held her breath, bracing herself for what Patrick had to say.

"I'm extremely worried about Aidan. It's been three weeks, and he's miserable, Emma. He doesn't sleep, and he barely eats."

The spiteful, vindictive side of her relished in the thoughts of Aidan's suffering. She gave Patrick a skeptical look. "I seriously doubt that. He's probably just vying for your sympathy and trying to turn you against me."

"No, I've seen it with my own eyes. He's been staying with me because he can't stand being alone."

Emma widened her eyes as her heart clenched in agony for Aidan. Although a very large part of her delighted in the thought of him hurting as badly as she was, another part of her pitied him. As much as she wanted to despise him, she couldn't. Every moment of the past three weeks, she had tried to bury her feelings and embrace the fact Aidan would never be completely emotionally available. To let him back into her life would be to walk barefoot over the shards of her broken heart. He would cut her again—it was inevitable.

But from the depth of her soul, she still loved him. There was a part of her that feared she always would—just like a part of her still loved Travis. She hated herself for feeling that way.

"Can you honestly say that nothing he has done in the past few weeks has softened your heart to him?" Patrick asked.

A tortured sigh escaped her lips. When Becky had said Aidan would try to win her back, she hadn't been kidding. Not even being forewarned could have prepared for the initial barrage of telephone calls, texts, and emails. He had even tried coming to her office, but she had asked the security guard to remove him. It had been quite a scene with Aidan scuffling with the guard to try to get

[19]

to her. He had then been warned by her manager never to come on her floor again.

Then he switched tactics. Her house soon doubled for a florist's with all the flowers he bought. Every bouquet and every dozen roses he sent had a separate card filled with his ramblings of remorse, how much he missed her, and how much he cared for her and the baby. Since there was still no profession of love, she gave him the silent treatment.

"Em?" Patrick questioned, jarring her out of her thoughts.

She twisted the hemline of her blouse in her fingers. "Don't you know how hard it's been with my feelings, coupled with my pregnancy hormones, to ignore him?"

"I would be lying if I said I wasn't impressed with his tenacity. Not even with Amy did he do something as heartfelt as that poetry book."

Emma pinched her eyes shut. That damn book! It had almost shattered her resolve. When she had opened the wrapped package and found an antique edition of love poetry by the Romantics, she had wept uncontrollably for an hour. The sight of John Keats, Percy Shelley, and Lord Byron brought thoughts not only of his nephews, but the glaring fact he remembered she loved their poetry. And while it was a book filled with sentiments of love, he still hadn't said the words himself. For Emma, that meant everything.

"I'm truly sorry he's going through so much. But I'm hurting, too," she finally said.

"I know you are, honey. But if I asked you just to talk to him for a few minutes, would you humor an old man?"

"Oh Patrick, don't you see. I'm scared."

"That he'll...cheat again?"

She bobbed her head. "With Travis, I never had to worry about him being unfaithful. He was totally devoted from the time we first started dating. I haven't dated a lot or been out in the world, so I don't know how to be with someone like Aidan and keep my sanity."

Patrick rubbed his chin. Emma could tell there was something he wasn't saying—something that held a piece of Aidan's puzzle. "I don't like to beg, but would you just consider sitting down with him and trying to hear him out? I know it would mean the world to him, and I think it would mean a lot to you, too."

A whoosh of air deflated her chest. "I guess I could try."

"That's my girl," he said, his face lighting up. "Good. Now that I've got that out of the way, I could use some dessert. Want something?"

As if on cue, Emma's stomach rumbled, and she grinned. "Even though I shouldn't, would you bring me back some more of that homemade pound cake?"

Patrick smiled. "Good choice. I was going after a piece myself."

She grabbed his sleeve. "Just make sure it isn't Mrs. Forrester's. I think she accidentally put salt instead of sugar this time."

He chuckled. "Oh lord. I do believe she has a screw or two loose."

"You shouldn't say that. You know she's sweet on you," Emma teased.

"And don't think I'm not going to keep running away from her. She'd probably kill me with food poisoning or something."

Emma laughed. "You don't have to run too fast. She's just one of your many admirers."

"Whatever," he grumbled. As he rose out of his chair, Patrick winced and rubbed his chest.

"Are you all right?" Emma asked.

"I'm fine," he murmured. But when he took another step forward around the table, he gasped and then collapsed onto the ground.

"Patrick!" Emma cried, leaping out of her chair. She raced over to him and knelt down, grabbing his hand in hers.

"My heart," he moaned.

"Someone call 911!" she screamed, trying to fight the rising panic that drummed in her chest.

"I will!" the bingo announcer replied, bringing his phone to his ear.

"Here give him this," a lady said, thrusting an aspirin in front of Emma's face. She took it from the lady and brought it to Patrick's lips.

"Swallow this."

He lifted his head and let her put the pill in his mouth.

"You don't have any other medicine with you to take? Like nitroglycerin?"

Patrick grimaced. "Left it in my other pants," he wheezed. At what must've been her horrified expression, he murmured, "Sorry."

"No, don't apologize. It's okay."

"Pray, angel." A shaky hand came up to tenderly touch her cheek.

Tears stung her eyes. "Of course, I will. I am. And you do too! Say a Hail Mary or whatever it is you Catholics do!"

Patrick chuckled and then winced. "Don't make me laugh."

"I'm sorry." She squeezed his hand tight and tried to give him a reassuring smile.

"If this doesn't go well—"

Emma's body tensed. "No! Don't you dare talk like that!"

He closed his eyes briefly before opening them. "Listen to me. If I don't make it, promise me you'll give Aidan another chance."

"Oh Patrick," she moaned.

"Promise," he urged.

The last thing in the world she wanted to do was lie to a potentially dying man. Somehow she found the courage to nod her head. "Okay, I promise."

"Good girl."

When firemen came barreling through the door, Emma said a thanks to God that the fire station sat just across the street from the VFW. Since most of them had EMT training, she knew they could help Patrick until the ambulance arrived.

"Excuse us, ma'am," a young guy said.

Emma reluctantly dropped Patrick's hand. The two firemen inched past her and squatted beside Patrick. Entwining her fingers, she brought them to her lips that were murmuring prayers. She watched as one man put an oxygen mask over Patrick's face while the other took his pulse.

Lost in her own thoughts, she didn't even hear the ambulance siren. The next thing she knew EMT's had arrived and were putting Patrick on a stretcher. "Em!" came his panicked cry through his mask.

"I'm right here," she called, pushing one of the firemen out of the way. Groping along the gurney, she snatched up his hand. "I'm here. You're going to be just fine."

The stretcher rumbled and shook along the uneven pavement as they wheeled him to the open doors of the ambulance. Emma had to fight to keep up with them, and she found herself winded as they started to load Patrick inside. His face crumpled when she was forced to let his hand go.

[25]

"I'm still here!" she cried, fighting the tears that scorched and burned her throat and eyes.

Emma felt a hand on her shoulder. A young fireman with kind eyes smiled at her. "Do you want to ride with him?"

"Please, can I?"

"Sure you can. Just come around to the front with me."

Emma stepped closer to the doors of the ambulance. "Patrick, I'm going to be right up front. I'm not leaving you. Okay?"

He bobbed his head. "I love you, and I'm right up front," she cried again, as the fireman pulled her away.

They walked around the side of the ambulance. He opened the passenger side door for her. "Up you go."

She braced herself on the doorframe and tried hoisting herself up. With her adrenaline depleted, she was too weak. Hands came around her waist and pushed her forward. She gasped as she flopped onto the seat. Once she collected herself, she turned around.

The young fireman's cheeks flushed crimson. "Sorry about that."

"No, it's okay. Thanks for the help."

He grinned before slamming the door. Emma turned in her seat to watch the EMT's working on Patrick. "See, I didn't leave you," she said.

The wail of the ambulance's siren starting up caused Emma to shudder. Like an electrical storm in the summer, long buried memories flashed in her mind. Although she gripped the sides of her seat, she was miles away from the chaos surrounding her.

With her hand wrapped firmly in her mother's, she skipped into the fire station. At the sight of her father, she squealed and ran forward. "Daddy! Daddy!"

"Hey baby," he said, hoisting her into his arms. She wrapped her legs around him as he squeezed her tight. "So you're finally getting to see my new station, huh?"

Emma nodded. She hadn't quite understood why they had left the mountains to come to the city. In fact, she had cried big tears from the back window of the car when she watched Granddaddy and Grammy waving goodbye. But Daddy had tried to explain he could make more money if he worked as a fireman in Atlanta, rather than in Ellijay. They could have nicer things. He'd even gotten her a puppy to try to make things easier.

"Let me wear your hat! Please Daddy!"

He chuckled. "Of course you can." When he sat the fireman's visor on her head, Emma's neck felt wobbly and weighted down. He walked her over to the gleaming red fire engine. "You want to hear the siren, angel?"

She squirmed in his arms. "Oh yes!"

He climbed onto the rig and sat her down on the seat. Her hands automatically went to the steering wheel, and she turned it back and forth, pretending to drive. He blared the horn. "Again, Daddy!" He grinned and honked it until the rest of the guys in the firehouse were ready to throttle him.

Like wispy shadows of fog swirling along rooftops and skylines, Emma's mind unveiled another memory just a short year later. *She was at school and sitting on the reading rug. With rapt attention, she listened to her teacher reading from a book about bears having a Halloween party where popcorn overflowed their house. The classroom door creaked opened, and Emma stared in surprise at Granddaddy standing in the doorway. She raced over to meet him, happily taking his hand. Out in the hallway, he pulled her into his arms and carried her outside. Grammy stood at the car hugging Nana, Daddy's mother. Emma peppered him with questions. "What's happened, Granddaddy? Why are you all here in Atlanta? Where's Mommy and Daddy?"*

For the first time she could ever remember, Granddaddy had tears in his dark eyes. "Emmie Lou, there was a bad fire, and your Daddy was trying to save these children. He got them out safely, but he..." *His voice choked off with emotion.* "Baby, your Daddy's gone to live with the angels."

That one statement sent her kicking and screaming out of his embrace. "No, no, no! Daddy wouldn't leave me! He's taking me to the circus this weekend." *Her fists beat into Granddaddy's belly.* "You tell the angels to bring Daddy back!" *she cried.*

The sound of the ambulance doors rattling open snapped Emma into another memory. *Once again she clutched her mother's hand as they weaved in between the tombstones in the cemetery. She had never seen so many people in all her life. People kept calling her daddy a hero. They sank down onto one of the velvet chairs under a green tent. Clinging to her mother's side, she jumped with every rifle blast of the Twenty-One gun salute. Then a man knelt before her mother with a folded flag. He glanced over to Emma and gave her a sad smile. She would never forget his soulful brown eyes.*

"Ma'am?"

Emma jolted back into the present. Glancing over her shoulder, she saw that Patrick's stretcher had already been taken from the ambulance. The EMT, who had driven them to the hospital, stood with the passenger side door opened, beckoning her with his hand. "Here let me help you."

"Thank you," she murmured. After she hopped down, he led her through the automatic doors. Pointing down the hallway, he said, "They took him to room two."

She nodded. "Thank you for everything."

Emma staggered down the white tiled floor. An antiseptic smell assaulted her senses. Men and women in blue and green scrubs hustled between rooms and patients. She gave the nurses station a fleeting glance before cutting across the hall to where Patrick was. When Emma started for the door, a nurse blocked her. "No, ma'am. You can't go in there. You'll have to go to the waiting room."

"How is he?"

"We don't know anything yet. They're running tests." The nurse gripped Emma's shoulder. "If you'll just go have a seat, someone will—"

Emma shook her head furiously from side to side. "Please, let me stay here. I won't get in the way, I promise. He didn't want me to leave him!"

The nurse took in Emma's swollen stomach, and her expression softened. She glanced over her shoulder before sighing. "Okay. Is there anyone else you should call?"

Emma had been so consumed by the ghosts of the past along with Patrick's condition, she hadn't even thought of calling Aidan or his sisters. Her hand flew to her mouth. "Oh God, I can't believe I didn't call his children!"

"It's okay, honey. I'm sure you've had a lot to process. Why don't you step right over there?" the nurse motioned to a table with a shiny black phone on top of it.

Emma nodded and walked away from Patrick's door. She eased down into the uncomfortable plastic chair. With Becky and Liz in Disney World and Julia living out of state, Aidan and Angie were the closest in distance of getting to the hospital. She tried Angie first, hoping she could get her to call Aidan. But she didn't pick up, so Emma was forced to leave her a voicemail asking her to call her as soon as she could.

With shaky fingers, she dialed Aidan's cell number. He answered on the third ring. "This is Aidan Fitzgerald."

The sound of the deep timbre of his voice vibrating her ear made her chest tighten. For a few moments, she couldn't process thoughts, and she certainly couldn't speak. "Hello?" he prompted.

"Um, it's me."

Aidan sucked in a sharp breath on the other line. "Emma…" The way he said her name caused her to shiver. It hummed with a mixture of both pleasure and pain. "God, it's so good to hear your voice." She remained motionless, unspeaking and unblinking. He was paralyzing her with just his voice. "Please say something. Please talk to me, Em," he begged.

Snap out of it a voice deep within her screamed. She shook her head. "I'm not calling because of all that. It's your dad. We're at the ER at Wellstar."

His tone changed over in an instant. "Wait, what happened to Pop?"

"I don't know yet. He had chest pains and collapsed at the VFW. They're running tests. He's conscious and breathing on his own."

"Fuck. I'm an hour away below Atlanta." He growled in frustration. "I'll be there as soon as I can."

"Okay," she replied. She hung the receiver up before he could say anything else.

She turned her attention back to Patrick's door. A slow eternity seemed to tick by as Emma waited for news. She paced back and forth outside. Every time another doctor or nurse entered,

[32]

her heart shuddered to a stop. Wringing her hands, prayers rolled through her mind continuously.

After trying unsuccessfully to get two nurses to give her an update, she leapt at the next person to come out of the door. Twisting her fingers into his white coat, she held on for dear life as the tears pooled in her eyes. "Please, please you have to tell me what's happening!" she demanded.

The doctor brought his hands to hers, and instead of shoving her away, he took them tenderly in his own. She glanced up into a pair of soulful brown eyes that radiated with empathy. "What's your name, sweetheart?" he asked.

"Emma."

A warm smile cut across his handsome face—one that in any other situation might have caused her heart to beat a little faster or even a stirring below her waist. His jet black hair fell in waves across his forehead, and his pearly white teeth contrasted against his dark skin. "Emma, I'm Dr. Nadeen. I need for you to take a deep breath and calm down, okay?"

She shook her head wildly. "But I—he—"

"Mr. Fitzgerald is going to be just fine. We have him stabilized while we're running some tests. But it doesn't appear that it is anything life threatening. He's in good hands. I promise."

The news caused her knees to buckle, and she would have dropped to the floor if Dr. Nadeen hadn't wrapped his arms around her. "Whoa, now." He glanced over his shoulder. "Come with me." With one arm firmly around her waist, he led her to the room across the hall from Patrick's.

"No, I need to stay with him," she protested as he eased her down onto the bed.

"You can see everything that goes on from here." He knelt down in front of her and brought his fingers to her wrist. "Your pulse is racing. You've got to calm down. Can I get one of the nurses to call your husband?"

Emma winced. "I don't have a husband." When he started to open his mouth, she shook her head. "Or a boyfriend."

"I know you're worried, but you have to look out for yourself and your little one." His gaze dropped to her belly. "How far along are you?"

"Twenty-three weeks," Emma replied.

"Ah, and do you know what you're having?"

"A boy." Her hand went to her abdomen. "A very active boy from the way he's kicking right now."

He chuckled. "That means he's strong."

Emma rolled her eyes. "I don't know if it's so much a strong child or a strong *willed* child. He likes to let me know when he thinks it's time for us to eat."

He opened his mouth, but he was interrupted by a nurse poking her head in. "Dr. Nadeen, we need you in Room Three."

He glanced over his shoulder and nodded. He then turned back to Emma. "I'm so sorry, but I have to go."

She smiled. "It was nice meeting you, Dr. Nadeen."

"No need to be so formal. I'm Alpesh, but you can call me Pesh." He grinned. "Now I want you to lie back and put your feet up for a bit. Just take it easy, okay?" Jerking his thumb across the hall, Pesh said, "He's going to be fine, and I'm sure he wouldn't want you worrying in your condition."

Emma couldn't help laughing. "My condition? I'm only pregnant."

He wagged a finger at her. "I mean it. I don't want to see you up again until I come back. Got it?"

"You're awfully bossy," she replied as she swung her legs up on the bed and smoothed her top down.

"They teach us that in medical school," he quipped before he headed out the door.

[35]

Emma shook her head before taking her phone out of her purse. There was little rest between fielding texts left and right. Julia, Aidan's second oldest sister, was on her way in from Alabama while Becky and Liz were packing up to cut short their Disney trip.

A nurse peeked her head in and caused Emma to jump. "I'm sorry. Dr. Nadeen said I should—"

The nurse smiled. "It's okay, honey. I was just wondering why Dr. Nadeen had put down this room was occupied, but there was no chart." With a knowing look, she replied, "But I can see why now."

"He's very kind."

"He's one of the best we have—the best doctor and the best bedside manner." She winked at Emma. "And by far the best looking."

With her cheeks warming, Emma replied, "That's nice."

"Take care then."

"Thank you."

The nurse hadn't been gone long when Pesh reappeared in the doorway. Emma quickly tried to hide her phone. Especially considering the sign that warned no cellular devices was right next to her.

She gave him a sheepish grin. "Sorry. I had to let everyone know how he was."

Pesh laughed. "It's okay, Emma. I'm not going to call security on you. I'm just glad to see you stayed put and aren't back to pacing." He strode over to the bed.

Clumsily, she pulled herself into a sitting position. Her eyes honed in on the plastic bag in Pesh's hand. When she gave him a puzzled look, he opened the bag to reveal a Coke, a bottle of water, a pack of peanut butter crackers and a bag of Doritos.

"What's all that?" Emma asked.

"Some of my secret food stash to feed your hungry little guy."

An inferno burned across her cheeks and neck, causing her to twist the hem of her shirt. "You didn't have to do that."

"He's hungry, isn't he?"

"Well, yes, but—"

Pesh smiled. "Then here. I don't mind sharing."

Instead of hunger pains, her stomach fluttered with butterflies as she took the crackers from him. "Ah, you must be a peanut butter fan, huh?" he remarked, as he sank down on the stool in front of her.

[37]

"Yes," she murmured, as she opened the package. Peering up at him through her lashes, she said, "I certainly hope I'm not keeping you from your patients."

"You're in luck. It's actually a slow day for us, considering most of the trauma patients get taken downtown."

Emma arched in her brows in surprise, considering all the rushing around she had seen earlier in the hallway. "Really?"

He nodded. "Besides, you may not have been officially admitted, but with you almost fainting and your pulse, I'm concerned about you. Therefore, I consider this a consultation."

Confusion flooded her at the somewhat amorous feelings crisscrossing over her at Pesh's thoughtfulness and care. After she bit into a cracker, he held out the Coke and water for her to choose from. When she reached for the Coke, he jerked it away. "Now Emma, you know better than that. Caffeine isn't good for you."

"No fair," she replied, with a grin.

Pesh winked at her. "You're right. I shouldn't have tempted you with such an elicit substance."

Emma's cheeks once again felt inflamed, so she took a swig of water to try and cool off. "How's Patrick?"

"Better. As soon as you finish eating, you can go see him."

[38]

"Really?" she asked, through a mouthful of cracker.

Pesh nodded. "He's been asking for you."

"He has?" She then crammed in another cracker as she stood up. Once she swallowed, she said, "Okay, let's go see him."

With an amused shake of his head, Pesh said, "I should have known not to say anything until you had finished eating."

"How about I promise to finish the crackers while I'm with Patrick?"

"I guess that sounds fair."

Emma grinned as they started out the door. "I can't thank you enough for the food and for looking out for me...and for Noah."

Pesh stuffed his hands into the pockets of his lab coat. "Ah, so our strong little guy is going to be named Noah?"

"Yes, after my late father."

He smiled. "He's very lucky to have you for a mother."

Emma couldn't help the heat that rose in her cheeks at his compliment. "Thank you. I'm going to try to be the best I can for him. I had a great role model in my late mother."

"You've lost both your parents?"

[39]

She nodded.

He shook his head. "So much sorrow." His hand touched her shoulder. "But just from the look on your face and the love in your eyes, I can tell how much joy this child is bringing you."

"Yes, he is," she murmured. She was almost overcome by the sincerity in his expression and voice.

"Dr. Nadeen to examining room five. Dr. Nadeen to examining room five," came a voice over the loudspeaker.

"I guess you'd better go," Emma said.

He nodded. "No rest for the weary around here."

She smiled. "It was very nice meeting you."

Pesh took her hand in both of his, tenderly stroking her flesh with his fingertips. "The pleasure was all mine."

As hard as she tried, she couldn't ignore the longing shiver that ran through her body at the touch of his hand on her skin. "Good-bye," she mumbled before stumbling into Patrick's room.

CHAPTER THREE

Aidan reached out his hand to flag down a passing nurse, but the sound of singing stopped him cold in the middle of the hallway. Strains of *Danny Boy* floated back to him—his father's favorite song. Only second generation Irish, Patrick had grown up with the songs of the old homeland like *Danny Boy* and *The Fields of Athenry.* Aidan couldn't remember a time in his life when his father wasn't humming one of them.

But it wasn't his father singing. The sweet harmony of this voice cut through to Aidan's soul, causing him to flinch.

It was Emma.

Her voice drew him nearer and nearer like a siren leading a man to his doom. His steps slowed to a crawl as his eyes honed in on the door down the hall from him. The last time he heard her sing was at her grandparent's Barn Dance. The night before he realized he was truly and completely in love with her—before he had broken her heart.

Pausing in front of the doorway, Aidan tried to still the rapid acceleration of his heartbeat. His father reclined back with Emma perched beside him on the hospital bed. She held his hand that was tethered to an IV pole in both of hers. Although Patrick had oxygen tubes stuck in his nose, he appeared to be feeling fine and was enjoying his impromptu concert.

When the last notes of the song echoed off the drab walls, Patrick applauded. "Beautiful, Emma! Absolutely beautiful!"

Even though she ducked her head, Aidan could see her usual flush of embarrassment that tinged her cheeks. "You're welcome."

"Without a doubt, you have the voice of an angel, sweetheart."

Emma leaned over and kissed his cheek. "You know there isn't anything I wouldn't do for you, and that includes singing a song with impossibly high notes in the middle of the ER." One hand flew to her abdomen while a smile spread across her face. "Noah must be a true Irish Fitzgerald. He's going crazy dancing right now." Taking Patrick's hand, she brought it to her belly. "See?"

Aidan sucked in a breath and staggered back. What the hell? His son had a name, and he hadn't even had a part in it. How could she do something as monumental as naming his child without asking him? He shouldn't have cared that Emma had bestowed her late father's name on their son, but he did. Anger pulsed through him. Stalking through the doorway, he blurted, "Excuse me? *Noah?*"

Patrick and Emma both turned to stare at him. Emma's face reddened from her ivory cheeks all the way down to her neck while her frantic gaze darted around the room as if looking for an escape. Scrambling out of the bed, she backed as far away from him as she could.

Although his attention should have been on his ailing father, Aidan couldn't take his eyes off of Emma. Any anger he felt for her quickly evaporated, and his heart constricted with love for her. God, he had missed her. He didn't realize just how much until she was standing right in front of him like a vision. She could have been one of Patrick's roses in bloom. Her breasts were fuller, her stomach was rounder, and her hips wider. He fought to catch his breath.

When Patrick cleared his throat, Aidan quickly gazed over at him. Patrick smiled. "Yes, Noah Patrick, after his grandfathers. Don't you think that's a fine name for your son?"

"Yes, it is," Aidan murmured, glancing back at Emma. When she finally dared to look at him, he bobbed his head. "Noah Patrick *Fitzgerald* is a very fine name."

Her eyes widened at the insinuation of his last name. Aidan braced himself for her to protest, but she started inching for the door instead. "Um, I'm going to go get something to drink."

"I'll get it for you," Aidan offered.

[43]

"No, no, I'm fine. You need to be with your father."

When she swept by him, Aidan fought to keep his arms pinned at his side so he wouldn't reach out and grab her to him. Her perfume filled his nostrils and invaded his senses. He closed his eyes in agony. Once she was safely out the door, his shoulders sagged in defeat. "She really hates me," he croaked.

"No, son, she doesn't." When Aidan snorted with self-contempt, Patrick shook his head. "As much as she would love to hate you, she can't. She's just gun-shy about you right now because of the dumbass move you pulled on her."

"Actually, it's me who should hate her." He grimaced. "Acting like I was diseased and naming our son without me!"

Patrick grunted. "Whenever you're done with your little tirade, might I remind you that I've been hospitalized?"

Aidan widened his eyes. "Shit, Pop, I'm so sorry. Seeing Em again knocked me on my ass." He closed the gap between them. "You look okay, but are you? I mean, was it a heart attack?"

Patrick started to open his mouth when a knock came at the door. A tall, dark-headed doctor smiled at them. After his eyes made a quick sweep over the room, his smile faded a little. "Hello again, Mr. Fitzgerald. You're looking much better now than when I first saw you today."

"I believe I have you to thank for that, Dr. Nadeen."

Dr. Nadeen strode into the room. "We have your test results back. It appears that you have two arteries that are eighty percent blocked. I've consulted with our head cardiologist, and just to be on the safe side, we feel it's best to keep you overnight and schedule an angioplasty for the morning."

Patrick grimaced. "Not one of those again?"

With a chuckle, Dr. Nadeen replied, "Yes, I noticed from your records you had the procedure before."

"Unfortunately, yes."

"You're going to have to start taking better care of yourself and maintaining a heart-healthy diet, so you won't be back here again."

Aidan snorted. "Good luck with that one."

Patrick chose to ignore him. "At least it's not something major like open heart surgery."

Dr. Nadeen nodded. "I'm sure this news will make your granddaughter feel better."

Patrick's brows furrowed. "My granddaughter?"

Dr. Nadeen ducked his head but not before Aidan caught a faint smile on his face and gleam in his dark eyes. "Emma—the beautiful redhead who almost passed out because she was so worried about you."

"She almost fainted?" Aidan questioned at the same time Patrick replied, "Aw, bless her heart, I sure hate that I upset her so much."

"It's okay. I got her to lie down for a while, and I got her little guy—I mean, *her,* something to eat."

Aidan's chest clenched not only at Dr. Nadeen's familiarity with Emma, but the mention of Noah. This dude was getting under his skin and fast. Even though Aidan was a guy, he knew competition when he saw it. It wasn't just the fact that Dr. Nadeen had the looks that made women's panties ignite, but the fucker was kind and considerate. Throw in the fact he was a doctor, and he was a triple threat.

Finally, Aidan found his voice. "That was very kind of you. I appreciate you taking care of her," he said, trying hard to speak without gritting his teeth.

A warm smile spread across Dr. Nadeen's face. "I was happy to do it for her. Your sister is a kind young woman—her spirit shines from within."

Aidan's mouth gaped open. What the hell? He thought Emma was his...*sister*? "Did you just say...?" Aidan sputtered.

Patrick shook his head. "Emma isn't my granddaughter, Doc."

"Oh, my apologies. You have a very sweet daughter then."

"No, no, she isn't even related to me."

"Ah, I see. Well, you're very fortunate to have someone in your life who cares that much about you."

Patrick glanced from Aidan to Dr. Nadeen. "Did I hear you call her beautiful?"

Pesh's expression turned apologetic. "I'm sorry. That was entirely too forward of me."

"It's all right, Doc." Rubbing his hands together, Patrick said, "Hmm, I can't help but play matchmaker while I'm laid up here. Would you be interested in dating Emma? She's single, you know."

Aidan glared at his father, which only caused Patrick to widen his grin. "What the hell do you think you're doing?" Aidan hissed.

"Forcing your hand." A mischievous gleam burned in his eyes, and Aidan knew there was no stopping him. He didn't know how after everything Patrick had been through that day he could still find the energy to goad his own son. He knew what a sore spot Emma was.

At the moment, she was more like a gaping hole in his chest. "You better be damn glad you're in the ER right now," he muttered under his breath.

Patrick ignored him and focused his attentions on Pesh who was staring strangely at the two of them. "Whatcha say, Doc?"

"Uh, well, I don't normally pick up women in the emergency room, Mr. Fitzgerald," Dr. Nadeen murmured, shifting uncomfortably on his feet.

"Oh please. This isn't picking up. It's a *fix-up*. That's totally different," Patrick argued.

"Pop," Aidan growled.

With a hesitant smile, Dr. Nadeen said, "Maybe we'll get a chance to talk again."

"She's six months pregnant!" Aidan countered.

Dr. Nadeen jerked back like he had been slapped. He cleared his throat before he spoke. "Yes, I'm well aware of that. It's what concerned me most when I met her. I didn't want her to get so upset in her condition."

Aidan grunted but didn't argue.

Dropping his gaze to the floor, Dr. Nadeen said, "After she assured me there was no husband or boyfriend to call, I thought I had surmised she wasn't with anyone. I apologize if my assumptions were wrong."

"Don't worry about my son, Doc." Patrick stared pointedly at Aidan. "He has no claims on Emma's happiness. Anymore."

A sense of understanding seemed to pass over Dr. Nadeen's face. "Oh, well, when you see Emma again, tell her to call me." He took a card out of his iPad case.

Aidan snorted and crossed his arms over his chest. "It'll never happen. Em's not the kind of girl who calls a man. She's very old-fashioned." His blue eyes narrowed at Dr. Nadeen's dark ones, silently taunting him to give the card to Patrick.

Dr. Nadeen smiled. He took a pen from his coat pocket. He then turned his attention to Patrick. "Mr. Fitzgerald, would you happen to have Emma's number? I'll be happy to call her myself." He held up a hand. "But only on the pretense of inquiring about her health after today's incident."

Patrick chuckled. "Why yes I do."

After Dr. Nadeen had scribbled the number down, he gave Aidan a fleeting glance before looking back at Patrick. "Thank you."

"You're welcome."

With a sheepish, grin, Dr. Nadeen said, "Now I suppose we should get back to business." He peered down at his iPad. "If you'll hang tight for just a few minutes, we should be ready to transport you upstairs. Surgery is set for…" he scrolled through something on the screen before wrinkling his nose. "Bright and early at seven am."

"I figured as much."

Dr. Nadeen laughed. "Well, I'll wish you the best of luck then, Mr. Fitzgerald." He leaned over and shook Patrick's hand.

With a wink, Patrick replied, "Same to you, Doc."

Cutting his eyes over to Aidan, Dr. Nadeen gave a slight nod before walking to the door.

When he exited the room, Aidan turned a wrathful gaze on Patrick. "After the last three weeks of experiencing my pure and total hell, how could you do that to me, Pop?"

"I didn't do anything to you."

Aidan gripped the rails on the hospital bed and leaned in closer. "Giving him Emma's number? Pawning her off on him?"

Patrick grinned. "I'm glad to see I got you fighting riled right now."

"Oh, I'm far from riled. I'm fucking livid!"

"Good. You need to be. It's important that you keep up your fighting spirit."

Aidan shook his head. "What will my spirit matter if she…" His heart shuddered at the thought of Emma being receptive to Dr. Nadeen's charms. After all, he was a good-looking doctor who wasn't even turned off by her being pregnant. That should be enough to make any woman swoon.

"There is not a doubt in my mind that Emma loves you, and while Dr. Nadeen's interest might be flattering, it will only serve one purpose."

"And what's that?" Aidan croaked.

"To show her there's no one else in the world for her but you."

They were interrupted by Julia sweeping through the door with her husband, Tim. While Becky, Angie, and Aidan favored their mother, Julia and Liz both took after Patrick with their dark hair and eyes. She gave Aidan a quick hug before wagging her finger at Patrick. "Pop, I can't believe it took a collapse at the VFW to finally get you checked out!"

Patrick rolled his eyes. "I was going to the doctor next week."

"Always a stubborn ass," Julia replied, pinching the bridge of her nose. "I'm just thankful you weren't alone. Thank God Emma was there, and you were so close to the fire station."

The mention of Emma's name heightened Aidan's senses. She had been gone an awfully long time to get a drink. "Speaking of Em, I better go find her."

"You do that, son."

"She was out in the hallway when we came in," Julia replied.

As Aidan whirled around, he stumbled over his feet, almost knocking Tim over. Julia grabbed his arm to steady him. "Easy, Little Brother. I don't think she's running away. *Yet.*" She then winked at Aidan.

"Thanks, Jules," he mumbled under his breath. When he stepped out into the hallway, he craned his neck left and right, but he didn't see Emma. Walking briskly, he smacked the button for the Authorized Personnel Only entrance and walked into the waiting

[52]

room. Slumped in one of the chairs, Emma's fingers texted furiously on her phone.

"Em?"

She jumped at his voice. "I, uh, I thought you and your family needed some space."

"That was sweet, but you could never be in the way," he said.

Emma held his gaze until her cheeks tinged, and she dropped her head. "I was just seeing if Casey or Connor could take me to get my car."

"I'll will," he offered.

Nibbling her bottom lip, he could tell Emma didn't like his proposal at all. "Well, since it's Saturday night, I can't seem to get either of them to answer, so…"

"Good. Then it's settled." He held out his hand to her. She eyed it warily. "Let's go tell Pop goodbye."

Hesitantly, she put her hand in his. Crackling electricity surged from his fingers all the way up his arm. From her stunned expression, he wasn't the only one to experience it. He refused to let go until she pried her grip from his. He didn't argue with her.

Instead, he pressed his hand into the small of her back, leading her to Patrick's room.

When they got to the doorway, they found the room was empty. "Oh, they must've already taken him upstairs."

The corners of Emma's mouth turned down in a frown. "I didn't get to tell him good-bye."

"I'll text Julia and get her to tell him I'm taking you home."

Emma bobbed her head in agreement.

As they started back down the hall, he turned to her. "I could pick you up in the morning, so you could see him before the surgery."

"Aidan, I—"

He grimaced. "Yeah, I guess I'm the last person on earth you want to spend time with, huh?"

She reached out and touched his arm. Once again, electricity pulsed through him, and he fought to catch his breath. "I just thought it would be better for me to drive myself, so you don't have the burden of taking me home tomorrow after Patrick's surgery."

"Trust me. Pop'll have my sisters fawning all over him." He swept a lock of hair away out of her face and pinned it behind her ear. "Besides, you could never be a burden to me." His fingertips feathered across her neck, causing Emma to shiver.

Her eyes widened, and she jerked away. "We should get going." She spun around and started power-walking back into the waiting room. Aidan almost had to break into a jog to catch up with her.

When she started out the door, he grabbed her arm. "Wait here. I'll go get the car."

"Thank you," she replied, ducking her head.

Aidan experienced a bounce in his step as he started into the parking lot. He had a chance to be with Emma again, and he was going to get her to see the truth if it was the last thing he did.

CHAPTER FOUR

Aidan had barely put the car in park by the curb when he hopped out. "What—" she began, but then she realized he was getting out to open the door for her. She couldn't help but cock her eyebrows at him. "My, my, aren't we the gentleman tonight?"

He gave her a tight smile. "If you'll really stop and think about it, I was always a gentleman." His body gave a slight tremor when she crossed her arms over her chest. "Well, for the most part, at least."

"I guess," she replied. He motioned for her to get inside. With the biting chill in the air, Emma gladly slid across the warmed leather seats of Aidan's car.

He closed the door and then hurried around to his side. "It's awfully cold for October, isn't it?" he mused.

Shivers went all down Emma's body like rivulets of rain. Immediately she thought of their parking lot conversation after Aidan first propositioned her at O'Malley's. He had been nervous then and talked of traffic. She knew now just how nervous he was since he had resorted to talking about the weather. The memory touched a raw nerve, sending a longing ache for the past through her.

To ease the chill of emotions, she rubbed her hands together. Aidan reached forward and turned the heater on. She glanced over at him. Her heart thumped wildly at his continued attentiveness. "Thank you."

"You wanna grab some dinner?" he asked.

"I'm not really hungry," she lied.

Aidan grunted. "Guess Dr. Nadeen filled you up, huh?"

Emma tensed at the jab. "He just brought me a snack."

"Well, you need to eat." He glanced away from the road to pin her with his stare. "For Noah's sake, if not yours."

She narrowed her eyes at him. "I'm well aware of what Noah needs, thank you."

He grimaced. "I'm sorry. I didn't mean for it to come out like that." He sucked in a ragged breath. "It's just I figured you needed to eat for him, even if you were still upset about what happened today with Pop."

The sincerity in his voice, along with his compassion, softened Emma. Her eyes took in his thinner frame. Patrick hadn't been exaggerating when he had said Aidan hadn't been eating. "From the looks of it, you could stand to eat as well."

His jaw tensed. "Maybe if you'll eat with me, I can."

[57]

Emma knew the last thing in the world she should do was agree to dinner. But she felt her resolve slowly fading as her traitorous stomach growled. She winced when it caused Aidan to smirk at her. "Hmm, so you are hungry? Was it just the company you wanted to refuse?"

She twisted her fingers into the hem of her top. "Let's not argue anymore, okay?" At his hopeful expression, she sighed. "Take me to dinner."

The corners of Aidan's mouth turned up, and Emma could tell he was suppressing a beaming smile.

When he pulled into a familiar parking lot, she couldn't help but gasp. "Here?" she squeaked at the flickering green and orange neon O'Malley's sign.

Aidan shrugged as he turned off the ignition. "It was the first place I saw. Besides we both like the food here and atmosphere, right?"

A rush of painful memories crashed against her like ocean waves in a turbulent storm. "I suppose," she murmured.

Ever the gentleman, he held the restaurant door open for her. For a moment, she was thankful not to see Jenny at the hostess stand. Then a piercing squeal caused her to snap her gaze toward the bar. "Emma!" Jenny screeched. Her face lit up as she hopped off her stool so fast it crashed to the ground.

After bounding over, Jenny threw her arms around Emma's neck. "Oh my God! I can't believe it!"

Warmth filled Emma's cheeks as well as her heart at Jenny's over the top enthusiasm. "It's good to see you, too."

Jenny pulled away. Her blue eyes flashed with happiness as she took in Emma's appearance. "You look absolutely stunning!" Her gaze honed in on Emma's protruding belly. "Man, I hope I look as hot as you do when I'm pregnant!"

Emma laughed and placed a hand on her stomach. "Thank you. I don't exactly feel hot at the moment."

"Trust me, you look it, sexy mama! Hell, you barely look pregnant, and you've got to be what, like six months now?"

Emma nodded.

"Congratulations on it being a boy."

"Thank you."

Jenny turned her attention to the hostess. "Why don't you take Aidan on back to a booth? I want to hear more about the baby."

With a nod, the hostess grabbed two menus and motioned for Aidan. He reluctantly followed her. He even threw a few cautious glances over his shoulder at Emma.

Jenny took Emma's hands in hers. Her once jovial expression faded into one of concern. "I just want you to know how worried we've been about Aidan. That first week my dad had to drive him home a few nights." Shimmering tears pooled in her eyes. "We were afraid we were going to lose him."

Emma sucked in a breath. Before she could respond, Jenny shook her head. "Look, I know he screwed up. I tried to warn him when he had the audacity to bring that skank in here."

"H-He brought her…"

Jenny bobbed her head. "Sometimes I wish I hadn't refused him a table. I think maybe if he had thought about it a little longer he would have never taken her home."

Over Jenny's shoulder, Emma saw Aidan staring expectantly at her. "I have to go." She started to pull her hands away, but Jenny squeezed them tight.

"I don't know what I would do in your shoes. I hope and pray I never have to. But I do know I've never seen a man more miserable over screwing up in my entire life. He's been so eaten with guilt and remorse that we've been afraid it would consume him."

Emma didn't know what to say, so she merely jerked her head in acknowledgement. On wobbly legs, she made her way over to Aidan. Thankfully, the waitress hadn't put them in the same section where they had been before.

Aidan had already ordered their drinks. Since she hadn't had any caffeine so far, she didn't ask for something different than the Coke that was already on the table. After taking a sip, she started scouring the menu. Glancing up, she asked, "What sounds good?"

Aidan shrugged. She could tell from the way he twisted his bottom lip back and forth between his teeth that he was struggling with something. She opened her mouth to question him when their waitress returned. "What can I get for you?"

Emma peered at the menu. "Hmm, I'm having a hard time deciding." When she looked up, she met Aidan's haunted eyes. She knew she needed to do something to ease the tension a bit. "Are you paying?"

His brows furrowed. "I can. Why?"

She grinned. "Good. I was torn between ordering something less expensive and then something more expensive. But if you're paying, I'll treat myself."

When she winked at him, a slow smile tugged at his lips. "Order the whole damn menu. I don't mind."

"I think I'll have the Ribeye, well-done, with the steamed vegetables. And I'd like a salad too with honey mustard on the side."

Nodding, the waitress scribbled down the order. She then turned to Aidan. "And what about you?"

"Just the beer is fine for me," Aidan replied.

The waitress started to leave for the kitchen, but Emma banged her fist on the table. "Oh no, you don't! You're not just going to sit there and drink like a fish. You better order something and do it right now! That was part of the deal, remember?"

"Em, I don't want—"

She swung her hostile gaze from him over to the waitress who had paled a little at the growing tension. "He'll have the Porterhouse steak, medium rare, with a loaded baked potato. You can also bring him a side of the garlic mashed potatoes because he's is addicted to carbs and potatoes. He'll also have a salad, but make his Caesar. And can you please bring a loaf of bread with lots of butter as soon as you can?" She cocked her head at Aidan. "He loves your bread so much he could make his meal just eating that."

[62]

He stared at her in shock. The waitress's pen hovered over the pad until Aidan bobbed his head in agreement. "Okay then. I'll put your order in and bring the bread."

"Thank you," Emma replied, handing her the menus. After taking a sip of Coke, she found Aidan staring at her. "What?"

"You remembered what I like," he murmured.

She slammed her glass down harder than she meant to. "Of course I do. The only thing predicable besides your outrageous libido is your stomach. You ordered the same thing each and every time we came here."

A ghost of a flirtatious smile played at Aidan's lips. "If I don't clean my plate, are you going to spank me, Mommy?"

Emma crossed her arms over her chest. "No, but I will force feed you myself like the damn petulant toddler you insist on acting like!"

He brought a hand to his chest. "Ouch, Em."

"Don't start with me, Aidan. You look like hell, and you need more nourishment than alcohol all the time."

He plopped his elbows on the table and leaned forward. "Doesn't seem fair, does it?"

"What?"

"That I look like such hell, yet you look so fucking beautiful." A pained sound came from deep in the back of his throat as he eyed her green maternity top. "And you're wearing green just like the first night I ever saw you." One of his hands reached out to brush against hers. "God, you were and still are the most beautiful woman I've ever seen."

She blew out a frustrated puff of air. "I don't want or need any of your pick-up lines or compliments, thank you very much!"

He shot her a wounded look. "Can't I tell the mother of my child how beautiful she looks? How pregnancy has made her blossom into an even more breathtakingly sexy woman."

Emma's heart stilled and then restarted at both his words and the passion in which he delivered them. The gleam in his eyes elicited a response between her thighs as well. She wanted to smack her traitorous body as well as the pregnancy hormones pumping through her.

"What I need more than compliments is for you to shape up, Aidan," she said, softly.

"What's that supposed to mean?" he demanded.

The waitress, armed with a basket of bread, hovered in front of the table. "Erm, here you go." She practically threw it at them before sprinting away.

Ignoring his question, Emma cut a piece of bread. After slathering it with enough butter to raise anyone's cholesterol level, she held it out for Aidan. He didn't protest. Instead, he took the slice from her, letting his fingers linger on hers longer than they should. After he swallowed the bread almost whole, she grinned triumphantly at him. "I knew you were hungry," she noted, as she fixed him another piece.

"Hungry for your company," he replied, in an agonized voice.

Closing her eyes, she shook her head. "Please don't."

"Look at me," he commanded.

Reluctantly, she opened her eyes to stare into his blazing baby blues. "It's the truth dammit! You don't know the hell I've been through because you wouldn't talk to me! You wouldn't let me apologize or talk this through. You fucking cut me off." He shuddered. "I've been dead inside the last three weeks. But now that I'm with you…"

"Let me guess. Now that you're back in my presence, you're like a butterfly emerging from a cocoon?" she snapped sarcastically.

"Keep talking that way to me, and I'll quit eating."

She gritted her teeth. "I'm glad to see you're still impossible."

He winked at her as he finished off his third piece of bread. She twisted her napkin furiously in her lap. "You act like you're the only one who's been suffering."

Aidan's face perked up. "You mean, you've missed me?" he asked, his voice vibrating with emotion.

"Of course I have! How could you even ask such a thing?"

His shoulders sagged. "I just figured when you wouldn't talk to me that your hate won out over anything else you felt for me."

"My hatred for you does fuel a lot of my emotions."

"Touche," he replied, tipping his beer up.

"Somehow you forget that what should have been one of the happiest days of my life was trampled and spat upon by the man I loved and the father of my child!"

Torment pulsed in Aidan's eyes as he slowly removed the bottle from his lips. "Jesus Em," he muttered.

His pained expression overwhelmed her, and her chest rose and fell in harsh pants. Finally she found her voice again. "I'm sorry, but it's the truth. Trust me, I may look more put together than you, but I'm not. I'm just as much a wreck on the inside. I can't shut down this time like when I lost Travis or my mom. I have Noah to think about." A bitter laugh rumbled from her chest. "So you may

[66]

think the last three weeks have been hell on you, but you can rest assured they have been for me just as much if not more!" Snatching her napkin from her lap, she dabbed the hot tears that pricked the corners of her eyes.

Aidan's chin trembled. "I swear to God and all that's holy I wish I could take it back," he whispered.

He reached out for her hand, but Jenny appeared with their salads. Emma's emotions suddenly switched gears, and she felt terrible that their outward animosity had scared the other waitress off. For a few minutes, they didn't speak. It seemed too much had transpired between them to say anything else. By the time Emma had daintily cut her lettuce, drizzled on her dressing, and taken a bite, Aidan had scarfed down his entire salad.

Emma's fork paused in midair at the sight of his fingers plunging in and out of his mouth. His tongue licked and sucked off every last bit of dressing. Assaulted with memories, her body trembled as she remembered what those fingers and that tongue felt like. Feeling enflamed, she tried looking anywhere but his delicious mouth. *What is wrong with you? The last thing on earth you should be thinking about is sex with Aidan!* The hormonal pregnancy roller coaster ride she was on seemed hell bent on careening off on a sex crazed course.

When he met her gaze, his hollowed cheeks flushed. "Sorry. I didn't mean to act like such a caveman."

"N-No, it's okay. I'm glad to see you eating so well. You're obviously very hungry."

He gazed up at her through his long lashes. "But too stubborn to admit it, right?"

She swallowed her bite of salad. "You never can admit what you should," she said softly.

"I know," he grumbled, as he snatched the last slice of bread.

She sighed. "I meant what I said about you needing to shape up. You have to take care of yourself. I don't like the excessive drinking—it worries me for your health and safety. Regardless of what we are or aren't, you're still going to be a father. I can't have a drunk in my--" she paused. "I mean, in *our* baby's life."

His tortured gaze held hers as he chewed. "So I can still be in Noah's life, just not yours?"

Not knowing how to respond, she pushed her salad around with her fork. "Em?" Aidan pressed.

"I would never keep you away from Noah if you truly wanted to be a part of his life."

[68]

Jenny interrupted them by bringing their plates. "Everything okay so far?"

Emma forced a smile at the almost loaded meaning of the question. "It's delicious thank you."

"I'd like some more bread," Aidan said.

Jenny nodded. "I'll take care of it."

They fell into silence again. "You need to eat your salad," Aidan finally said.

"Oh, so now you're telling me to eat?"

"You're supposed to be eating a lot of green, leafy vegetables for the folic acid."

She arched her brows in surprise. "And just how do you know that?"

Through a mouthful of baked potato, he said, "*What to Expect While You're Expecting.*"

Her heartbeat thundered in her chest so loud she was sure he could hear it. "You actually read the book I gave you?"

He bobbed his head as he shoveled in a bite of steak. "Read some others too," he muttered between chewing.

She stared at him in disbelief. When he finally looked at her and not his plate, he grinned. "So eat your salad."

Pursing her lips, she glared at him for a moment before picking up her fork. Once she filled her mouth with an enormous bite of lettuce, she mumbled, "Happy?"

"Mmm, hmm. Eat your steak too. Noah needs his protein."

Emma snorted exasperatedly but did as she was told. When she cleaned her salad plate, Aidan clapped for her. She laughed in spite of herself. "I don't think two people have ever been so obsessed with one meal," she mused.

"I guess we both benefit from having someone take care of us."

"Maybe," she murmured.

After pushing his empty plate out of the way, Aidan's expression grew grave. "I need to tell you the truth about what happened with Amy."

"I already know." At Aidan's puzzled expression, she replied, "Becky told me about how you tried for a year to get her back. How you became an alcoholic…had to go to therapy. It really doesn't affect us."

Aidan cringed. "Yeah, well, that's only half of the story."

A chill ran over Emma, causing her to shudder. "What do you mean?"

"Only Amy, Pop, and I know the real truth." He downed the rest of his beer and shook the bottle at the waitress as she passed by.

"So tell me," Emma prompted.

"After all of our years together, Amy was desperate for us to get married." He drew in a ragged breath. "She was so desperate that she went as far as to try to trap me into marrying her."

The world tilted and spun around Emma. "You mean…"

"Yes, she was pregnant."

Her hand flew to her mouth. "Oh my God."

"The second time we got back together we weren't swimming competitively, so she started broaching the subject of not doing double the contraception anymore. After awhile, she finally wore me down. She was on birth control, so I figured that was enough. I stopped using condoms."

Emma arched her eyebrows at his admission. "You told me I was the first woman you'd ever been inside of without a condom."

He scowled at her. "Yeah, well, excuse me if I thought it would have totally fucked up the moment by admitting that after going off condoms just twice, my ex-girlfriend got pregnant." He gave a bark of a laugh at Emma's gasp. "Yeah, I'm pretty potent, huh? That's how I knew I would be a good candidate to knock you up."

"That's a disgusting way of putting it," Emma hissed.

Aidan's expression softened. "I'm sorry. I didn't mean for it to come out like that."

"Anyway, so Amy got pregnant on birth control?"

A bitter smile then twisted on his face. "Oh no. An accidental pregnancy? That would have been easy to forgive. After all, the fucking directions on the box even admit it's only 98% effective." His fingers ripped at the label on his beer. "Nope. A year into us being back together and me running like hell from any commitment, she stopped taking her birth control without my knowledge."

"Oh Aidan," Emma murmured. She didn't know what else to say. "So you're trying to tell me you have a child out there somewhere?"

The angry expression drained off his face and was replaced by one of absolute sorrow. "I wish that were the case."

Emma couldn't help but reach across the table and take his hand in hers. "What happened?" she prodded.

[72]

The waitress returned with his beer, and Aidan drowned half of it before speaking again. "A few weeks before I found out she was pregnant, Amy and I had been out partying with some friends, and I got plastered. That night as I was digging around in the medicine cabinet for some Advil, I accidentally knocked her birth control in the sink. You can imagine how surprised I was when it was unused, not to mention the prescription hadn't been refilled in two months. When I confronted her, she admitted she'd stopped taking it because she thought a baby would solidify our relationship."

Aidan shuddered. "I was furious. I packed my things and left for my parents. I refused to talk to her or see her." He leaned forward on his elbows. "Kinda like what you've been doing to me."

Emma rolled her eyes. "Finish the damn story, Aidan."

He held up his hands. "Fine then. She eventually came to my office and showed me the pregnancy test." He gave Emma a sad smile. "The fact that the Amy I thought I knew and loved had betrayed me by trapping me into getting married was terrible, but the worst part was the fact I was scared out of my freaking mind at the prospect of being a father at twenty-four." He took two long pulls from his beer. "I'm sure you can imagine what happened next."

Her stomach turned at the prospect. "Go on," she instructed.

He sneered at her. "You want me to actually say the words?"

"Fine. That's when Amy caught you screwing another woman."

"Yes," he croaked.

Emma narrowed her eyes. "Wow, I guess we have a lot in common. Maybe we should get t-shirts that say, 'We were both fucked over by Aidan Fitzgerald'!"

"Em, please," he begged.

She huffed out an exasperated breath. "Fine. Continue."

"Amy threw me out of the house that night. The next morning I went back over and tried to reason with her. I told her I was sorry, that I loved her, and that in spite of what had happened between her trying to trap me and then me screwing someone else, I still wanted to marry her. She wouldn't have it. She got into the car and sped away."

Emma's brows shot up in surprise at the tears sparkling in Aidan's eyes. "She ran a stop sign in the subdivision trying to get away from me. A car smashed into the driver's side. Thankfully, she walked away with just a few scrapes and bruises." His chest rose and fell in harsh pants. "But she miscarried later that day."

Involuntarily, Emma reached out and took Aidan's hand in hers again. His expression, his tears, and his words broke her heart. All the pieces of his puzzle finally fell into place.

"All these years you've felt guilty about the baby, haven't you?"

He nodded, swiping the tears from his cheeks. "I never wanted it, and then I…killed it." He started sobbing then. Emma chewed her lip and fought herself from rising out of the booth and going over to him. Her better judgment lost out, and she found herself cradling him in her arms. The old Aidan she knew would never have cried, least of all in public. He was absolutely broken by the ghosts of the past and present.

She rubbed wide circles over his back. "You're not to blame for what happened with the baby, Aidan, any more than Amy is just because she was driving too fast and ran the stop sign. Accidents happen."

Raising his head, he swiped the tears from his cheeks. "Accidents may happen, but people never forget them…or forgive them."

Emma ignored the double meaning of his statement in regards to her. "I'm sure time has helped to heal any bad feelings Amy had for you. I'm sure she's struggled with her own guilt over what she did to you by trying to trap you."

[75]

He shrugged. "I hope so. She certainly helped to screw me up for every other woman." His blue eyes honed in on hers. "Maybe it's me who can't forgive. If it hadn't been for her, maybe I wouldn't have fucked things up so epically with you."

"Maybe," she murmured.

His fingers came to grip her chin. Tilting her gaze up to meet his, he shook his head. "For the most part, our proposition was about me getting the chance to have sex with you, and I did promise my late mother I would one day have children. But it was also about being able to find redemption with myself…and with God. I thought if I could help you bring a baby into the world, it might take away the hurt of the past."

Emma's mouth dropped open in surprise. For a few moments, she could only stare at him in utter and complete shock. All this time he really had possessed a deeper, more admirable desire for wanting to be her sperm donor.

"Do you hate me now because of that?"

She shook her head wildly back and forth. "No, how could you even think that?"

"It's just you were staring at me and not saying anything. I thought you might feel used or deceived."

"That's not it at all. In fact, I was thinking much more highly of you because of what you told me."

"Really?"

"I'm glad having Noah is a way you feel you can repent for what you did. It's never too late for redemption, Aidan."

A hopeful look entered his tortured eyes. "I'd give anything and everything in this world to redeem myself with you. Just please, please give me the chance."

Emma couldn't hold the intensity of his desperate gaze any longer. Staring down at her lap, she fought to breathe. Her mind whirled with trying to process her out of control thoughts while her chest heaved with emotion. Did she really want to give him the chance to redeem himself? Could she actually do that to herself and her heart? And if she denied him, how was she even to have him a part of Noah's life without letting her feelings get in the way?

"Please, Em," he begged.

"I guess I can try," she finally replied. When she glanced back up at him, his blue eyes shone with determination. "I'm not making any promises."

He smiled. "I can take that—I can take whatever you're willing to give me."

Jenny interrupted them by bringing over their check. "Would you like some dessert?"

Emma laughed when she appeared to be asking her more than Aidan. She patted her very full belly. "No, I think I'm good."

Aidan swept his hand inside his jacket pocket for his wallet. Without even glancing at the bill, he stuffed a wad of cash in the envelope. When Jenny started to protest at his generosity, he shook his head. "I owe a lot more than that to you and your dad for taking care of me in the last few weeks."

"We were happy to do it." Jenny leaned over and gave Aidan a quick hug. "Just promise to take care of yourself, and we'll call it even, okay?"

He nodded as his eyes burned into Emma's. "I'm already feeling like my old self again."

She cocked her eyebrows at him. "Let's hope that's not every aspect of your old self," she said, rising out of the booth.

"Damn, Em, do you always have to shred me with those freakin' claws of yours?" he grumbled as he stood up.

Jenny threw a worried glance between the two of them before forcing a smile to her face. "Well, I hope to see you guys again soon."

Emma gave Jenny a reassuring smile. "Thanks you." After giving her a quick hug, she started out of the bar. Aidan hurried to catch up with her. He stepped in front of her just before she could open the door.

"Thank you," she mumbled, trying to ignore the little zap of electricity she felt when his body touched hers. She edged away from him as they started back to his car. The drive over to the VFW was silent except for the muted sound of the radio playing love songs that were like spikes to her broken heart.

When they pulled up to her abandoned car, she didn't want to leave him. Her brain screamed for her to pick up her hands and feet and get going. Finally, as her hand reached for the door handle, Aidan grabbed her shoulder. "Wait!" he cried.

CHAPTER FIVE

Aidan's chest tightened at the prospect of letting Emma out of his sight for even a second. They had come so far in the last few hours he was afraid it might all fade like a dream if they didn't remain together. He was desperate for anything to keep her with him. A thought flashed in his mind, and he blurted, "Can I see Beau?"

Emma stared down at her lap. He could tell she was raging a battle within herself about whether to let him come over. "Please?" he pressed.

Her shoulders sagged, but she raised her head and smiled. "Of course. I mean, he does miss you."

Aidan gave a bark of a laugh. "I doubt it. He chose you over me, didn't he?" He was then assaulted with the painful memory of the night Emma caught him with Heather. The sight of Beau running after Emma, nudging her stomach and whining to go with her, cut through to his heart the same way it did that night. Shuddering, he forced a smile to his face. "I'm sure he's too busy eating table scraps and lying around on your couch to miss me."

"No, he really does. After all, you were his daddy for two years."

"Good because I've missed him." He leaned over the gearshift towards her. "I've missed him every moment of every day." Her green eyes widened both at his proximity and the fact that they both knew he wasn't talking about Beau anymore. The electricity crackled all around the two of them.

"You can follow me home."

"Thank you."

He waited until she was safely in her car and cranked up before he pulled out of the parking space. On the way to her house, his fingers drummed anxiously against the steering wheel. Even though it wasn't more than ten minutes, he couldn't seem to get there fast enough. Hope pulsed through him that she might finally forgive him and fully let him back into her life.

As he started to pull into the driveway, a yard sign caught his eye. Squinting in the darkness, he gasped at the recognition of the realty sign. The words *For Sale* sent a stake through his heart. Animosity overwrought the amorous feelings he had pulsing through him.

He screeched to stop barely off the road. His blood pounded in his ears as he clambered out of the car and slammed the door. He was at Emma's side before she had time to close hers. "YOU'RE MOVING?"

Shrinking from his anger, she pressed herself against the car. "Yes," she whispered.

Shame washed over him that his reaction had frightened her. "I'm sorry for shouting at you, but how could you not tell me?"

"I was going to," she argued

"When? The day the moving van came? Christ, Emma, we've been together all night! I unveiled my heart and soul, yet you couldn't manage to tell me this one little detail?"

"I'm sorry."

He was afraid to ask the next question because deep down he already knew the answer. "And just where are you going?"

"I'm moving back home—to Ellijay. I'm going to live with Grammy and Granddaddy for a while until the house sells, and then I might find a place of my own close by them. They're getting older. Granddaddy fell off a ladder a week ago and just had to have hip replacement surgery. They need me, but more importantly, I need them."

He shook his head. "I won't let you take my son from me!"

Emma's green eyes narrowed into angry slits. "Don't you dare threaten me like that! You know I would never keep you from Noah. Just because I don't live here, doesn't mean you won't get to see him."

"Ellijay is a fucking hour and a half away! How will I get to see him when he's that far from me? Are you going to put me on some visitation schedule? Like every other weekend or some bullshit?"

She rubbed her temples. "I don't know what I'm going to do. I just know I can't stay here anymore. Alone."

"Dammit, Emma, I can't believe you could be so cold."

She jerked her chin up and glared at him so hard that he took a step back. "You asshole! How dare you accuse *me* of being cold! I'm not the one who cheated and ruined everything between us!"

"I didn't sleep with her," he protested.

Emma threw her hands up. "The fact you couldn't get it up or I interrupted you is irrelevant to the point, Aidan! You brought some stranger into your home on the pretense of screwing me out of your heart and mind!"

He grimaced. "I've said it a million times in a million different ways that I'm sorry!"

"I know you have, but just like I told you back at O'Malley's, I would work on forgiving you, and it's going to take a hell of a lot of time. So don't expect me to fall into your waiting arms like nothing ever happened any time soon. I had a life before you, and I'm going to have one after you!" She turned and stalked away.

"Em, wait!" When she kept on walking, he called, "Fine, you want even more grand gestures? Here's another one." He sank down onto his knees on the sidewalk.

When Emma whirled around, her eyes grew wide. "What are you doing?"

He gazed around them. "What the hell does it look like I'm doing? I'm on my knees—totally and completely begging you to forgive me."

"Get up!" she hissed when a couple walking their dog paused to stare at them.

"Not until you forgive me."

She growled in frustration. "I said it would take time, so quit being dramatic."

He shrugged. "Fine, call me a Drama Queen. Call me any fucking name in the book! Just get all the anger and hate out of your system, so you can work on forgiving me tonight." He opened his arms wide. "I said it on cards, in text messages, and voicemails, and even in that fruity book of poetry I sent you. But now I'm going to say it to your face in case it's the only other chance I have."

Suddenly in that moment Aidan didn't feel so sure of himself. He drew in a ragged breath. "I am *sorry*, Emma. I'm so sorry for breaking your heart. I'm sorry for being an utter prick and being afraid of my feelings for you. Most of all, I'm sorry for screwing up the perfect life we had by pushing you away and cheating on you."

Emma's face flushed with warmth as the woman on the sidewalk gasped. Aidan turned to her. "Yeah, that's right. I'm one of the countless assholes who break women's hearts. I couldn't tell Emma I loved her, and I almost screwed another woman trying to push her away." He smacked his palms hard against his chest. "But from the depths of my heart and soul, I'm so, so sorry!"

"Jesus dude, have you lost all your pride?" the man questioned, which caused the woman to punch him in the arm.

Aidan chuckled. "Yeah, I have. Because I'm willing to do whatever it takes to win *her* back," he pointed to Emma and smiled at her.

When Emma strode over to him with a determined look, Aidan felt his hope rising. It quickly faded as she grabbed him by the hair and yanked his head up. "Get off my front walk this minute,

[85]

or I'm going to call the cops!" She shook her head maniacally. "I can't believe you just embarrassed me in front of my neighbors like that!"

"I thought you wanted a man who would say how he truly felt?"

She rolled her eyes. "*This*," she said, motioning wildly to him, "is not what I had in mind."

"Fine," he said pulling himself off the ground. He leaned closer to her and cocked his eyebrows. "But can you honestly say you weren't the tiniest bit impressed by that?"

The corners of her lips pulled up, and he could tell she was fighting not to smile. "Maybe a little."

"Aha, I knew it!"

"Come on. Let's go inside before you can be more of a twatwaffle tonight."

He burst out laughing. "What did you just call me?"

"It's one of Casey's words."

"Hmm, let me guess. It's probably one of Casey's words for *me*?"

She nodded as she unlocked the front door. "Yes, but with some stronger expletives along with it."

"I figured as much."

"Have a seat. I'll go let Beau out of the basement."

When Aidan eased down on the couch, a memory flashed in his mind of making love to Emma in the very same spot before they went to see her grandparents for the first time. He heard Beau long before he saw him racing around the corner.

"Hey boy!" he cried, rising up off the couch.

At the sight of Aidan, Beau went into full freak-out mode with his whole body wiggling while he whined and cried. He barreled into Aidan, knocking him back down onto the couch. Then he went to licking Aidan's face, hands, and any other body part he could get his tongue on.

Emma laughed. "See, I told you he missed you."

Beau barked a few times as if in agreement, and then went back to slurping his tongue over Aidan's face. "Okay, boy, I missed you, too." Aidan rubbed over Beau's back and then patted his head.

"Now sit down, Beau, and be a good boy," Emma instructed.

[87]

To Aidan's surprise, Beau obediently slid down onto the floor and sat stock still for Aidan to pet him. "Damn, I can't believe you've gotten him to obey."

"It's taken some time."

"Did you take good care of Mommy while I was gone?" Aidan asked, scratching Beau's ears. At her sharp intake of breath, he glanced up at her and winked.

"He's been wonderful company. Especially at night," she replied softly.

"I can imagine. The nights alone have been hell on me."

Emma opened her mouth to say something, but then suddenly wagged her finger at Beau. "Stop that licking, or I'm going to put the cone of shame back on you."

Aidan laughed as he patted Beau's back. "Don't be so uptight, Em. He's just a dog. Let him lick himself if he wants to."

She shook her head. "If he keeps licking like that, he's going to cause an infection with his stitches from his surgery."

"Surgery?" Aidan repeated lamely. "What happened to him?" When Emma didn't respond, Aidan glanced up to see her flushing and ducking her head. Oh no. She couldn't have gone there. She wouldn't have done that. Taking Beau by the collar, he

[88]

turned him slowly around. At the sight of his lost manhood, he sucked in a breath. "You had him fixed?"

Emma nibbled on her bottom lip. "The vet suggested it. He said it would help calm Beau down and make it easier for him to get acclimated when Noah's born."

Aidan rose off the floor. "Jesus, Em, first you wanted my balls on a skewer, and now you had to take my dog's!"

"I never wanted your…balls!" she huffed in protest.

"Symbolically you did."

She rolled her eyes. "But look how much calmer he already is."

Aidan glanced at Beau. As much as he hated to admit it, he was way more relaxed. "Yeah, well, you should have consulted with me first. He's *my* dog!"

She winced as if in pain. She took a few slow steps before easing down into the chair. "Whoa, wait a minute. Don't walk away. We're not through discussing this."

"Em?" When she didn't respond, he walked around the side of the chair. He squatted down in front of her. His heart jolted to a stop and restarted at the anguished expression etched on her face. "Em, what's wrong?"

[89]

"I'm…cramping." She closed her eyes, and her chest rose and fell in harsh breaths. "It hurts really bad."

Fear crashed over Aidan's head. "Come on. Let's get you to the hospital." Before she could protest, he took her hand and helped her out of the chair. She whimpered and clutched her abdomen. "I'll carry you if you need me to," he said.

"No, I can make it," she replied.

He wrapped his arm around her waist to steady her. "Stay Beau," he called over his shoulder. Beau whined, but reluctantly, he sat down in the foyer. When they started out the door, Emma froze. "My purse."

"I'll get it." He whirled around and went to snatch it from its place on the floor. He then returned to Emma's side to help her out of the door and down the porch steps. "You want to take your car since it's closer? I can move mine."

She shook her head. "No, no, yours is fine."

"How's the pain?"

"Intense," she panted.

"Are you bleeding or do you think your water broke?"

"No, it's just the contractions."

[90]

A tiny flicker of relief filled him. "It's going to be okay, Em. We'll get you to the hospital, and whatever it is, they'll fix it."

His heart shattered when she stared up at him with eyes pooling with tears. "I hope so."

"Have faith."

He opened the car door and eased her down onto the seat. As soon as he shut her door, he sprinted over to the driver's side. He climbed inside and cranked up. After pealing out into the street, he glanced over at Emma.

Her eyes were closed and her brows furrowed while she bit down on her lip. Taking one of his hands off the steering wheel he grabbed up one of hers. Her eyes flew open, and she stared over at him. "I'm here for you, Emma."

"Thank you...I'm glad." She squeezed his hand tight. Refusing to let go, she used her other hand to dig her phone out of her purse. She thrust it over at Aidan. "Call Casey," she murmured.

Keeping one hand on the wheel, he used his other to scroll through Emma's contacts. He braced himself for the wrath to come as his finger pressed dial. Casey answered on the third ring. "Hey Hot Mama, sorry I haven't had a chance to call you back yet," she said without a hello.

"Um, this is Aidan."

A long pause came on the line. "What the hell are you doing with Em's phone? Please don't tell me you've done something truly insane to try to get her back? Because if you have, I will make sure that you go to jail for a long, long time where a very large and hairy man can make you his bitch!" she shrieked loud enough for even Emma to hear.

"Casey, listen to me. I haven't kidnapped Emma. We're on our way to the ER at Wellstar."

Casey gasped. "Oh God, what's wrong?"

Aidan glanced over at Emma whose eyes were once again pinched closed while her jaw was clenched in pain. "She's having some contractions."

"She's not bleeding is she?"

"No, just the contractions."

Aidan heard who he assumed was Nate talking in the background. "It sounds like a good sign that she isn't bleeding. Nate thinks it might just be Braxton Hicks, but we'll be there just as soon as we can."

"Okay. Can you call Connor, too?"

Emma's eyes flew open, and she looked at him in shock. Aidan figured she was amazed that he didn't have to be told to do everything, and he could actually be considerate of her feelings.

"Yeah, sure."

"Bye."

Casey merely hung up, so Aidan cut the call off. "Anyone else you want me to call? Virginia?"

Emma shook her head. "I don't want to worry Grammy yet in case it is something like Braxton Hicks."

"Okay, if you're sure."

They made the rest of the drive in tense silence. After screeching into the hospital parking lot, Aidan wheeled up to the curb at the emergency room and killed the engine. When he got out and started over to Emma's side, a security guard hustled over. "Sir, you can't park there."

"Look, my..." he trailed off when he realized he didn't know what to call Emma. She certainly wasn't his wife and their relationship status didn't qualify as girlfriend either. "*She's*," he finally emphasized, "having early contractions, so I'm getting her inside. If you don't like it, then tow my fucking car!"

The security guard held up his hands. "Sorry sir. Once you get registered, please come out and move the car. A nice Mercedes like that will get knocked to hell at the impound lot."

Aidan growled with frustration as he held his hand out to Emma. "Fine. But I'm not coming back out here until I know both she and my kid are okay!" With his free hand, he dug a hundred out of his wallet. "Watch it for me, okay?"

The guard looked left and right before he hastily snatched the money. "Yes, sir."

Turning his attention back to Emma, he helped her out of the car. She grimaced as she stepped onto her feet. "Lean on me," Aidan instructed as she took a tentative step onto the curb.

With one arm wrapped around her waist, Aidan led Emma through the mechanized double doors and into the ER lobby. She gripped his hand tighter and from the expression on her face, he could tell the pain was worse. "Just a little further, Em," he said.

At the registration desk, he eased her down into a chair. When the clerk didn't come up immediately, he banged his fist on the desk. "Excuse me, but she might be in preterm labor here!"

The receptionist nodded to a nurse. "We'll go ahead and take her on back."

"Thank you," Aidan said.

A nurse came out of the doors with a wheelchair. Aidan helped Emma to her feet and then helped her over to sit down in the wheelchair. When he started to go back with them, the receptionist called to him. "You can't go back until we have all of her medical information."

"I'm already pre-registered here through my OB/GYN," Emma muttered, through teeth gritted in pain.

"Then he'll have to stay until we get the insurance information."

Aidan stared helplessly at Emma as she handed him her purse. "My cards are in my wallet."

He raced through the paperwork. Most of it he left blank, hoping they already had it since he didn't know it. The irony wasn't lost on him that Emma may be carrying his child, but he had no idea if she had ever had any major surgeries or childhood illnesses. Just as he started to punch the button to open up the doors, someone cleared his throat.

It was the security guard. "Fuck!" Aidan cried. Several people in the waiting room looked up at him. Digging his keys from the pocket, he sprinted past the security guard and to his waiting car. Tires squealed as he pulled around the entrance and back-tracked it to the available parking deck.

When he got back inside, he punched the button on the Authorized Personnel Only doors. His gaze spun desperately around the hallway of rooms. Feeling an odd sense of deja vu from earlier in the day, he was just about to flag down a nurse when Dr. Nadeen appeared before him, his face tense with worry. "She is in room five," he said.

Although he hated to say it, Aidan mumbled, "Thank you."

He threw open the door to find the curtain pulled. The sound of a baby's heartbeat echoed off the walls. "Em?" he cried.

"I'm here."

He raced forward, throwing the curtain aside. At the sight of Emma in stirrups and a doctor between her legs, he froze. "Aidan," she urged, motioning him to her side. The insistent tone in her voice caused him to move quickly. He sidestepped the doctor and went to her side. He grabbed up her hand and squeezed.

"I'm sorry. I had to fill out all this paperwork and then go move my car."

"It's okay."

He shook his head. "No, it's not. You shouldn't have had to be back here alone. You needed me." He gazed down at her. "I needed to be with you."

"You're here now. That's all that matters."

Aidan couldn't stop himself from leaning over and kissing her forehead. He would have to give the hospital props. They had been there barely twenty minutes, and Emma was already outfitted in a hospital gown and was being seen by a doctor. He couldn't help but wonder if it was not only the seriousness of her condition, but also Dr. Nadeen that helped matters along.

The doctor, whose white coat had "Dr. Pendleton" embroidered in blue, rose off his stool. "You can come out of these now." Emma eased her legs out of the stirrups as Dr. Pendleton slid the table back down for her. After he tossed his rubber gloves in the trash, he turned to face them. "Even though you were experiencing preterm labor, you're not dilated, and your cervical plug is still intact."

At what Aidan assumed was his blank expression, Dr. Pendleton said, "Those are good factors. I'm going to have a nurse come in and administer Turbutaline, which will stop the remaining contractions you're experiencing. I'll come back in and do an ultrasound to see how your baby looks. From his heartbeat, he seems to be a little agitated, but that could be from the uterine walls contracting." He turned to go to the door. "Since you're condition is now stable, I'll be back in a little while to check on you."

Aidan's legs didn't feel like they would support him any longer, so he collapsed into the chair by the bed. Relief washed over him. For the moment, it appeared that Noah was going to be okay, and in turn, Emma was as well.

"Thank you God," Emma murmured.

A commotion came outside the door. "What the—"Aidan began before Casey and Connor burst inside the room.

CHAPTER SIX

"Em!" Casey cried, hurrying over to the bedside. She wrapped her arms around Emma and squeezed tight. "What's the verdict?"

"For now, I'm okay, and Noah's okay. Some preterm labor, but they're able to stop it."

Casey and Connor both exhaled noisily. "Thank goodness," Connor said.

A nurse interrupted by coming in to administer the shot of Turbutaline. She eyed everyone before shaking her head disapprovingly. "You really shouldn't have such a crowded room. You need rest and relaxation."

"Please don't make them leave. They are relaxing to me," Emma protested.

She tsked before sticking the needle into Emma's IV. "Dr. Pendelton won't like all these people in here, disturbing you, and he's about to come back in to do your ultrasound."

"We'll step outside for a bit," Casey said diplomatically.

"Yeah, we don't want to get you in trouble," Connor agreed.

When Aidan didn't budge, Casey shot him a look. "I'm staying with Emma and my son," he replied tersely.

"Whatever," she snapped before starting for the door. She and Connor were about to go out when Dr. Pendleton swept inside. They pressed themselves up against the far wall. Without a hello or an admonishment to the over-capacity room, he proceeded to do the ultrasound. Emma felt slightly comforted seeing Noah's form on the screen. His heart rate had thankfully calmed down. "He looks like he's planning on staying inside for awhile," Dr. Pendleton remarked before turning off the machine.

He stood up. "While everything appears to be improving, I'm going to insist on strict bed-rest for at least the next week to two weeks. You may lie down or sit, but your feet are only to touch the ground to use the restroom. I'd advise that you use a seat in the shower, too. Is that clear?"

Emma gasped. "But my job—"

Dr. Pendleton held up a finger to silence her. "Ms. Harrison, I know it seems that since we have the situation under control at the moment that all is well, but the future stability of your pregnancy rests on the care you give yourself in the next ten days."

"I understand," she murmured, trying to calm the rising panic that pricked its way like needles over her body.

"As for your job, I'll fill out the necessary paperwork for you to take a leave of absence. The most important thing right now is for you to rest and limit your stress level. We don't want any more premature labor."

"How long do I have to stay in the hospital?" Emma questioned, her voice wavering.

"I want to keep you over night, and then you're free to go home. Let me go check on the status of moving you upstairs."

After Dr. Pendleton exited the room, Emma's emotions spiraled out of control. She tried fighting with everything in her not to totally and completely lose it at the prospect that Noah's life might still be in danger. It was too much to bear, and she couldn't stop the floodgates from opening. A strangled cry erupted from her lips, sending both Casey and Aidan racing forward to comfort her. Somehow Casey elbowed Aidan out of the way, blocking him from getting to her.

A frustrated grunt came from Aidan. Casey ignored him and grabbed Emma's hand. She squeezed it tight and gave her a reassuring smile. "Don't cry, Em. It's all going to be fine. Lots of women have to go on bed rest for a while, and then the rest of their pregnancies are completely normal."

Between hiccupping sobs, she replied, "I hope so."

"I know so. And I'll take you to Grammy's first thing in the morning, and she'll get you through this."

Emma shook her head as the tears slid down her cheeks. "I can't go to Grammy's. Granddaddy had hip replacement surgery a week ago, and she's already ragged from taking care of him. I can't put any more stress on her at her age."

Aidan cleared his throat and sidestepped Casey to stand in front of Emma. "You're coming home with me. I'm going to take care of you."

A hiss erupted from Casey. She jerked her hand away from Emma's to jab a finger in Aidan's chest. "Over my dead body!"

Aidan's eyebrows shot up. "Excuse me?"

Casey's nostrils flared. "You've got to be out of your fucking mind! *You* take care of her? You're the very reason she's in this condition."

He winced. "With Pop's episode, Emma's had a lot of stress on her today as well as in the last few weeks."

"Don't you dare try to pawn this off on someone else!"

"Look we all know I fucked up! Royally. Even though I'd give anything to take it back, I can't. But I can make it right, and

[102]

one way to prove to Emma how much I care about her is to take care of her when she needs me most."

Emma sucked in a breath at Aidan's words. She was sure one of the countless monitors she was hooked up to was about to go haywire with her accelerating heartbeat. Shock reverberated through her that he had even suggested taking care of her, least of all that he actually meant he'd do it. While deeply touched, she couldn't imagine how her frayed nerves could allow her to be so close to him. Finally, she shook her head. "I don't think—" she started.

His blue eyes blazed with a steely determination. "This isn't up for discussion."

Casey snorted. "Oh hell yes, it *is* up for discussion. If anyone is going to be taking care of Em, it's me, fuckwit!"

Aidan's face clouded over with fury, and Emma feared he was about to truly lose his temper. His jaw clenched as he leaned closer to Casey. "You seem to forget that's *my* child she's carrying. He is my responsibility. You can sure as hell believe that nothing else matters more to me in this world than *my* son."

Glaring back at him, Casey countered, "Too bad you weren't thinking about Noah when you almost screwed that skank."

At Aidan's growl, Connor squeezed between them. "Okay, enough!" He shook his head. "Damn, you two have got to chill with the pissing contest about Em. Would you stop for a minute and think about how much you're upsetting her?"

Both Aidan and Casey snapped their gaze from Connor and stared at Emma. Their attention caused her cheeks and neck to flush.

Aidan's expression softened. "I'm sorry, Em. I don't want to upset you. I just want…" He ran his hand through his sandy hair. "I just want you to let me take care of you and Noah."

The sincerity in his words sent her heart fluttering again, and she hated herself for it. After nibbling on her lip, she questioned, "What about your job? You can't possibly travel like you have been and take care of me."

"I'll just take a leave of absence like you are."

Emma couldn't help widening her eyes. "You would do that?"

"Of course I would. You need me," Aidan said, edging closer to the bed.

"But with your position, will they even consider granting you one? I mean, it's not like we're married."

Aidan shrugged. "If they don't, then I'll just quit. You and Noah mean more to me than a job."

Casey crossed her arms over her chest in a huff. "And what if your libido kicks in one night after seeing some slut in a short skirt? Are you just going to run out on her again?"

"Case," Emma pleaded at the same moment Aidan snarled, "Don't fucking go there!"

"I cannot believe you're honestly considering letting him do this. He broke your heart, Em!" Casey cried, throwing her hands up in frustration.

Emma sighed. "Yes, I'm well aware of what he did. But at the moment, I don't see any other choice but to accept what he's proposing." She then turned her gaze to Aidan. "My house is a wreck with the move. I'd have to stay with you."

His beaming smile thawed a little of the remaining chill towards him in her heart. "Of course you can. I'll put you up in my bedroom since its downstairs and the bathroom is closest."

"Thank you. I'll need some of my things. Casey, can you go with Aidan and help him pack up what I'll need?"

Casey's eyes bulged like Emma had just asked her to help Satan achieve world domination. "I can't stand being in the same room with him, least of all help him paw through your things!"

Emma rolled her eyes. "Fine then, be an immature ass about it. I'm sure Connor will be happy to do it."

"Sure thing, Emmie Lou," Connor replied, stepping forward to thump Aidan's back. From the way he winced, Emma was sure Connor had hit him a little harder than necessary.

"I appreciate that Connor," Emma replied. Staring pointedly at Aidan, she said, "Just the essentials. I won't be staying very long."

The corners of Aidan's lip curled into a self-satisfied smirk. "We'll see."

"You're impossible," she muttered.

"Okay, then, guess we better head out and get started. That way everything will be ready for you when they discharge you in the morning," Connor said.

Aidan nodded. "Sounds good."

After a long, drawn out sigh, Casey said, "Fine. I'll go with you."

"Seriously?" Connor and Aidan said at the same time.

"Yes," she snapped.

Connor held his hands up. "Fine. It's your funeral."

"Let's face it. Considering I'm the only one out of the three of us who has a vagina and knows what Em would want, you're going to need me."

With a snort, Connor said, "Yeah, well, I've known her longest and—"

"You've practically got a vagina?" Casey teased with a smile.

"Har, fucking, har!"

Emma laughed. "Would you guys knock it off and get going?"

"Man, you're already bossing us around," Connor said, with a grin. He nudged Aidan. "You're in for a fun two weeks, Slave Boy."

Aidan chuckled. "I don't mind. Emma can use and abuse me to her heart's content. As long as she's happy and healthy, I'll do anything she pleases."

Connor stared at Aidan for a moment and then shook his head. "Yep, you've got the love-bug bad, dude. Very, very bad." He turned back to Emma and winked. "See you tomorrow, Emmie Lou." He leaned over and gave her a hug and a kiss. Before he pulled away, he whispered in her ear. "Work him hard, Em, but give him a chance too."

"I'll try."

Connor swapped places with Casey who also gave Emma a big hug. "When I'm done, I'll come back and stay the night with you," Casey said.

Emma shook her head. "No, no, I'll be fine. It's just one night. It's not like I haven't spent a few nights in the hospital. It's just I'm usually on the other side of the bed."

"Are you sure? Nate's pulling an all nighter tonight, so I don't mind."

"I'm positive. You can come in the morning or to the house tomorrow."

Casey's body went taut at the prospect of Aidan's house. "We'll see."

When Casey turned to go, she swung her massive purse around, nailing Aidan in the balls. With a groan, he doubled over, puffing out a few breaths and then sucking them in. Once he recovered, he jerked his head up. His blue eyes narrowed into slits of fury.

Casey gave him a sweet smile. "Oh, I'm so sorry. My bad."

Aidan muttered under his breath, but he didn't challenge Casey. "Come on," Connor said, taking Aidan's arm. Once Aidan and Connor had gone out the door, Emma called, "Case?"

Glancing over her shoulder, Casey said, "Yeah?"

Emma gave her a tight smile. "Be nice to him, please?"

Casey sniffed a frustrated breath. "How can you ask that of me? You know how I feel about that…douchenozzle!"

"I know, but there's more to what happened than you understand. So give him a little bit of a break."

Whirling around, Casey threw up her hands. "Dammit, Em, why do you have to be so nice and forgiving?"

"I didn't say I was forgiving him. I just understand more now." At Casey's continued doubtful expression, Emma said, "Just trust me on this one."

"Fine, I'll be civil, but I can't be nice."

"Does civil mean you won't nail him in the balls again?"

Casey gave an evil grin. "It means I'll try."

"Try hard, okay?"

She nodded.

"Thank you."

Casey blew her a kiss before heading out the door. Throwing her head back against the pillows, Emma blew out a puff of air. Her hand went to her abdomen as she continued gazing up at the ceiling tiles. "Please God, please watch over Noah and don't let anything bad happen to him. Nothing else in the world matters as much as delivering him healthy into this world at the right time." Closing her eyes, Aidan's face flashed before her, sending her eyes popping back open. "And if Aidan is truly the one, soften my heart to him...or give me a sign I should move on."

Her prayers were interrupted by a nurse and an orderly. "Time to move you upstairs."

The orderly brought the wheelchair over, and Emma swung her legs out of the bed. After she sat down, she smoothed the hospital gown down over her legs. They took a quick trip up the elevator to the 3rd floor. She couldn't help but wonder which floor Patrick was on. She made a note of her room number, so she could text it to Casey...and to Aidan.

A sweet-faced middle aged nurse came in just as she was getting settled in the bed. "I'm Connie, and if you need anything, you just let me know."

Emma smiled. "Thank you. I appreciate that."

Once Connie and the orderly left, Emma turned on the TV to try to get her mind off of things. She was enjoying some old reruns of *I Love Lucy* when a gentle rapt came at the door.

"Yes?" she called, her brows furrowing at who would possibly be knocking.

It cracked open before Pesh stuck his head in. "Hey there."

Emma inwardly groaned. He was the last person on earth she expected to see. Shooting up in the bed, she smoothed her ruffled bed hair and hoped she didn't have leftover raccoon eyes from crying. "H-Hi."

Wagging his finger, he made a tsking noise as he stepped into the room. "Just couldn't let Mr. Fitzgerald be outdone, huh?"

Emma laughed. "No, I don't suppose so."

Motioning to the chair next to the bed, Pesh asked, "May I?"

"Sure."

His jovial expression suddenly grew serious. "You can't imagine how horrified I was to see your name come across the computer screen." He shook his head. "So I was right in thinking you needed to take better care of yourself?"

"Unfortunately yes. But it's not only today though." Emma glanced down at the standard order hospital blanket. "The last three weeks have taken their toll, I suppose."

"Does it have anything to do with your relationship with Mr. Fitzgerald's son?"

Emma jerked her gaze from the blanket over to Pesh. "W-Wait, how did you…"

He gave her an understanding smile. "It's a long story."

"So is mine," she replied, with a mirthless laugh. At the tension in the air, Emma desperately sought to change the subject. "I thought you had gone home for the day. When I was brought in, I was hoping you would be my doctor. Dr. Pendleton's bedside manner is quite lacking."

"I apologize for that."

"It's not your fault he's so gruff."

"No, but it's my fault that you had to see him."

"What?"

A sheepish grin curved on his lips. "You were assigned to my caseload, but I asked him to see you instead."

Emma gasped. "But why?"

[112]

Ducking his head, Pesh replied, "Because I knew I wanted to see you personally in the future, and that would be too uncomfortable for both of us if I had to…" He drew in a sharp breath as pink tinged his tan cheeks. "Well, if I had to examine you physically."

Understanding crashed over Emma as she thought of how thoroughly Dr. Pendleton had examined her. "Oh," she murmured.

He leaned forward in his chair, his dark eyes taking on a pleading glint. "I don't want you to think I'm a creep or something for wanting to get to know you better. It was Mr. Fitzgerald who first broached the subject."

Emma widened her eyes in horror. "He actually did that? I'm going to give him a piece of my mind when we're both better!" When his shoulders sagged in defeat, Emma felt terrible that he appeared insulted by her words. "Oh Pesh, I'm so sorry. It's not that I wouldn't want to go out with you."

His dark eyes lit up with hope. "Really?"

"Yes. I just can't believe that Patrick would do such a thing."

"Because of what was once between you and his son?"

"Yes that and the fact he was laid up in the emergency room. It's not the most opportune time to be playing matchmaker."

"I guess I planted the seed when I called you beautiful."

Emma's cheeks warmed at his compliment. "Thank you."

Staring down at his hands, Pesh said, "I want you to know that taking your phone number from Mr. Fitzgerald, saying that a total stranger is beautiful—that's not who I am. I'm sure none of my colleagues would believe I had done such a thing."

"Really?"

Pesh nodded. "The truth is I haven't reacted to a woman like I did with you in a long, long time."

"Oh?"

He peeked up at her through his long, dark lashes. Sorrow radiated in his eyes. "Eighteen months ago I lost my wife to an aneurysm."

Emma gasped. "I'm so sorry."

"You can't imagine what a helpless feeling it is to be a physician, and you can't save the woman you love most in the world."

"How old was she?" Emma tentatively asked.

"Only thirty-five."

"That's so young."

Pesh nodded. "Jade was adopted when she was just three. Her adoptive parents didn't know anything about her medical history. From what I've been able to gather, it could have been preventable had we known the signs and symptoms of what to look for."

At his anguished expression, Emma reached out for his hand. With a grateful smile, he slipped it into hers. "I know what it's like to lose the love of your life."

Pesh's dark brows arched in surprise. "You do?"

She nodded. "Five years ago my fiancée was killed in a car accident."

"I'm so sorry." An awkward silence filled the room. Finally, Pesh gave a short shake of his head. "Hmm, between your lost fiancée, your breakup, and me being a widower, I suppose we would make a tragic pair, wouldn't we?"

"People do move on," she said softly. But when she uttered the words, she was thinking more of Aidan than of Travis. Was Pesh the sign she had prayed about? Or had everything that had been thrown at her in the last three weeks just confused her too much?

"In the eighteen months since I lost Jade, I could never imagine ever wanting to date another woman again." He smiled at her. "Until today."

"But why me?"

"Why not?"

"You do realize I'm six months pregnant right?"

"I'll tell you the same thing I did Mr. Fitzgerald's son when he mentioned it."

Emma's cheeks burned at the mention of Aidan. She didn't even want to begin to imagine what the conversation had been like between Patrick, Aidan, and Pesh. Her mortification was interrupted by Pesh squeezing her hand. "The fact you're pregnant has no bearing on how beautiful you are outwardly or the kindness that radiates from within you."

Unblinking and not breathing, she stared at him in disbelief. How was it possible that a handsome, successful, compassionate man was interested in dating her when she was six months pregnant with another man's child? "Pesh, I'm very grateful for your flattering compliments, but my life is so very complicated at the moment."

"And I'm not helping matters with my amorous declarations, am I?"

She gave him a sad smile. "You've been through so much that you deserve true happiness. I have to be totally honest when I say I just don't know if I have anything to give you at the moment."

Pesh tilted his head to one side in thought. "What if we just tried getting to know one another as friends and see where it goes? I know you're not going to be able to get out and about much in the next few weeks, so I could come and do house calls. You know, check your vitals." He momentarily grimaced. "That sounds completely stalkerish, doesn't it?"

"No, I—"

"It's been so long since I was in the dating game. I'm sure I'm saying and doing everything that is a major turn-off."

Emma gazed at his drop dead gorgeous face and wondered how he could ever turn any woman off. "I would love to have you come and check on me."

His eyebrows shot up in surprise. "Really?"

She nodded. "I'm sure after a few days stuck inside, I'd love the company as well as the medical expertise."

A pleased smile cut across Pesh's face. "I would like that very much."

"Me too."

The pager on Pesh's belt went off. "Guess that means I better head out." He rose up from the chair. "So I look forward to seeing you sometime this week."

"But how will you—"

Pesh held his hand up. "Mr. Fitzgerald has already taken care of that."

Emma rolled her eyes but smiled in spite of herself. "Why am I not surprised?"

He laughed. He once again took her hand in his and then brought it to his lips. "You better promise to take very good care of yourself."

Finding it hard to breathe, she could only murmur, "I will."

He then turned and went to the door. Just before he slipped out of it, he gave her one last wave. Once she heard the door click shut, her head fell back against the pillows. Shaking her head, she couldn't believe the insanity of the day's events. If anyone had told her the day before a gorgeous man would be asking to go on a date with her, she would have told them they were out of their mind. The same could be said for everything that had transpired at dinner with Aidan from his admission about Amy to his desire for her forgiveness.

Exhausted from the day's events, she closed her eyes and tried to block out all of her out-of-control thoughts and fears.

CHAPTER SEVEN

Around three in the morning, Emma's full bladder woke her up. As she swung her legs out of the bed, she froze. Warmth spread through her chest at the sight of Aidan fast asleep in the chair. Sometime during the night he had come back so she wouldn't have to stay by herself. Her heartbeat accelerated at how much he truly cared for her. Any thoughts of Pesh vanished from her mind as she sat on the bedside staring at Aidan.

His neck hung forward at a precarious angle, and she knew he would have a terrible crick in it. She stood up on her wobbly legs and leaned over him. "Aidan," she murmured, bringing her hand to his cheek.

"Hmm?"

"Wake-up."

His eyes snapped open, and he sprung up so fast he almost lunged into her. "What's wrong? Are you okay?"

She smiled. "I'm fine. I just needed to go to the bathroom, and you were about to break your neck sleeping that way."

Wincing, he rolled his shoulders. "You should get a nurse to do a bed pan and stay off your feet."

She snorted. "I'm not that helpless, thank you very much."

Amusement twinkled in his eyes. "Want me to carry you?"

"Absolutely not! The last thing I need is my soon-to-be caregiver to get a hernia from trying to lift me."

"Em, you would not give me a hernia," he replied.

"Whatever," she murmured before padding into the bathroom. After she finished and washed her hands, she came out to find Aidan already asleep again and snoring slightly.

Shaking her head, she slipped back into bed. She felt like she had barely closed her eyes when she felt someone's breath warming her cheek. "Em, wake-up sweetheart."

Fluttering her eye-lids, she saw Aidan hovering over her. "What time is it?"

"Six. I wanted to let you know I was going upstairs to be with Pop before his surgery."

"Okay. Tell him I love him, and I'm praying for him."

"I will." He hesitated a moment before leaning over to kiss the crown of her head. "I hate to leave you."

"No, you need to be with your dad."

"I'll be back just as soon as I can."

Emma nodded. When he turned for the door, she said, "Aidan, wait."

He whirled around with his eyebrows cocked, waiting for her response. "I just wanted to say thank you for staying with me last night. It really means a lot that you didn't leave me alone."

He smiled. "Although you don't need to say thanks, you're more than welcome."

When he closed the door behind him, Emma laid her head back against the pillows. In no time she was asleep again until the morning breakfast trays came rumbling around on their carts. Along with the morning meal came another nurse to check her vital signs. Emma was forcing down some of the hospital's rubbery bacon and overcooked eggs when her hospital room door swung open. "Morning sunshine!" Casey said, sweeping inside.

"Good morning."

"I brought you something comfortable to go home in…well, I guess I should have said something to go to the douchenozzle's place."

Emma rolled her eyes. "How did it go last night?"

"Fine. I managed not to maim him or draw blood."

[122]

"I'm glad to hear you didn't cause anymore physical harm. Did you spare him emotionally as well?"

Casey grunted as she plopped down in the chair. "I probably said five words to him tops." Gazing around the room, she asked, "Speaking of, where is the douchecanoe this morning?"

Emma grunted in frustration before replying, "He's with his sisters waiting to see how Patrick's surgery goes."

"Ah, I see."

She had just opened her mouth to tell Casey about Aidan staying the night when Pesh entered the room. "Morning. I just wanted to check in to see how you were feeling before I started my shift."

Emma bit down on her lip to keep from laughing at Casey's expression. Open-mouthed and wide-eyed, Casey drank in Pesh's appearance from his head down to his toes. When he glanced at her, he thrust out his hand. "I'm Dr. Alpesh Nadeen."

"C-Casey Turner," she replied.

"She's my best friend," Emma informed him as Casey kept staring.

"It's very nice to meet you." Side-stepping Casey, he came to Emma's side. "I'm hoping you won't think it was completely inappropriate, but I snuck a little peek at your chart this morning."

"You're a total stalker," she teased.

Pesh grinned, causing dimples to appear in his cheeks. "Well, with that said, everything looks good. I think once you take it easy these next fourteen days, you'll be fine for the rest of your pregnancy."

"I hope so."

"Have faith. It's all going to be just fine." Once again his pager interrupted them. He glanced down at it and scowled. "Guess I better get downstairs."

"Thank you so much for coming by."

He nodded. "I'll talk to you tomorrow, and we'll iron out our dinner plans."

"Dinner?"

He cocked his dark eyebrows at her. "You didn't think I would just come check your vitals and run out the door, now did you?"

Emma felt her cheeks warming at the insinuation. "Well no, but—"

He held up a hand and smiled. "We'll talk about it later." He turned to Casey. "Nice meeting you."

"Yes, nice meeting you too," she replied, her gaze honing in on his ass as he walked out the door. Once they were alone, she whirled back to Emma. "Holy shit, Em! You have precisely five seconds to fill me in on who the hell Dr. McDreamy Bollywood is!"

Emma laughed and then she proceeded to tell Casey everything. Once she was finished, Casey shook her head slowly back and forth. "Wow...I mean...just *wow*."

With a dreamy sigh, Emma said, "Tell me about it."

"So are you going to give him a chance?"

Emma shrugged. "Maybe."

"I think a man like that warrants a little more than a 'maybe'." Casey gazed longingly at the door Pesh had only moments ago exited. "I mean, incredibly good looks aside, the man is compassionate and caring...and completely the opposite of the commitment-phobic dirt-bag."

"I'm already too stressed, Case. I can't throw in a potential new man to the mix right now." When Casey started to protest, Emma shook her head. "Besides, I'm still not sure I'm ready to move on from Aidan."

[125]

Casey rolled her eyes. "Seriously? You're going to let your feelings for the douchenozzle screw up a potentially amazing soul-mate?"

"Aidan is the father of my child. I'll always love him for that fact alone, but there's still so much between us." At Casey's tight-lipped expression, Emma said, "There's no easy black and white here, Case. It's all grey. Besides what I still feel about him, his actions in the last twenty-four hours are very endearing. He's risking his job to take care of me. He came back last night so I wouldn't be alone. He's begging and pleading for my forgiveness. I can't just ignore that."

Casey's shoulders drooped in defeat. "I just don't want to see you get hurt."

"I know you don't. And trust me, neither do I. But I have to at least let him try and see this thing through, or I'll always regret it."

Casey started to protest but was interrupted by Emma's phone buzzing. She glanced down at it. "Aidan's on his way up."

Casey wrinkled her nose. "I better get a move on, or I'll be late to work."

"Hold down the fort for me while I'm gone."

She grinned. "Will do. You just make sure to take extra good care of yourself and Mr. Noah, so you can get back as soon as you can."

Emma smiled. "I sure will try."

Casey leaned over and gave Emma a quick hug and a kiss. "I'll be over to see you soon."

"Good."

As Casey started out the door, Aidan breezed in. He flinched and pushed himself as far away from her and her pocketbook as he could. "Easy Big Papa, your boys are safe this morning."

He sighed in relief. "I'm glad to hear it. They're still a bit traumatized from last night."

Throwing a glance over her shoulder, Casey winked at Emma. "Bye."

Emma waved before turning her attention to Aidan. "How's Patrick?"

"Good," Aidan replied.

Emma sighed in relief. "Thank God."

"You'll be happy to know the first thing he did when he got back to his room was ask about you."

[127]

Tears welled in Emma's eyes. "Really?"

Aidan nodded. "He said to give you and Noah his love, and he would be over to see you just as soon as he got sprung out."

Emma laughed and wiped her eyes. "That's so sweet."

"Yes, sweetness runs in the Fitzgerald DNA, especially with the males," Aidan mused.

She shot him an exasperated look. "Isn't it a little early for you to be this cocky?"

Aidan chuckled as a nurse came into the room with Emma's discharge papers. Once she had signed everything, Aidan said, "Guess that means we get to hit the road, huh?"

Emma nodded and started to get out of the bed. "As soon as I change clothes and run a brush through my hair."

Aidan's brows furrowed. "Don't stand too long while you're changing. Sit on the edge of the tub or the toilet seat."

Emma huffed out an exasperated breath. "Are you going to be this overprotective when we get to your house?"

He bobbed his head. "Yep, at least until I know you and Noah are out of the woods."

Her frustration evaporated a little at his sincerity. "Okay, okay, I'll sit down while I get dressed."

After she padded into the bathroom, she happily tore off the hospital gown and then threw on the yoga pants and long sleeve shirt Casey had brought. She then slid her somewhat swollen feet into the size bigger tennis shoes she recently had to purchase. She pulled her long hair back into a ponytail.

When she was done, she came out to find a nurse waiting with a wheelchair. She eased down in it while Aidan grabbed the bag Casey had brought along with her purse. The nurse then wheeled her down the hallway to the elevator. "Make sure you read your discharge papers about what to do and not to do. It also indicates when you need to go back to see your doctor."

Before Emma could respond, Aidan replied, "I'll make sure she does."

The nurse gave Aidan a big smile. "I bet you're going to take very good care of her."

"Yes, ma'am. I'll be giving her lots of TLC."

When Emma cocked her head at him, he winked. Once they got to the lobby downstairs, the nurse said, "We'll wait here while your husband goes and gets the car."

Emma made a slight strangled noise while Aidan skidded to a stop. "Um, okay," she finally squeaked.

Aidan cut his eyes over to her before jogging out to the parking lot. It didn't take him long to return with the car. "Good luck," the nurse said before she closed the car door.

"Thanks," Emma replied. She quickly buckled her seat belt and turned to Aidan. "Okay then."

As they pulled out of the parking lot, Aidan said, "There's someone else who is very anxious to see you."

"Oh?"

He took his gaze off the road and grinned at her. "Beau."

Emma laughed. "I hope you brought him home last night."

"I thought his home was your house?"

"His original home."

"Ah, then yes, I did. Of course, he kept circling through the rooms looking for you."

"Poor baby."

"I'm sure he'll be more than ready to share your bed and your leftovers when you get there."

She grinned. "I hate sleeping alone, so I'll be thrilled to have him as my bed buddy again."

Aidan opened his mouth to say something but then closed it.

"What?" she asked.

"Nothing."

Since she sensed his comment dealt with offering his services as her bed buddy, she decided to drop it. When they turned on Aidan's street, Emma's chest clenched as she was enveloped by a mixture of both happy and painful memories. As he pulled into the driveway, she couldn't help but flashback to the night she had found both his car and another's.

When he killed the engine, he glanced over at her. "Why don't you sit tight while I go unlock the door, so you don't have to wait?"

She shot him a look. "Aidan, I think I can stand for two seconds while you open the door."

"Fine," he grumbled.

She couldn't believe how extreme he was taking her bed rest. One minute it was infuriating and the next it was endearing. She just hoped her hormones would allow her to appreciate him rather than verbally berate him.

The next thing she knew Aidan had moved like lightning from the car and through the garage, so by the time her slow-moving form reached the door, he had it unlocked and opened. "Nice footwork, Speedy," she remarked.

"You're welcome."

Beau came yipping into the kitchen. "Hey boy, did you miss me?" He whined and then nudged her belly. "Aw, we're both okay. I just have to take it easy," she informed him.

"Speaking of taking it easy, let's get you on to bed."

"You're so bossy," she replied as she padded down the hallway.

When she entered Aidan's bedroom, she gasped. The quilt Grammy had made her when she was a little girl was draped over the bed while the antique silver framed pictures of her parents sat on the nightstand. Her glider and ottoman rested to the right side of the bed. She turned back to him, unable to hide her surprise. "Did Casey suggest this?"

"No," he murmured.

Her heartbeat broke into a wild sprint. "You mean, you did this? For me?"

"Yeah, I did." Aidan rubbed his neck furiously when she continued staring at him. "Casey got your essentials and all, but I thought you needed some things to make you feel more at home here. Even if you say you aren't staying long."

She couldn't breathe, let alone speak. Oh God, why did he have to be so amazing? Every time he did something caring and compassionate, it almost broke her heart, instead of warming it. It was like throwing it in her face once again that besides the one glaring mistake he had made, at his very core, he was a good man— one who deserved to earn her forgiveness.

Emma took a few tentative steps over to him. Standing before him, she stared into his questioning blue eyes. She leaned in and gave him a hug. "Thank you, Aidan. This means so much to me."

He quickly wrapped his arms around her. She closed her eyes and let the feeling of comfort and even love wash over her. His warm breath tickled the skin on her earlobe. "I'm glad you like it. I want to do anything and everything I can to make you happy."

"Well, this was a wonderfully amazing start."

"You're welcome." She could hear the pleasure vibrating in his voice. "So do you want to rest for awhile? Or I could fix you an early lunch."

"Actually, I'd kill for a shower. I feel pretty disgusting."

Aidan nodded. "I picked up the seat from the medical supply store. Let me go get it ready for you."

"Great, I'm going to feel eighty years old," she grumbled, trailing behind him into the bathroom. She skidded to a stop at the sight of her favorite robe hung over the door and all her toiletries and makeup laid out on the counter.

Aidan put the toilet lid down and motioned for her to sit. "You don't need to be on your feet, remember?"

With a sigh, she obliged him and sat down. It didn't take Aidan long to get the seat set up. After he turned on the water and adjusted the temperature, he glanced over his shoulder at her. "Okay then. You're all set."

"Thank you."

When Emma didn't move, Aidan's brows creased in worry. "You need some help?"

The very thought of him seeing her naked again sent a stinging rush of warmth across her cheeks. She shook her head back and forth furiously. "I can handle it."

"Fine," he replied. When the door closed behind Aidan, Emma's fingers went to the hem of her shirt and then froze. Her gaze honed in on the shower seat. A flashback of the later days of her mother's cancer battle assaulted her. Her mother's ravaged form trying desperately to get in and out of the shower flashed in her mind, and she shuddered.

That vision coupled with everything she had been through in the last twenty-four hours sent her emotions careening out of control. Most of all, fear still hung heavy around her. It was like a silent specter in the room, mocking her that her perfect dream of having a child would actually come true. Just the thought of losing Noah sent a chilling shiver reverberating through her.

Burying her head in her hands, she wept unabashedly. Even though she knew she shouldn't, she let the sobs roll through her. At the bathroom door cracking open, she froze.

"Em, are you all right?"

"I'm fine," she replied forcefully, but her wavering voice betrayed her.

Aidan stepped inside. She tried to hide the trembling of her body as he tentatively walked across the tiled floor. Peeking up at him through her fingers, she took in his worried expression at the sight of her still sitting on the toilet. "Why aren't you showering?"

"I, uh…"

Kneeling down in front of her, he took her chin in his fingers, raising her head to meet his gaze. "Em, you've got to stop crying. It isn't good for you or Noah."

"I'm sorry," she whispered hoarsely.

He brought his other hand up to cup her face. "You don't need to apologize. You're here with me now, and everything is going to be okay."

Furiously she shook her head. "But don't you see? Everything is *not* okay!"

"I know, but—"

"It's easy to stand there and tell me not to get upset, but you have no idea what I'm going through at the moment!" she shrieked.

He cast his blue eyes downward. "I realize that, Em."

She swiped her cheeks with the backs of her hand. "Every minute, every second, I can't help thinking of it all falling apart. I'm so scared something bad is going to happen to Noah. I've lost everyone I've ever loved. I can't lose him, too." Her chest heaved as another racking sob rolled through her.

Without hesitation, Aidan drew her into his strong embrace. She should have shrugged him away. Being close to him when she was so emotionally broken was playing with fire. But she was so very tired of being alone all the time and having to bear every burden on her own. Aidan had enough strength for the both of them, and just being held in his arms sent comfort pulsing through her.

Grabbing him around the back, she fisted his shirt in her hands, hanging on for dear life. Aidan's lips warmed against her ear, causing her to shiver. "Shh, please, sweetheart. Don't cry," he crooned in her ear. "I'm here for you, and we're going to get through this together."

His words reassured her, and for both him and for Noah, she tried composing herself. When her cries begin to quiet, Aidan pulled away and stared intently at her. His blue eyes blazed with intensity. "Listen to me. You have every right to be scared, but I want you to believe me when I say that Noah is going to be *fine*. He's blessed with some strong as hell genes." Placing his hand on her belly, he smiled. "He's part Fitzgerald, and for generations, the men of my family have been known for being tough, scrappy fighters with a will of iron to survive."

"Really?" she questioned with a hiccup.

Aidan nodded. "But even more than the fighting Irish Fitzgerald blood pumping through him, he's inherited the most amazing DNA from his mother. She's the strongest person I've ever known."

His words, coupled with the sincerity in which he spoke them, caused a burning wildfire in her chest. "Oh Aidan," she murmured.

He brushed her hair out of her face. "You just have to keep being strong, Em. That fire that burns so deep within you—the one that's seen you through the darkest times—you've got to stoke it to burn a little brighter."

"I'll try."

"Good. I'm glad to hear it." He rose up off the floor. "Now come on. All the hot water is going to be gone before you get cleaned up."

When he tore his shirt over his head, she widened her eyes. "What are you doing?"

"Taking my shirt off. I don't wanna get drenched helping you take a shower."

Her head shook wildly from side to side. "I don't need your help."

"You're exhausted, Em. Just let me help you, okay?"

"I don't think that's a good idea."

"And why not?"

Heat flooded her cheeks. "Because you'll see me…"

A playful grin curved on his lips. "Have you forgotten that I'm well acquainted with every beautiful inch of your body?"

She stared down at her hands in her lap. "No, but it was different then. *We* were different then."

The feel of his intense stare made her finally look up. "And it's different now because I'm not going to devour you when I see you naked. I'm going to take care of you. There are more levels of intimacy than just sex, Emma."

"I know," she whispered.

"So let me help you."

She exhaled a defeated breath and nodded. "Will you turn the chair around, so I'm not facing you?"

An amused glint twinkled in his eyes. "Yes, Miss Modest, I can."

"For your information, there's more of me than the last time you saw me," she argued as he adjusted the seat.

He turned around and shrugged. "I doubt that. Besides, you're still just as beautiful as the first time I saw you."

"Always the flirt, aren't you?" she replied with a grin.

[139]

"Just stating facts, ma'am." Aidan's hands then reached for the hem of her shirt. Instead of protesting, she let him pull it over her head. His gaze hovered over her cleavage a little longer than it should have before he tossed her shirt onto the wicker hamper. "Stand up," he instructed.

"You're so bossy."

"And you're so damn stubborn," he countered as he pulled her pants down.

Left in only her underwear, she shivered. As if to even the playing field, Aidan's fingers went to his fly and took his pants off as well. His eyes met hers as she brought her arms around her back and unfastened her bra. After it slid to the floor, she wrapped her arms around her breasts.

"Oh Em, seriously? Quit acting like I'm some pervert getting off at this."

That little flicker of hellfire sparked within her at his exasperation. Her hands then went to the waistband of her underwear, and she ripped the panties down her thighs as best she could with her belly getting in the way. Meeting his surprised gaze she strode over to the shower and sat down on the chair. "I'd like my vanilla body wash please and the pink sponge. Thank you."

His chuckle echoed off the bathroom walls. Sticking his hand in the shower, he gave her the body wash. "I already put your shampoo in there." He closed the shower door behind him. Emma didn't dare glance back to see if he'd dropped his boxers or not. "Want me to wash your hair?"

"You seriously want to do that?"

"Of course. Besides it's not like you're going to let me wash the good parts anyway."

A giggle escaped her lips. "I thought you were going to behave," she protested.

"I am. That's why I want to keep my hands busy with your hair."

"Fine then."

Taking the shower nozzle, he brought it to her head, soaking her hair. Once it was fully wet, he squirted the peach smelling shampoo in one hand and then worked up a lather.

She couldn't help moaning as his fingers massaged her scalp. "Oh God, that feels so good."

"I'm glad you like it. If I end up getting fired for taking this time off, maybe I have a future in cosmetology."

[141]

Emma laughed. "I can't quite see you doing hair for a living."

"Me either."

"You know, you washing my hair like this reminds me of *Out of Africa* when Robert Redford washes Meryl Streep's hair," Emma remarked.

"My mom loved that movie."

"Really?"

Aidan laughed as he started rinsing her hair. "Yeah, she loved anything with Robert Redford. She used to say he reminded her of a blonde haired version of Pop."

"Oh my God, now that I think of it, Patrick does look a little like Robert Redford!"

"I can't believe he hasn't already mentioned it to you. It used to give him a big head."

"Hmm, an inflated ego? Sounds like a Fitzgerald family trait."

"Ha, ha," he replied. When Aidan's fingers ran over the ridge of her scar, she tensed. "Em, what's this?"

The sponge she had been bathing with fell from her hands and onto the tile floor. "It's nothing. Just an old war wound."

"It doesn't feel like nothing." Aidan's hand left her head and came to rest on her shoulder. "Tell me."

She hugged her arms around her chest. "It's a reminder of a very painful time in my life when I did something very stupid." When Aidan's hand remained frozen on her shoulder, she sighed. "After my mother died, I was so alone. My grief for Travis was still very fresh. There was no husband, no father, no mother...I couldn't see through the dark clouds that I still had Grammy and Granddaddy."

A tremble ran through her body as she let the skeletons of her past dance precariously around her. "One night when I was in the mountains, I got up in the middle of the night and got into the car. I started flying over those curvy roads, hoping another car would come along, and I could end it all."

"Oh God," Aidan muttered, his hands squeezed her shoulders tight.

She glanced back at him. "I slammed into a tree instead. And even though it totaled the car and gave me that horrific scar, I walked away."

"Was that the only time you tried to…" She could tell he couldn't bear to say the words.

Emma gave a quick nod. "After that night, I knew it was meant for me to stay alive—to try to live a happy life for my parents and for Travis. I found a really good therapist, and she, along with my family and my faith, helped me through it."

"Thank you for sharing that with me." He leaned over and planted a kiss on the crown of her wet head. "You're the most amazing woman I've ever met."

"I don't know about that."

"You really are."

"What I did was really stupid and selfish and —"

Aidan shook his head. "I'm not going to judge you, Em. I've never had to go through the hell that you have. I'm just glad you're here."

"Thank you."

He turned off the water. Glancing back at her, he asked, "All clean?"

She laughed. "Yes, all clean."

He opened the shower door and went over to get her a towel and her robe. She was glad to see he still had on his underwear. Although with it soaked through, she had a very fine view of the imprint of his ass.

Rolling her eyes at her out-of-control hormones, she turned her gaze back to the tile. When he handed her the towel, she started drying off her arms and legs. He pulled her hair up and wrapped another towel around her head.

"Are you getting hungry?"

"Umm, hmm," she murmured as she slid into her robe.

"What sounds good?"

She arched her brows in surprise. "You'll fix anything I want?"

"Yep. Or go out and pick it up."

"How about some of your shrimp scampi?"

Aidan nodded. "While you're drying your hair, I'll fix it and bring it to you."

"Are you going to bring it on a silver tray with a rose bud in a crystal vase?" she asked, with a grin.

"Always that mouth," he muttered as he headed out of the bathroom.

Emma giggled as she got out her hair dryer. She eased down on the toilet seat before Aidan could order her to do it. Once her hair was dry, she slid into a pair of pajamas and got into the bed. Beau happily climbed up beside her.

She eyed a stack of books on the nightstand before reading through the titles. They were predominantly nonfiction, self-help books. She picked up one of her favorites, *Tuesdays with Morrie*, and began rereading.

Aidan appeared a little while later with a tray with two plates and two drinks but sans the crystal vase and rose. She sniffed appreciatively. "Oh God, that smells so good!"

"Thank you."

She eased up in bed and took the tray. As Aidan grabbed his plate, she motioned to the nightstand. "What's up with the reading material?" she asked.

Pink tinged his cheeks. "Oh, um, well, those were recommended by my therapist."

Emma choked on the bite of scampi she had taken. Once she recovered, she asked, "You're in therapy?"

[146]

He nodded, turning his head from her intense gaze as he sat down in the glider. "How long have you been seeing a therapist?"

Staring at his plate, he nudged a piece of shrimp around with his fork. "Do you even have to ask?"

"Yes," she whispered.

He snapped his gaze up to meet hers. "I made an appointment the morning after I epically screwed up my life and yours."

"I see."

"I really like Dr. Leighton. She's really helping me work on a lot of things."

"How often do you go?"

"Three times a week."

Emma gulped. "That often." Even when she was dealing with her immense grief, she only went twice a week.

He gave her a sheepish grin. "I asked for the most intense program because I wanted to fix myself as fast as I could…for you and for Noah."

She couldn't still the rapid beating of her heart. He wanted to be a better man for her—to right all the wrongs he had done, and most of all be everything she wanted and needed him to be. Part of her wanted to reach over and hug him tight—to tell him that her heart still belonged to him and always would. But she couldn't. She was too gun-shy.

"Wanna watch a movie?" he suddenly asked. When she gave him a skeptical look, he grinned. "Your pick, I promise."

Her mind whirled with the possibilities. *"The Sound of Music."*

Aidan winced. "Christ, do we really have to watch a musical?"

"You said my pick!" she countered.

"Fine, fine," he muttered, digging into the mammoth box of DVD's he had brought from her house. Once he found it, he popped it into the player and then grabbed his plate. He eased in the bed beside her rather than back in the glider.

"How's the scampi?"

"Mmm, delicious." She grinned at him. "I sure hope you made more."

He chuckled. "In your condition, I figured it was best to double the recipe."

"Oh my hero," she replied.

[148]

"Let me guess. Your hero is going to be marching his happy ass back to the kitchen in a minute to get you another plate."

She batted her eyelashes at him. "Yes, but I'll be sweet and at least wait until you finish eating first."

"Angel of mercy," he muttered through a mouthful of scampi.

Giggling, she flipped on the TV. As the opening credits began and Julie Andrews started twirling and singing on the mountaintop, Emma snuggled the blanket closer to her and sighed with contentment.

"You really dig this shit, don't you?" Aidan asked.

She glanced over at him. "What if I were to tell you I played Maria my senior year in high school?"

Aidan swallowed hard. "You mean you wore a nun's costume?"

"Of course I did."

He licked his lips. "Damn, that's hot."

She rolled her eyes. "You're impossible."

Aidan chuckled. "Sorry babe, but every man has his fantasies."

"You fantasize about me in a nun's costume?"

"Actually you in anything…or nothing," he replied with a wink.

"Whatever," she mumbled as she fixated her gaze on the screen and not him.

After another plateful of scampi, her eyes grew heavy. When she glanced over at Aidan, his eyes were glassy, but she wasn't sure if it was from exhaustion or being forced to watch a musical. She nodded off just before the Von Trapp's escaped into Switzerland.

When she woke up, it was dark outside. Glancing over her shoulder, Aidan wasn't beside her anymore. The sound of the shower running alerted her where he had gone. Peeking at the clock on the nightstand, it was just after six.

Yawning, she stretched her arms over her head before pushing herself into a sitting position. Shifting her body made her bladder scream for release. Nibbling her lip, she gazed at the closed bathroom door. There were two options: bust in on Aidan's shower or be a coward and go down the hall to the half-bath in the foyer.

She shook her head at the thought of walking so far. With a heavy sigh, she hoisted herself out of bed. Beau slid off beside her. "Hang tight, boy. I'm not going far."

He ignored her and continued by her side as she padded into the bathroom. Steam enveloped her and momentarily clouded her vision. Just as she started for the toilet, Aidan shut off the water and stepped out of the shower in all his naked glory. Her eyes met his shocked baby blues before her gazed dropped below his waist. Her pregnancy hormones kicked into overdrive at the sight, and she licked her lips.

"Are you done ogling my package?" he asked, amusement vibrating in his voice.

She reluctantly jerked her gaze up to his. "Wait, what?" she asked. Then mortification rocketed through her, and she quickly ducked her head. "I'm sorry. I needed to pee." She sidestepped his dripping wet, naked form and headed for the toilet.

Aidan laughed at her embarrassment. He grabbed a towel, but instead of wrapping it around him, he took his time drying off his arms and chest. Emma ignored him and focused on relieving her bladder. Once she was done, she went to the sink to wash her hands. She rolled her eyes when Aidan still hadn't covered up.

"What sounds good for dinner?" he asked.

Keeping her gaze on the vanity, she said, "Anything. I'm starving."

"Seriously?"

She laughed. "You better get used to feeding my out of control appetite."

"I can try," he mused as he finally wrapped a towel around his waist. "How does pizza sound?"

"Mmm, heavenly."

"Then I'll order in some pizzas."

She giggled. "Yes, you better make them large. Ooh, and get some Cinnamon Bread too!"

"Okay then, I will."

"Can we watch more movies?"

Aidan shuddered. "More chick flicks?"

Emma poked out her bottom lip. "Pwease?"

He rolled his eyes. "I guess so."

"Aw, thank you, thank you, thank you!" she cried, throwing her arms around his neck.

With her mouth inches from his, she quickly turned her head and kissed his cheek. He stared intently at her for a moment. "All right. Enough of that. Get back into bed and off your feet."

"Yes Drill Sergeant," she sighed.

As she started out of the bathroom, he popped her ass playfully. When she glanced at him over her shoulder, he shook his head. "Always you and that mouth!"

CHAPTER EIGHT

Emma woke up a little before one, and after using the bathroom, she slipped back into bed. Aidan was dead to the world, snoring softly. She had just covered back up when her phone buzzed on the nightstand. She leaned over and picked it up.

It was a text from Casey. *Checking in on you, Em. Hope you're resting & feeling all right. Call me in the am.*

Emma smiled at Casey's concern. *I'm fine. Thanks for asking. Btw, what are you doing up so late?*

I might ask you the same question.

Had to pee.

Ah, gotcha. I'm waiting for Nate to get home and bang me!!!

Rolling her eyes, Emma typed *Poor guy. No rest for the weary with your libido around!*

Lol. True. Speaking of resting, where's the assclown?

Emma giggled as her fingers flew over the keys. *He's asleep beside me.*

WHAT THE FUCK? ARE YOU INSANE?!!!

Yeesh with the shouting! It's not like we were doing anything. We fell asleep watching movies.

I sure hope you punished him with some epic chick flicks.

She glanced over at Aidan's passed out form and almost felt sorry for what she had inflicted on him. Almost. *Lol, let's just say I gave him a trifecta of estrogen with <u>The Sound of Music</u>, <u>Steel Magnolias</u>, and <u>Fried Green Tomatoes</u>. I think he actually cried in Steel Magnolias...but I think it was more about him being stuck watching them instead of football.*

He didn't have to stay and watch them, Em. He wanted to be with you...the fuckwit.

Emma couldn't help grinning at the screen. *It doesn't matter if he wanted to be with me. I'm still not sure I need to be with him.* Regret filled her the moment she finished typing. She wasn't sure that statement was entirely true.

Hmm, does your change of heart have anything to do with Dr. McDreamy Bollywood?

Nibbling her bottom lip, Emma hesitated before typing, *Maybe...maybe not.*

When's the hot date?

It's not a date. He's just coming over to check my vital signs.

[155]

He's bringing dinner, Em. It's a date.

Whatever.

Emma could imagine Casey rolling her eyes and huffing with frustration as she typed. *Look, just don't count Dr. McDreamy Bollywood out just because Aidan's grown a vag and become all caring and considerate.*

Aidan has not grown a vagina!

It wouldn't hurt him if he did. Maybe he'd think with his dick a little less!

Case….

Fine, fine, I'll quit running down the douchenozzle.

Thank you

Actually, I think you need to test out my theory about Aidan's considerate vag.

What?!!

You need to send him to get you something to eat. Aren't you craving something?

Emma pursed her lips in thought. She craved both bacon and ice cream constantly, even at breakfast she could eat the two together. *I could go for a double Baconator from Wendy's and a Frosty.*

Ha! Good one. They're open til two. Send him out. ASAP

Case, he's dead to the world.

Oh for fuck's sake! Wake him up and let him show off his shiny new vag!

Emma huffed out a frustrated breath. *Fine. Ttyl*

Night! Don't think I won't check back in to see if you really did it.

You're evil

But you love me!

Yes, I do.

Love you too.

After she tossed her phone back onto the nightstand, she glanced over at Aidan. He was in his favorite non-sexual position—on his stomach with his arms wrapped tight around the pillow cushioning his head. With his face turned towards her, he looked so peaceful. She felt terrible waking him up—even if she really was hungry and not just trying to prove something to Casey.

With a sigh, she poked his back. "Aidan?" He stirred a little. "Wake up."

"Em?" he questioned drowsily.

"Yeah, um, I hate to bother you, but I kinda have a craving."

With his eyes still shut, he yawned. "Want me to get you something from the kitchen?"

She nibbled her bottom lip. "Actually, I wanted something from Wendy's."

His eyelids flew open. "Seriously?"

She nodded.

"What time is it?"

"One."

"You want me to go out and get you something to eat now?" he asked incredulously.

"Please?"

He stared at her for a moment, unblinking and unmoving. She could only imagine the thoughts racing through his mind. Just when she thought he might tell her to go back to sleep, he rose up into a sitting position and rubbed his eyes. "What do you want?"

"A double Baconator, fries, and a chocolate frosty."

"Christ, at this time of night?"

"I could eat bacon and ice cream all day."

"Remind me to buy some at the store tomorrow," he said as he got out of bed.

"So you're really going?"

He waved his pants at her. "Of course I am."

"Guess you have grown a vag," she murmured.

Pausing with one leg in his pants, Aidan said, "Excuse me?"

"Oh, nothing."

Once he zipped up his fly, he leaned over the bed towards her. From the light trickling in from the bathroom, she could see the amusement on his face. "I could have sworn you just said I had grown a vag."

"No, I said that you really had grown a lot. You know emotionally," she lied.

"Uh-huh."

Before he could pull away, she leaned up and kissed his cheek. "Be careful and thank you."

He grinned. "I will." When he got to the bedroom door, he turned back. "Just make sure Casey knows that I wear my alleged vagina with pride, not because she took my manhood with that purse of hers, but because I want to be a better man for you."

Emma widened her eyes. "How did you—"

He chuckled. "When I started gathering all the personal stuff to bring here, Casey accused me of growing a vagina. I figured there was no one else you would be texting at one in the morning besides her."

Shaking her head, Emma said, "Whatever. Just go get my food please."

"Me and my vagina will be back in twenty minutes. Tops."

And with a wink, he was gone.

CHAPTER NINE

Emma woke the next morning to the shrill ringing of her cell phone in her ear. Squinting at the clock with one eye, she groaned. It was barely seven in the morning, and she knew only one person would be calling her that early.

Fumbling for her phone, she grabbed it and pressed the button. "Good morning, Grammy," she murmured drowsily.

"Hey sweetheart. How are you feeling?"

"Sleepy."

Grammy laughed. "I'm sorry to wake you, but you know that Granddaddy and I think sleeping past five is too late."

"That's a travesty when you guys could sleep in."

"Listen honey, I wondered if Aidan could come up here today? I took some things out of the freezer that I thought you would like, and I'm about to start fixin' some casseroles for him to heat back up later on."

"Grammy, you should be taking care of yourself and Granddaddy, not me!" Emma protested.

"Oh, what's a few casseroles? Most of it I'd already cooked and put away. Besides, I can't rest if I think you and the baby aren't getting good, healthy food."

"Aidan's actually a really good cook, Grammy."

She harrumphed into the phone. "Not like me."

Emma laughed. "That's true."

"So you think he'll be up here after while?"

Glancing over her shoulder, Emma was surprised to find Aidan still in the bed beside her. "I'll ask him when he wakes up."

He popped one eye open. "I'm awake," he muttered.

"Does that mean you're going up to Grammy's to get us some food?"

"She's cooking?"

Emma nodded.

He grinned. "Hell yes. I'll get my clothes on right now."

With a laugh, Emma replied, "He'll be up there around noon." At Grammy's sigh, Emma said, "He needs to fix us breakfast first and get a shower."

"All right then. I love you, baby girl."

[162]

"I love you, too."

Once Emma hung up the phone, she cradled it to her chest. She wanted more than anything to feel Grammy's arms around her. No matter what was going on in her life, somehow just being in Grammy's embrace made everything all right.

"You miss her, don't you?"

She tore her gaze over to Aidan and then nodded. "Will you give her a great big hug and kiss for me when you get up there?" she asked.

Aidan laughed. "I don't think Virginia would let me past the front door without hugging and kissing me."

Emma giggled. "That's true. But give her one anyway, okay?"

"I will. And then I'll be sure to come back home and give you her love too."

"Thank you."

Collapsing back against the pillows, Aidan groaned. "Jesus, my first real day I can sleep in from work, and I'm awake at seven-thirty."

"You don't have to get up now. We can try to go back to sleep."

"Sure you're not hungry?"

Emma wrinkled her nose. "No, I still get a little nauseated in the morning."

"Will you set the alarm for ten?"

She cocked her eyebrows. "You're really planning on snoozing late, huh?"

"Mmm, hmm," he murmured.

When she pushed back under the covers, Aidan scooted over in the bed. His arm snaked around her waist as he spooned against her. Nuzzling his face into her neck, he said, "Warm me up."

Her breath hitched as she glanced over her shoulder at him. "Are you really that cold?"

He popped one eye open and gave her a sly grin. "Maybe."

"Uh-huh, well, just watch it, mister."

They had just settled back down when Noah struck up a kicking frenzy. "Oomph," Emma said, shifting to the right.

"Seriously, Em, I'm not trying to cop a feel!"

She giggled. "I know you're not." She took his hand and brought it to the place on her stomach where Noah's foot was thumping.

Aidan sucked in a breath. When she glanced back at him, he wore an expression of pure wonderment. He met her gaze and smiled. "Is he always so active in the mornings?"

"Sometimes. Usually, he really gets going after I eat."

"Ah, like he's on a sugar rush or something?"

"I guess so."

Even after Noah settled down, Aidan kept his hand firmly against her belly. Although Emma should have protested, she didn't. It felt too good with his arm around her. And within a few moments, she fell into a contented sleep.

***

After the alarm went off at ten, Aidan hopped out of bed. As Emma rose up, she figured he was headed for the shower, but instead, he reached for his phone.

"What are you doing?"

"Calling Becky."

"Why?"

"Besides going to Grammy's, I need to go to the grocery store and run a few errands. It might turn out longer than I expect, and I don't want to leave you alone that long."

She rolled her eyes at him. "I think I can make it from the bed to the bathroom just fine, thank you."

He shook his head as he stepped out of the bedroom. "Hey sis, can you do me a favor?" she heard him ask. He wasn't gone long before he came back inside. "Becky's coming over."

"Fabulous," she muttered.

Aidan's brows furrowed in confusion. "I thought you liked her?"

"I do. In fact, I love her like my own sister. It's just I feel so overprotected at the moment—like I'm in a fishbowl."

"I'm sorry, but I can't help worrying about you, Em."

Her chest clenched at the earnest expression on her face. She didn't know why she had to fight him so much. She should just stop and enjoy the fact he was being so attentive and caring. So instead of arguing, she threw up her hands in defeat. "All right, all right. Becky can come baby-sit me."

He grinned. "Good considering you didn't have a choice."

"Aidan," she warned.

He leaned over to kiss her cheek. After he pulled away, his lips hovered close to hers. When she looked into his eyes, she saw the longing burning bright. Part of her wanted to reach out and kiss him, but the other part knew what an explosive land mine that was. Putting her hand on his chest, she gently pushed him back. "You better go get a shower. Grammy will be standing on her head and blazing the phone lines if you're not there right at twelve."

Hurt momentarily flashed in his eyes before he bobbed his head. "Okay then."

Emma's heart clenched as she watched him march defeated into the bathroom.

CHAPTER TEN

Aidan made the trek out of the city up to the mountains. It was just after noon when he pulled to a stop in front of Earl and Virginia's house. He drew in a breath of trepidation as he started up the front walk. He had just started up the porch steps when Virginia threw open the front door. "Well hello there handsome! Good to see you again."

Relief flooded him that at least one of Emma's grandparents didn't hold a grudge. Of course of the two, he had worried the least about Grammy. The worst she could do was frail him with a frying pan—Earl was the one of the knives and shotguns.

He smiled. "Hello Virginia. It's good to see too."

Just like he expected, she wrapped her arms around him and squeezed him tight. "How's my sweet girl holding up?"

"Right now she's mad as hell that you're cooking for her and not taking it easy," he replied as he pulled away.

Virginia cocked her silver head at him, and he grunted. "Even though she wants me to tell you she's fine, I can't lie."

"I figured as much."

"Physically, she's doing fine, but it's the emotions that are killing her...and me." Shoving his hands in his pockets, Aidan rocked back on his heels. "I wish I knew what to say or do to make her feel better. I hate to see her cry, and it kills me to see her scared like she has been."

Virginia rubbed his arm. "Aw, honey, I'm sure you're doing a fine job taking care of her. Being pregnant is hard enough without throwing in pre-labor and bed-rest into the mix."

"What does it matter how well I'm taking care of her when it's my fault she's where she is?"

"Now you can't think like that."

"It's the truth, isn't it?"

Virginia shook her head. "I'm not here to judge you or chastise you about what happened, Aidan. That's between you, the good Lord, and Emma. And if I know my baby girl like I do, the greatest stress on her came with what happened to your daddy. Riding in that ambulance, hearing those sirens, I know it brought back everything that happened with Emma's daddy." She cupped Aidan's chin. "So don't run yourself down so much, okay? If you're in the pits, no one is going to be there to bring Emma up."

A hesitant smile played at his lips. "I guess so."

"Well, I know so." She waved him towards the house. "Come on in and let's get the food. I don't want to keep you away from Emma too long."

"Not that she would care," he muttered under his breath.

Virginia cast a knowing glance over her shoulder at him. "She cares a lot more than you think she does."

That sentiment made Aidan's heartbeat accelerate and gave him a little more hope. As he stepped into the living room, he locked eyes with Earl who was lounging in the recliner. He gulped and steadied himself in anticipation for a showdown. "Hello, Earl."

"Howdy Aidan," Earl said, muting the television.

"How are you feeling?"

Earl shrugged. "I'm getting around a little better."

Virginia huffed out a frustrated breath. "He's trying to do too much, and he's going to land himself back in the hospital."

He shot her an exasperated look. "I hate sitting on my ass all day and being waited on hand and foot," Earl lamented.

"You sound like Emma," Aidan mused.

"Bless Emmie Lou's heart," Earl said.

As Virginia swept by Earl, she kissed his cheek. "Trust me, darlin', no one wants you up and about more than I do."

Earl grinned up at her. "You're an angel, Ginny."

An almost girlish giggle escaped her lips before she turned to Aidan. "Sugar, you just have a seat, and I'll go pack up everything."

Aidan glanced uneasily between her and Earl. "Are you sure I can't help you?"

She shook her head. "Nope. I need to take out one last casserole from the oven."

After she headed into the kitchen, Aidan reluctantly eased down onto the couch. He swallowed hard when he eyed the gun cabinet only a few feet away.

The sound of Earl's voice caused him to jump. "What's wrong with you?"

"N-Nothing." When Earl's brows shot up questioningly, Aidan sighed. "I was actually contemplating how much of a jumpstart I could get on you if you went for the gun case."

Amusement twinkled in Earl's eyes. "Son, I'm not going to shoot you for what you did to Emmie Lou."

"You aren't?"

[171]

He shook his head. "First off, I want my great-grandson to have a daddy, and if you were maimed or six feet under, that wouldn't do him much good."

Aidan gave a shaky chuckle. "No, I suppose not."

Earl glanced past Aidan to the kitchen before turning his attention back to him. "Second off, I'm a lot of things, but a hypocrite ain't one of them."

"Excuse me?"

With a deep sigh, Earl said, "Let's just say when I was young and stupid, I made a mistake much like you did."

Aidan couldn't keep his mouth from dropping open in shock. "So you, um…"

Earl rolled his eyes. "How plain you want me to make it for you? I was a cocky twenty-five year old bastard who just because Ginny couldn't give me all her attention anymore because of our two sons, I let some cheap floozie almost ruin my marriage."

"Yeah, that's pretty plain."

"Thankfully for me, Virginia gave me a second chance, and I've spent the last fifty years making it up to her."

Leaning forward, Aidan asked, "How long did it take her to forgive you?"

[172]

"A long, long time."

Aidan exhaled in frustration. "I just hope Em will be that forgiving."

"Depends on how much work and effort you put into it."

"Seriously? I swear that I'm working my ass off."

Earl harrumphed. "Trust me, until you've dug ditches in ninety degree heat to earn the money to buy your wife the pearls she's always wanted, you ain't got no room to talk."

With a wince, Aidan said, "I guess not."

Virginia's voice echoed from the kitchen. "Okay, honey, it's ready."

When Aidan stood up, Earl held up his hand. "Listen, son, you just gotta keep tryin'. Emmie Lou comes from a long line of stubborn, hard-headed women. But I do know that she's crazy bout' you, so if you really want her, then you just keep on tryin' to win her back."

Earl's comforting words sent a smile stretching across Aidan's face. "I sure as hell will."

***

Once he got back into Atlanta, Aidan made a grocery stop and finished up a few errands before heading home. When he swung the car in the driveway, his heart shuddered to a stop. Becky's car was gone. His mind whirled with out-of-control thoughts. What if Emma had started having contractions again, and Becky had rushed her to the hospital? Tumbling out of the car, he didn't bother closing the door. Instead, he rushed through the garage door and skidded into the kitchen. "EMMA!" he cried.

The sound of gunfire and explosions assaulted his ears. Craning his neck, he saw John and Percy sitting on the couch each with a game console in their hands. "Where's Emma? Where's your mother?" he demanded without even a hello.

John glanced up and rolled his eyes before looking back down at his game. "Dude, hold your ball-sack. Mom got called to some emergency department meeting at the university, so we're babysitting Emma until she gets back. Georgie's back in the bedroom with her now watching *Finding Nemo* or some shit."

Aidan's relieved emotions were too jumbled to call John out for his mouth. "Oh, well, good." He jerked his thumb towards the garage. "Can you guys come and help me get in all the groceries and stuff from Em's Grammy's?"

"Seriously?" John asked.

Aidan grunted. "Yeah, I'm serious. Call it payback for mooching off my pool all summer."

"I thought you let us use your pool because we're your favorite nephews?" Percy questioned, rising obediently off the couch.

Aidan chuckled and ruffled his hair. "I guess that's true." When John still hadn't budged, Aidan reached over and took his game away.

"Hey!" John started to protest.

"Move your ass and you might live to play it again."

Huffing, John got off the couch and stalked through the kitchen. Aidan and Percy followed behind him. Aidan popped the trunk and leaned in to start handing some of the bags to the boys.

"Uncle Aidan?" Percy began.

"Yeah?"

"Don't you think you ought to marry Emma?"

Aidan jerked his head up, slamming it against the trunk lid. "FUCK!" he shouted as he saw stars before his eyes. A few more expletives escaped his lips as pain raged through his skull.

"Nice mouth you got there," John chided.

[175]

Gritting his teeth, Aidan rubbed his aching head. "You mention that one to your mom, and I'll tell her about your ball-sack comment."

John's eyes widened. "Dude, that is *so* not cool!"

"Yeah, well, deal with it." Aidan started to resume gathering up the bags when he noticed Percy staring expectantly at him for an answer. Aidan sighed. "Perce—"

His blonde brows knitted together. "Don't you love her?"

"Oh Christ," Aidan muttered, raking his hand through his hair. He winced as pain once again shot through his head. "Did your mom put you up to this or something?"

"No. When I asked her the same question, she just said that you were a cad." Percy shrugged. "I don't even know what that means."

"I'm pretty sure it's a dude who acts like a douchebag to women," John said.

Aidan glared over at John. "I am not a cad!"

John held his hands up. "I didn't say it. Mom did."

Leave it to his sister the English professor to resort to name calling him something from the nineteenth century. He handed

Percy one of the box's from Earl and Virginia's. "Perce, it's complicated because—""

"You're a cad?" John asked.

Ignoring him, Aidan said, "I was stupid and did something that hurt Emma's feelings pretty bad. It's going to take her some time to forgive me and let me back into her heart."

Percy shifted the box he was carrying to one hip. "You're having a baby with Emma, so the responsible thing to do would be to marry her," he said sensibly.

Aidan blinked a few times at Percy. "Did I hit my head harder than I thought, or did you actually just sound like a mature adult, rather than a kid?"

Percy shrugged. "Maybe. Dad always says I'm an old soul."

Aidan laughed. "I think he called that one right." He glanced over to John who wore an amused smirk. "Of course, anything you say has to sound light years above this one," he said, jerking his thumb at John.

"Whatever," he grumbled.

Aidan picked up a light bag and handed it to John. "What's this?" he asked, peering inside.

Aidan quickly snatched it back. "Erm, that's for Emma."

[177]

"Doesn't quite look like her size," he mused with a wicked gleam in his eyes.

"That's because it's for Noah, smart ass." He motioned to the trunk. "Go on and bring those in. I'm going to go check on Emma."

John grabbed a few more bags while Aidan and Percy started in the house. He left the boys in the kitchen and started down the hallway. The sound of Emma's laugher warmed his heart. Then in a sing-song voice, he heard Georgie call, "Noah…Noah! Kick for me Noah!"

Standing in the bedroom doorway, Aidan surveyed the scene with a smile. Emma held a flashlight to her baby bump. Hovering close to her, Georgie stared expectantly at Emma's stomach as if waiting for something earth shattering to happen.

Emma glanced up to see him and smiled. "Hey. You're back."

"Grammy sends her love and the promise she'll be down within the week."

Emma huffed out a frustrated breath. "And Granddaddy?" she asked tentatively.

"Is still in a lot of pain, but he's doing pretty well. And he managed not to verbally or physically assault me."

[178]

Emma's brows raised in surprised. "That's good news."

He motioned at her and Georgie. "What are you guys doing?"

"Trying the flashlight trick," Georgie replied, not taking his eyes off Emma's belly.

"Flashlight trick?" he repeated, as he walked over to them.

Emma nodded. "Since a baby's eyes start to open in the sixth month, supposedly pressing a flashlight to your belly will make him move." She smiled down at Georgie. "He's never felt a baby kick, so he wanted to feel Noah."

Aidan chuckled. "Any luck?"

Georgie's lips turned down. "Nope."

"He's showing his true Fitzgerald stubbornness by not cooperating," Emma said.

"Hey now, I think he's equally inherited some of that from you too," Aidan argued.

"Kick Noah!" Georgie ordered.

Aidan laughed at his determination. "Did you ever think that maybe you're making him mad or something? How would you like someone sticking a flashlight on you and shining it in your eyes?"

Grabbing Georgie by the ankles, he slid him down the bed. "Let's see how you like it, huh?"

Georgie giggled when Aidan snatched his shirt up and pressed the flashlight to his stomach. "Stop it, Uncle Aidan!" he said, when he could catch his breath.

"Did your baby start kicking?" Aidan asked.

Georgie pushed his shirt down. "I don't have a baby in my belly, silly!"

"You don't?"

"No, only mommie's have babies in their bellies."

"Oh, I see." He tickled his fingers up Georgie's sides, causing him to laugh and squirm again.

"Quick Georgie!" Emma cried.

Aidan grabbed Georgie's waist and hoisted him back up to Emma. She took his hand and brought it to her belly. His eyes widened. "Uncle Aidan, Noah's kicking me!"

Emma grinned. "He must like the sound of your laugh because that's what got him going, not the flashlight."

Georgie dropped his hand to lean over and kiss the spot where he had been feeling. "I love you, Noah!"

[180]

Aidan smiled when tears sparkled in Emma's emerald eyes. He was getting used to her hormonal waterworks at the drop of a hat.

Georgie, however, peered up at her in surprise. "Why are you crying, Aunt Emma?"

"Because you're such a sweet boy," she replied, drawing him into her arms. She kissed the crown of Georgie's head as she hugged him. It didn't escape by Aidan how Georgie had called Emma 'aunt', and she hadn't protested.

"I gotta go pee-pee," Georgie said, squirming away from Emma and hopping off the bed.

As he swept by Aidan, Emma's gaze honed in on the bag at his side. "What's that?"

"Oh, um…" He rubbed his jaw and shifted on his feet. He didn't know why he was nervous about giving her the gift. It was just a stupid onesie. "It's something for Noah."

Emma's green eyes instantly lit up. "Really?"

"It's nothing much. I just saw it in the store and thought of him…and you."

With a grin like a kid on Christmas morning, she snatched the bag from his hands. Her fingers dug inside to pull out the onesie.

[181]

She unfolded it and peered at the writing. "I'm cute, Mommy's cute, and Daddy's..." She tore her gaze up to meet his.

"Daddy's lucky," he finished for her.

"Oh Aidan," she murmured. Tears once again welled in her eyes, but a pleased smile curved on her full lips as she ran her fingers over the onesie. She tilted her head up at him. "Thank you. This is too adorable and sweet. And I love that the first article of clothing anyone has gotten for him is from his father."

"Besides his christening gown," Aidan reminded her.

"Oh, you're right. But still."

"If I knew you were going to get that sentimental about it, I would have bought him something nicer," he mused.

"It's not just the onesie, Aidan. It's what it says," she said softly. Her eyes met his, and his heart leapt at the love he could see burning in hers. If he could only bottle moments like these, he could then give them back to her whenever she tried to doubt her love for him.

"Aunt Emma?" Georgie asked, squirming back up on the bed.

"What honey?"

"I was just wonderin' how did Noah get in your belly?"

[182]

"Um, well…"

"Mommy says he's Uncle Aidan's baby, so did he put it there?"

Emma's eyes bulged as she stared up at Aidan. "Uh, well…"

John and Percy then appeared in the doorway. "You know, I'm a little fuzzy on that one too, so maybe you can explain it to us all," John said, with an amused smirk.

Aidan turned to scowl at John. "Georgie," he began, "where babies come from is really something you need to ask your mom and dad about."

Georgie's blonde brows furrowed. "Why? Is it a secret?"

"No, it's just, um, well…" Aidan rubbed the back of his neck while trying to come up with an answer. Finally, he remembered what his own mother had told him when he was just a kid and his sister Angie was pregnant. "It's like this. When a man and woman love each other very much, the love grows inside the woman and makes a baby."

Rubbing his chin, John asked, "So I guess that means you love Emma, huh?"

Aidan shot him a death glare before turning his gaze back to Georgie. Wonderment flickered on his face at the explanation.

"That's so cool that I grew as my Mommy and Daddy's love," he murmured.

When Aidan dared to look at Emma, she stared wide-eyed, open-mouthed back at him. Although he insinuated it every day, he still hadn't managed to actually say the words. Maybe now was the perfect time to say it and seal the deal between them.

"Hey guys, there's some homemade brownies from Emma's Grammy in the kitchen if you want some."

Georgie scrambled off the bed while John and Percy hightailed it down the hall. Once they were alone, he smiled at Emma. "How was my explanation?"

She sucked in a breath. "Good…and sweet. And he totally bought it."

"But did you?"

"What do you mean?" she whispered.

His heartbeat pounded in his ears. This was it. It was now or never. He took a tentative step forward and opened his mouth.

"Aidan Fitzgerald, what are you doing giving my sons chocolate before dinner?" Becky demanded from the doorway with a hand on her hip.

Fuck! His moment had been totally ruined. He whirled around to glare at Becky. She gave him a funny look. "Between John and Percy, I'm not sure if you have any brownies left for Emma."

He raked a hand though his hair and sighed resignedly. "I'm sorry, Sis. They helped me lug in the groceries, so I thought they could use a snack."

She grinned. "I guess you're forgiven then." Becky then turned her attention to Emma. "Everything go okay while I was gone?"

Emma nodded. "They were the best baby-sitters I've had so far."

Becky laughed. "I believe they've been your *only* ones besides my little brother here."

With a teasing smile at Aidan, Emma said, "Oh, he's so much more than just a baby-sitter."

He arched his brows at her. "Oh, really?"

"Mmm, hmm. You're a cook, a house-keeper, and an entertainer."

Aidan shook his head but laughed in spite of himself. "Yes, I am all those things."

"Well, I guess I better round up the boys and head out," Becky said. She came over to the bed and gave Emma a kiss. "Take care of your self, Mama."

"I will…and Aidan will."

At the loving expression on Emma's face, Aidan couldn't help smiling. "Of course I will."

"Work him hard then," Becky said. She gave Aidan a playful nudge before kissing his cheek.

"You can bet she will," he mused.

"Bye then," Becky called with a wave.

Aidan stared at Emma for a moment. Should he go ahead and say it now or wait until a more opportune moment? Emma's phone going off confirmed that he might as well wait.

CHAPTER ELEVEN

The next few days rolled along in a monotonous rhythm. Before long, Emma had completed her first week of bed-rest. She read, she watched TV and movies, and she visited with Casey and Connor as well as Aidan's sisters. True to her word, Grammy came down for a day, and neither Emma nor Aidan could keep her from cooking them a huge meal along with a dessert. Emma especially enjoyed when Patrick came by. She was so glad to see him looking healthy and a complete opposite from when she had seen him last. They were both on the road to recovery, and she was so grateful.

Fortunately, Aidan's leave of absence had turned into more of a work from home situation. Emma liked the fact he was kept busy so he wouldn't be hovering over her 24/7 acting like a deranged mother hen. It wasn't that she didn't enjoy having him around. She loved the fact he was willing to do anything and everything she asked him to. He was good company with the fact he ate all his meals with her and usually fell asleep watching movies, which meant he ended up sleeping by her side.

Every day they seemed to grow closer and closer. But worry gnawed deep in the pit of her stomach. She feared her hormones and the close quarters of her bed-rest situation were making her blind to the truths of Aidan's character. After all, she'd been fooled by him once before. Could she really ever trust him completely again? Could she emotionally withstand building a life with him only for it to all fall apart if he cheated again?

On Monday afternoon, she had just settled in to watch a marathon of one of her favorite old series, *Dr. Quinn Medicine Woman*, when her phone buzzed beside her. At the name on the screen, her heartbeat accelerated so fast it threatened to beat out of her chest.

It was from Pesh. *Would it be presumptuous of me to inquire about checking on you tonight?*

She shook her head as she read and reread his text. Not only did he always sound so different than the men she knew, but he was always so kind and thoughtful. He had already called twice to check on her, but he had yet to broach the subject of coming by.

Sure. That sounds great.

I've even secured a portable ultrasound machine, so we can check on Little Man.

At the mention of Noah, Emma's heart melted. *Aw, thank you so much.*

Is five too early? I have to go in at nine tonight.

That's fine.

Wonderful. Do you like Indian food?

Emma nibbled her bottom lip before responding. *Actually, I've never eaten any.*

Seriously?

Yep.

Wish you could see how far my mouth is hanging open right now.

With a giggle, Emma typed *Sorry. Diehard Southern girl raised in the boonies.*

We'll have to remedy that. I'll bring you several courses from my favorite Indian restaurant.

That sounds wonderful.

Just text me the address, and I'll see you in a little while.

As her fingers punched out the street number of Aidan's house, revulsion flooded through her. Was she seriously about to bring another man into Aidan's house? A man whose very presence had the ability to confuse her about the depth of her feelings for Aidan? "Ugh, you're a hateful, awful person, Emma Harrison!" she moaned, her head falling back against the pillows. Why did everything have to be so complicated?

She knew what Casey would say. It became complicated because Aidan almost banged another woman and broke her heart and her trust. If he hadn't made such a mistake, she wouldn't even be entertaining the idea of Pesh. But at the same time, Aidan had been trying so hard to win her forgiveness, and she couldn't ignore the fact he was her child's father.

"Heartless bitch," she muttered as her internal monologue worked on overdrive of calling herself out.

But in all honesty, it wasn't like she was inviting Pesh over to have sex with him. He was coming in a medical capacity for goodness sake. Just because he happened to be bringing dinner didn't mean it was a date or anything special. She had told him at the hospital that she wasn't sure she had anything to give him, so it wasn't like she was leading him on…or being unfaithful to Aidan.

Now all she had to do was figure out a way to tell Aidan about Pesh coming over. Her stomach churned at the prospect. Fortunately, she didn't have to wait long. He appeared in the doorway only a few moments later as she still sat staring at her phone screen.

"You need anything?"

She forced a smile to her lips. "No, I'm good."

"Listen, I know you hate me hovering and all, so would it be okay if I ran some things down to the office? They don't seem to understand this whole 'leave of absence' thing."

"No, no, that's fine."

"I may run by the gym after that. I shouldn't be gone more than two hours. I can pick us up some dinner on my way in."

"Oh, um, that won't be necessary."

Aidan gave her a funny look. "Won't you be hungry then?"

"Actually, Pesh is coming by for a house call in a little while. He's bringing dinner with him."

Emma sucked in a breath as Aidan's blonde brows disappeared into his hairline. "You're having a date with Pesh tonight?"

"It's not a date!" she protested.

Aidan crossed his arms over his chest and countered, "He's not just stopping by to take your pulse, Em. The fucker is bringing dinner."

She winced. "No, it's not like that. Pesh knows that I'm not looking to start anything right now. He's just checking on me to be nice. You know, friendly and all."

"It sure as hell doesn't sound like that to me."

At his harsh tone, Emma stared down at her quilt. "Look, this is your home and your hospitality I'm imposing on. So if you really feel that strongly about Pesh, I'll tell him not to come."

When she dared to look up again, Aidan's expression momentarily softened. "You mean you would do that? For me?"

"Of course I would. Give me a little credit for considering your feelings."

After jerking a hand through his hair, Aidan gave a frustrated grunt. "And you're sure you're not trying to start something up with him?"

"The last thing I need right now is more stress in my life, and any relationship, especially a new one, is always stressful."

"Even with me?"

She cocked her head at him. "I wasn't the one who caused the stress in our relationship, remember?"

Aidan cringed. "I'm well aware of what I did as it continuously comes back to bite me in the ass. Like with this foreign fucker sniffing around you."

Emma rolled her eyes. "He has a name, and it's Pesh. If you would take the time to get to know him, you would realize he's not the type of man trying to take advantage of me or get in my panties."

"No, it's worse because he isn't," Aidan grumbled.

"What?"

"I'd rather he be some douchenozzle trying to get in your pants because you'd be totally repulsed by that and tell him where to get off—just like you did me at first." Aidan grimaced. "But it's worse because he's some honorable dude who doesn't care that you're pregnant with another man's child. He reeks of commitment for God's sake. Hell, you'll probably be engaged by the time he leaves tonight!"

After taking in Aidan's words, Emma remained speechless. When they had stared each other down for a few agonizing seconds, Aidan sighed. "Fine. Let him come by and check you out."

"He's not checking *me* out. He's checking my vital signs. He even has a portable ultrasound to check on Noah."

"Fabulous," Aidan muttered before starting to the door.

"You're not being fair," she said.

Aidan whirled around, fire burning in his eyes. "Excuse me?"

"Can't you at all empathize with what I'm going through? All this confusion I'm feeling about you and about us and all the uncertainness—you felt this too, didn't you?"

"Are you insinuating that what you're going through right now is the same thing I did about committing to you?"

"No, it's just—"

Aidan held up a hand. "I'd think long and hard about making any comparisons, Em. Because in the long run, my confusion led me to screw up the most wonderful thing I ever had." He shook his head sadly at her. "I wouldn't want you to have to go through the same thing."

Her chest caved in at his words, and she had to suck in a few harsh breaths. Was Aidan right? Was she throwing away happiness with both hands because of her stupid uncertainty?

His voice brought Emma out of her thoughts. "How long should I be gone tonight?"

"Aidan, you don't have to leave. You can stay right here and see that there's nothing going on."

"I may be a masochist but only to a certain extent," he replied bitterly.

Emma sighed. "He's coming at five, and he has to go into work at nine."

Aidan bobbed his head in acknowledgement. "I'll have my phone if you need me."

Without another word, he left her. When the back door slammed shut, she jumped. Beau came into the bedroom and gave her a WTF look. She rolled her eyes. "Yeah, yeah, it's all my fault, right?"

Beau barked and came over to the bed. Emma sat up and leaned over to scratch his ears. "Come on. I need to get ready. We're having company this afternoon."

Beau's ears perked up at the mention of company, but she shook her head at him. "But I'm sure you're not going to like Pesh very much. You'll get all territorial, which means I probably need to put you in the basement."

He whined and backed away, causing Emma to giggle. "Not now, silly. Just before the company gets here."

She then got busy getting ready for Pesh's arrival. After she showered, she put on a small amount of makeup. To prove to herself and to Aidan it wasn't a date, she didn't bother putting on one of her nicer maternity dresses or outfits. She maintained her daily wardrobe of stretch pants and a long-sleeve shirt.

[195]

After banishing Beau to the basement, she was lounging on the couch with a book when Pesh rang the doorbell. "Come in," she called.

Pesh pushed through the door. His gaze scanned the room for her. When his eyes met hers, he gave a beaming smile. "Well hello. Don't you look wonderful?"

Emma glanced down at her clothes and then back up to him. "Seriously?"

He chuckled. "I don't mean your attire. I meant that your color looks very good. Your bed-rest appears to be agreeing with you because you have a healthy glow."

"Oh, well, thank you. That's good to hear."

"You aren't starting to feel a little stir-crazy, are you?"

She grinned. "Maybe a little. I've only been out of the house once to go to the doctor. Nothing exciting."

"Well, speaking of the doctor, let me get my bag and the monitor, and we'll check to see how you're doing."

"That sounds good."

Pesh disappeared out onto the porch for a moment before returning with a black medical bag and a large box with a handle. He sat them down on the side of the couch. He then glanced around the living room, taking in the décor. "You have a very beautiful place."

"Thank you, but I can't take the credit since this isn't my house."

He eased down on the couch beside her. "I should have realized you were staying with someone."

Nibbling her lip, Emma replied, "Actually, this is Aidan's house."

Pesh grimaced. "I'm alone with you at *his* house."

Emma's cheeks warmed. "I'm sorry if it makes you uncomfortable. He's the only one who could take care of me."

"It's fine." He placed his hand on top of hers. "I'll go anywhere if it means getting to spend some time with you."

She met his intense gaze. "Thank you," she murmured. Everything that she had argued with Aidan about being interested in Pesh seemed to fly out the window when she stared into his soulful, brown eyes.

He flipped over her wrist and began taking her pulse. "A little fast, but it seems good," he noted.

Leaning over, he started digging through his medical bag. He stuck the stethoscope buds in his ears and brought the silver disc to her chest. His demeanor was all professional as he instructed, "Breathe normally." As he shifted the disc across her chest, his arm brushed across her breasts, and she stiffened. If Pesh noticed her reaction, he didn't acknowledge it. Instead, his brows furrowed as he listened to her heart and lungs.

Pesh's closeness caused her heartbeat to accelerate. His woodsy smell, the heat from his body, the tousled dark hair she wanted to run her fingers through—it drove her to distraction. Breathing normally like he had requested was completely out of the question. Instead, she managed to draw in several harsh pants. Pesh's dark eyes swept from the stethoscope up to hers. He took the buds out of his ears and smiled knowingly. "Either I'm making you nervous, or you need to get back to the hospital for your erratic breathing and heartbeat."

She felt a warm flush creeping across her cheeks. "No, it's you," she murmured.

He cocked his eyebrows. "So you're saying if Dr. Pendleton were here taking your vitals you wouldn't be reacting this way?"

Laughter sputtered from her lips. "Of course not."

Shifting his body, he leaned in closer to her. His dark eyes penetrated hers. "Why do I make you nervous, Emma?"

Her mouth ran dry, and she licked her lips. "Because…" *You're so damn good-looking, and your fabulous body kicks my pregnancy hormones into overdrive, making me think things about you I normally wouldn't. But more than the lust, you're kind and compassionate, and if given the chance, I could see myself falling for you.*

Emma exhaled the breath she had been holding. "I told Aidan that there was nothing between us, and that you knew I couldn't give you more. But now that you're in front of me, looking at me…" She shuddered. "You confuse me."

"I confuse you?"

Staring down at her hands, she said, "I still care very deeply for Aidan, but when I'm with you, I start to feel…differently."

"I could argue that it's merely biological, and that your body is just seeking out a mate to protect you and your child."

She raised her to head. "If that's the case, then I would only feel for Aidan, right?"

Pesh's expression grew serious. "So I at least have a chance to woo you?"

"To woo me?"

He laughed. "Not a word you would usually use?"

"Not exactly."

He tilted his head in thought. "Hmm, a chance to win you over by romancing you? To wine and dine you?"

Emma smiled and pointed to her belly. "There will be no wining, and with my bed rest, our dining is going to be a little limited."

"Ah, but that's why I brought food to you." He rose off the couch. "Let me go get it, and we'll commence our wooing."

When he winked at her, she laughed. "Okay."

Pesh stopped when he got to the door and turned around. "As long as I have a chance to win your heart, Emma, I'll take whatever you can give me."

Emma tried not to be overwhelmed by his words. All she planned on giving him was her friendship, and that was it—nothing more and nothing less. Regardless of what her traitorous body wanted to feel that was going to be it.

He carried two large food bags when he swept back through the door. "Goodness. I don't eat that much you know!" Emma teased.

Pesh laughed. "I know, but I just wanted you to get a good flavoring for different Indian courses and dishes." He glanced around. "Should I take these to the kitchen?"

"No, just put them here on the table. We'll have a picnic of sorts."

"Sounds good to me." Once he sat the bags down, he turned back to her. Rubbing his hands, he said, "Before we dig in, let's check on Little Man."

Emma laughed at his enthusiasm. "Okay."

"It's hard to believe technology has come so far that we actually have portable ultrasound machines."

"It's crazy."

Pesh set up the device and then turned to lift her top. Emma instinctively reached out to knock his hand away. His eyebrows shot up in surprise. "I'm sorry. I was just—"

"I know. I was being ridiculous."

She then eased her top up over her belly and lamented the fact Pesh had to see her like this. If he managed to see her swollen stomach and didn't appear totally repulsed, maybe he really was worth giving a chance romantically. She quickly shook the thought out of her head when he squirted the cold jelly on her skin.

[201]

He ran the wand over her stomach, and Noah's grainy image appeared on the screen. "There he is. Looking good too, I might add."

Emma focused in on Noah. His arms and legs flailed a bit as the wand seemed to disturb his resting. In fact, he gave two enthusiastic kicks to prove he wanted to be left alone. "His heart rate is normal, and everything looks good with the placenta." Pesh glanced up from the monitor to meet Emma's gaze. "No more contractions or pain?"

"Nope. Everything has been fine."

He smiled. "Such a blessing to hear. I'm sure once you're off bed-rest in the next week, you can look forward to a happy and healthy remainder of your pregnancy."

"That's what I've been hoping and praying for," Emma replied.

Pesh patted her hand reassuringly. "Just believe it." He then put away the wand.

Emma glanced down at her sticky belly. "Do you mind grabbing me a hand towel from the kitchen?"

From his medical bag, he produced a towel. "I always come prepared."

She laughed. "Well, thank you then."

"While you get cleaned up, I'll go get us some plates and silverware."

"Sounds good."

As Emma swiped herself clean of the jelly, she heard Pesh opening and closing cabinets. He had started into the living room when a bang at the basement door caused him to jump and almost drop everything. His wide-eyes met Emma's as scratching and howling persisted at the door. "Is Aidan keeping someone hidden in the basement?"

She giggled. "That would be our…um, well, Aidan's very spoiled dog, Beau."

Pesh nodded as he set down the plates. "Want me to let him out?"

"I guess so. I wasn't quite sure how he might react to you."

"Animals usually love me, so we'll see if I can win him over." When Pesh opened the basement door, Beau came bounding in. He raced over to Emma and licked her hand. "Hey good boy."

Then his ears perked up, and he swung around to take in Pesh. A low growl erupted in his throat. "No, no, Beau. Pesh is our friend," she said, grabbing his collar.

Pesh slowly walked over to the couch. Tentatively, he stuck his hand out for Beau to smell. After Beau took it in, he still stared hard at Pesh. "I would almost think Aidan had warned him about me before he left tonight," he mused.

Emma laughed. "He's usually really good around strangers, but I was afraid this might happen with Aidan gone."

"He's just being a good, territorial dog. Since he doesn't know me, he's protecting you and the baby." Pesh tilted his head to the side. "Hmm, let's see if I can make friends." He dug his hand into one of the bags. "Let's see if a piece of Samosa might seal the deal." He reached out to Beau with the piece of what looked like a tortilla.

Beau glanced back at her. "It's okay. You can have it." Reluctantly, he inched forward and snatched the bread out of Pesh's hand.

"What exactly is that?"

"It's a wrap of potatoes and spices."

"Oh jeez, then he'll be in heaven. He loves potatoes almost as much as his daddy does." When she realized what she had said, she couldn't fight the flush filling her cheeks.

"So while I get things unpacked, do you want to tell me what happened with you and Aidan?"

[204]

Emma grimaced. "Do I have to?"

"Not if it's going to upset you. I would never want to cause you any pain."

She groaned. "No, I guess it's only fair that you know what you're dealing with."

"Or what I'm up against?"

"I guess," she murmured.

"So, you and Aidan were dating, you got pregnant, and he couldn't commit?" Pesh suggested, as his hand delved into one of the bags.

Oh God. How could he be further from the truth? "Not exactly."

Pesh drew his attention away from the containers he was taking out and looked at Emma. "I'm sorry. I shouldn't have asked."

"No, it's just at the hospital when I said it was a long story, I wasn't kidding." After drawing in a deep breath, she proceeded to tell Pesh everything from the start of wanting Connor to father her child to Aidan's betrayal.

When she finally finished, Pesh shook his head. "You're right. That was a really long story." At his teasing, Emma smacked his arm playfully, and he grinned. "Thank you for sharing that with me. I know it couldn't have been easy unburdening yourself of all that pain."

Emma cocked her head at him. "Do you always talk so proper—so worldly?"

"My parents like to say I'm an old soul. I guess that's why I sound the way I do."

"Were you the oldest?"

Pesh nodded. "Yes, you could say I'm the classic oldest child stereotype. My baby brother…well, he's a whole other story for another day."

Emma laughed as Pesh started pouring out some soup into a bowl. She sniffed appreciatively at the bowl. "Hmm, what's this?"

"Rasam or tomato soup."

She took a tentative bite. "That's really good."

"I thought you might like it. It's very healthy too. Good for digestion."

Emma laughed. "The restaurant should hire you to do PR for them."

"You think?"

She nodded. "I should know. I mean, I do work in advertising."

After taking in a few spoonfuls of the soup, she eyed another container Pesh was opening. At her apprehension, he said, "Just take a bite of the Daal Makhani." When she gave Pesh a skeptical look, he laughed. "Trust me. It's good for you. It has a lot of protein and fiber in it."

The moment she thrust the spoonful into her mouth she knew she had made a mistake. "That's hot."

"Seriously?"

She bobbed her head while waving her hand in front of her mouth. "I guess I should have mentioned I'm kinda a wuss when it comes to spicy foods."

"Oh, well, then. Why don't you skip out on that and take the Butter Chicken instead." Pesh put some orange looking chicken on her plate.

"So tell me about your family," Emma said. It was hard to talk considering her tongue was still enflamed.

"Well, my father came to America with his parents when he was just a teenager. He wanted to leave India behind and become Americanized." Pesh shook his head. "He even changed his name to Charlie."

[207]

"Really?"

Pesh grinned. "Yes, no one I know except my mother and my late grandparents called him by his real name."

Emma pushed her fork around the plate, uncertain of what to eat next. "What about your mother?"

"She's the reason why I'm not completely Americanized, or have a name like Bill or something."

Emma giggled. "I can't quite see you as a 'Bill'…William maybe, but definitely not Bill or Billy."

"Me either." Pesh wiped his mouth with his napkin. "She came over to marry my father when she was just eighteen. They had known each other as children, but it was very much an arranged marriage."

"Oh," Emma murmured. She took a tentative bite of the lesser of the spicy evils. "Was your marriage arranged?"

"No. In fact, Jade was the first non-Indian girl I ever dated."

"Was your mom angry?"

He bobbed his head. "At first. But Jade very much wanted to acclimate herself to my life and my customs. Over the years we dated, she slowly grew on my mother." He grinned at Emma. "As for my father, the traitor to his culture, the thoughts of a blonde hair, blue eyed daughter-in-law was a dream come true!"

Emma laughed. "I can only imagine." When she glanced up from her plate, she saw that Pesh's expression had turned serious. "What?"

"I can only imagine he would be thrilled with an auburn haired beauty with sparkling green eyes."

Her fork clattered noisily onto the floor. She and Pesh both leaned over to retrieve it, and they ended up bumping heads. "Oomp," Emma muttered. She brought her hand to her head and rubbed her aching hairline.

"I'm sorry I upset you," Pesh said softly.

"You didn't upset me. It's just that…" She nibbled her lip, unsure of how to proceed. "When you say things like that, I feel like I'm leading you on. I don't want you to get hurt."

"Emma, I am a grown man. I'm fully capable of taking care of myself and my feelings. I'm also well aware of how plain you've made your intentions to me."

She shook her head. "Then why bother wasting your time on me if I'm all closed off?"

"That's the same question one might pose to Aidan. Why should he bother pursing you after what he's done and how you still feel about him?" He gave her a hesitant smile. "Because you're worth fighting for."

"Oh God," she moaned. She covered her face with her hands.

"Did I say something wrong?"

From behind her hands, she replied, "Oh no. That's the problem. You never say the wrong thing. Everything you say and do is absolutely wonderful."

Pesh laughed. "I'm sorry for confusing you, Emma. I really am."

She peeked through her fingers at him. "Really?"

"Well, I could lie and say yes, but the truth is I'm glad I'm slowly breaking down your walls. I want you to be able to see that whenever you're ready and if you really want me, I'll be here."

"You would say something like that," she grumbled.

Standing up, Pesh stretched his arms over his head. "Okay, I think it's time for a conversation change and for me to clean up."

"Oh no, you don't have to do that."

"I wouldn't dream of overstepping your hospitality by leaving a mess."

"There you go with that worldly talk again," she remarked.

He wagged his finger at her. "Okay, so I talk worldly. What's something unique about you?"

"Hmm, well…"

"Oh come on. I know there has to be tons of unique things about you."

"Okay then, I'm a singer."

His dark eyebrows shot up in surprise. "You are?"

She nodded and then told Pesh all about growing up singing at her cousin, Gary's, bar.

"You sang at bar called 'Doc's'?" Pesh asked, the corners of his lips turning up in amusement.

"Yes, I did. That was Gary's nickname."

"Hmm, I like the irony."

When Pesh winked at her, she shook her head. "Okay, so I'm a singer. What's something else unique about you?"

Scratching his chin, Pesh said, "Well, I own and fly my own plane."

Emma widened her eyes. "You do?"

"Yep. Actually, it isn't entirely my own plane. My father and middle brother also have their pilot's licenses."

"Wow, I've never been up in a small plane before."

"Then I'll have to take you some time."

Emma's heartbeat fluttered at the insinuation. As if he read her confused thoughts, Pesh grinned. "Are you sure you're done eating?"

Considering her stomach was already churning from the mixture of spices and dishes, she knew she couldn't eat another bite. "I'm good. Thank you."

"You won't mind if I take the left-overs in for the other doctors and nurses?"

"No, no. Go right ahead."

Pesh grinned. "So I didn't sell you on Indian food, huh?"

Emma laughed. "I think from now on I better stick with one dish instead of sampling them all."

Pesh had just finished cleaning up when his pager went off. "Seriously?" he grumbled.

"What's wrong?"

"They need me in a little early tonight. Full moon has all the crazies coming out I guess."

"Really?"

Pesh glanced up at her and smiled. "Which part? Them needing me to come in or that a full moon really brings out the craziness in people?"

She giggled. "Both I guess."

"Oh yes. Full moon nights in the ER are something out of a horror movie."

"Then I'll keep you in my prayers."

"Please do." He glanced at the bags around him. "I think I'm going to have to make two trips. Be right back." He grabbed the food bags and his medical bag and headed out the door. Beau started to follow after him.

"No boy. Come here."

He immediately came to Emma's side. The look he gave her brought a smile to Emma's lips. "No, I'm not running off with him. Your bed buddy and provider of table scraps is staying put."

Beau wagged his tail at her comment. When Pesh came back in the door, Beau stiffened. Pesh eyed him as he came around the couch for the ultrasound machine. "Hmm, guess that Samosa didn't cement our friendship, huh buddy?"

Beau proceeded to jump on the couch and lay his head down on Emma's lap. Pesh laughed good-naturedly. Wagging a finger at Beau, he said, "You take good care of her and the Little Man, okay?"

Emma smiled. "He will."

"Thanks for letting me come over tonight."

"No, it's me who should be saying thanks for the fact you were willing to check on me and for bringing dinner."

"It was my pleasure, and one I hope to repeat in the future. But I think I'll wait until you're off bed-rest to commence more of my wooing."

"Okay, I guess we can do that."

Pesh stroked his chin in thought. "Do you like the opera?"

"Oh, yes, I adore it. I'm a big fan of the cultural arts."

After digging his wallet out of his pocket, Pesh produced several tickets. "These are for next week's performance of *Aida*. You should be off bed-rest by then. Would you like to go?" At her hesitation, Pesh said, "Just as friends, Emma."

She exhaled in relief. "Thank you. I would enjoy that."

"Then I look forward to seeing you again next week for our non-date to *Aida*."

"Me too."

Pesh grabbed the machine and then leaned over to tenderly kiss Emma's cheek. Beau raised his head and gave a low growl. "Beau!" Emma admonished. He ducked his head and gave her his best sad hound dog face.

"I guess that's my cue to be going."

"I'm sorry about him."

Pesh shook his head. "Don't be sorry about anything, Emma. For Beau, for not enjoying dinner…" His face hovered inches above hers. "Most of all, don't be sorry for what I might've made you feel tonight."

She stared up at him, unblinking and unmoving. "I won't."

"Good." He then stood up, and with a final wave, he walked out the door.

Once they were alone, Beau whined and snuggled up to her. "Oh give me a break, would you? It's not easy being a big, pregnant ball of hormones!" She then fell back against the pillows and turned on the TV.

CHAPTER TWELVE

At a little after nine, Beau raised his head and woofed happily. "Hmm, I guess that means Daddy is home?"

Beau wagged his tail as he raced to the kitchen. The beep of the house alarm alerted her of Aidan coming in the back door. "Hiya, boy. You hold down the fort for me while I was gone?"

Aidan came into the living room with Beau still yipping at his side. "I sure hope he didn't do anything embarrassing like pee on you to mark his territory while your date was here."

"No, he didn't," Emma snapped.

"Speaking of, how was your date?" Aidan asked, tossing his keys on the table.

"It wasn't a date," she muttered.

"Excuse me, Miss Testy." He inhaled sharply. "Ugh, what stinks in here?"

"Pesh brought Indian food for me to try." Emma's stomach rolled at the thought of ever eating again, least of all anything with spices. "Where have you been?" she asked, trying to change the subject.

"I had me a hot date."

Emma jerked her head up to stare at him. She couldn't stop her eyes from widening in shock or her mouth dropping open. He had been with another woman? After everything he had said to her before he left? Her nausea revved into overdrive at the prospect, and she fought the rising bile in her throat. "Y-You did?"

He nodded and plopped down on the coffee table. His knees knocked into hers, and she fought the urge to pull away from the closeness of him. He leaned in on his elbows. "Picture this outfit. Cut-off, Daisy Duke's with the ass cheeks hanging out—"

"Short shorts? It's late October!"

Aidan held up his hands. "I'm not finished."

Crossing her hands over her chest, she huffed out a frustrated grunt. "Fine."

"Anyway, so like I was saying, there were the Daisy Dukes, cowboy boots, and to top it all off there was the halter top with the bare mid-drift…" He closed his eyes and shook his head. "Man, *I* was looking good!"

His eyes snapped open, and then he winked at her. Emma stared at him in disbelief. "There wasn't a girl wearing that…you mean you…"

[218]

Aidan laughed. "I was just teasing you, Em. I went over to Pop's, and we watched the game. I sure as hell wasn't out with a woman."

The prospect of him being on an actual date had worked her into such an emotional firestorm that along with the relief she felt, she also knew she was going to be sick. She had only a moment to panic about whether or not she would make it to the bathroom before she leaned forward and threw up in Aidan's lap.

He gazed from his soiled pants back up to her eyes. "Damn, Em, I know my joke was bad, but did you seriously have to puke on me?"

Tears of mortification stung her eyes. "I-I…I'm sorry."

His expression turned from amusement to compassion when she burst into tears. He reached over and rubbed her arm. "Hey, don't cry. You're not the first person to puke on me. I did belong to a fraternity back in the day. Nothing is worse than drunk guy vomit."

"I can't believe you're being so nice about it," she sobbed.

"Well, it's not like you did it on purpose." He raised his eyebrows at her. "Did you?"

"No! I would never do that!"

He rubbed her cheek with his thumb. "I know. I was only teasing you again, Em."

"I don't think the food agreed with me—too many different spices and sauces," she replied, wiping her nose with the back of her sleeve.

"Hmm, I think that speaks volumes about the company as well, don't you?"

"Aidan," she warned, her embarrassment fading into anger at his assumptions.

He cocked his head at her. "Sounds to me like Noah is trying to tell you something. I'm glad the Little Man already has his dad's back."

She narrowed her eyes at him. "I've never eaten Indian food before. It has nothing to do with my feelings or Noah's. It's my digestive system speaking, thank you very much," she snapped.

Aidan grinned. "Ah, there's those lovely pregnancy mood swings I love so much."

She sniffed in a frustrated breath. "Come on. You need to get cleaned up, and I need to go back to bed."

When Aidan stood up, vomit slid down his pants legs. He made a face. "Jeez, I think that's seriously about to trigger my gag reflex." His hands went to his button, and he unzipped his pants. He quickly stepped out of them and balled them up. "I better throw these in the washer."

Emma leaned forward to get up off the couch just as Aidan turned. Her face grazed across his crotch. At his sharp intake of breath, she jerked back. "Uh-sorry," she mumbled.

"This night just keeps getting better and better," he grumbled. Before he started to the bedroom, he turned back and offered Emma his hand. Her heart kick-started at the small gesture.

"Thanks."

"You're welcome. Listen, I'll grab my stuff and hit the shower upstairs so you can have mine."

Her hormones went into overdrive. "Aw, that's so sweet," she murmured.

Aidan gave her a playful smirk. "Damn, babe, it doesn't take much to impress you, does it?"

She rolled her eyes. "Excuse me for being grateful for your kindness," she huffed before stalking into the bathroom and slamming the door.

Aidan poked his head in just as she swept her top off. She squeaked at the sight of him. "Um, you do remember I need to get my shit from in here, right?"

"Yes, go ahead."

Only in her bra, Emma began brushing her teeth. Once Aidan swept up his shampoo and body wash, he leaned to grab his toothbrush before bestowing a kiss on her bare back. Longing shuddered through her. If Aidan realized her reaction, he didn't say anything. "Now don't stay on your feet too long."

Giving him a salute, she mumbled through a mouthful of toothpaste, "Yes sir."

He shook his head. "Always you and that mouth."

She grinned at him before he headed out the door.

***

When Emma finished showering, Aidan was still upstairs. Exhausted from the emotional rollercoaster ride of the day, she fell immediately into a deep sleep. But it wasn't restful. Dreams plagued her. First, she had one where Aidan and Pesh were fighting over her with a duel to the death like in the olden days. Then she dreamed that when Noah was born, he looked just like Pesh, rather than anything like her or Aidan.

Finally, her mind reeled into another dream—one that was all too surreal since it had once happened.

Cool water lapped against her bare neck and shoulders as she kicked her legs to stay afloat in Grammy and Granddaddy's pond. She could almost touch the bottom if she let the water cascade over her head. As she treaded water, Aidan swam up to her with a predatory gleam in his eyes. A shiver of anticipation ran through her.

"Are you cold?" Aidan asked.

"A little," she murmured.

"Then let me warm you up." He pulled her into his arms and brought his lips against hers. "Mmm, you taste sweet...a little sweeter than usual."

She grinned against his mouth. "I might have made a pit-stop for some cake before I came to your room."

Aidan chuckled. "Midnight craving for food and sex, huh?"

"Yep."

"I think it's time we fulfilled that second craving, don't you?"

"Please."

"Wrap your legs around me, babe."

She did as she was commanded. Aidan grunted as he started walking them through the water to the shore. "Am I too heavy?"

"No, not at all," he murmured through gritted teeth.

She laughed. "Aidan, I can make it myself. You don't have to carry me."

"It's not that you're too heavy. It's just this is harder than I thought it would be in the water."

"Aw, but you're my hero now for sure!" She then brought her lips to his cheek. She kissed a trail down to his jaw before nipping and licking her way over to his lips. She moved her hips against his groin.

"Damn, Em," he murmured gripping his hands tighter against her ass.

"Am I getting you worked up?"

"Oh hell yes."

"Good." She thrust her tongue into his mouth, seeking out his warmth. She let his dance teasingly over hers. Then like a flick of a switch, they turned from teasing each other to ravaging each other's mouths.

Once Aidan stepped out on shore, he held Emma tight as he sank to his knees, causing her to squeal as she was pitched back. "You okay?" he asked. She glanced up at him. The full moon cast a halo around his head, making him appear momentarily angelic.

"I'm fine now." She widened her legs to allow him to ease between them. "Make love to me, Aidan."

He stared intently into her eyes, and she knew the fact she had used the term making love had not been lost on him. "Whatever you want, babe," he replied with his usual cocky smirk.

When he thrust into her, she cried out and gripped his shoulders tight. He moved slowly, tenderly within her. His tongue mirrored the movements of his languorous strokes while his hands cupped one of her breasts, bringing the nipple to a hardened peak.

Just as she was so close to coming, he changed his pace and began rocking harder and harder against her, causing the sand and twigs beneath her to dig into her back. He shook her in his arms. "No, not like that. Be gentle with me, Aidan," she murmured.

Slowly she was sucked out of making love on the shore and back into Aidan's bedroom. Someone was shaking her. No, *Aidan* was shaking her.

"Em, wake up."

Her eyelids fluttered open to stare up at his concerned face. "What happened?"

His hand left her shoulder to cup her cheek. "You were moaning. I think you were having a nightmare or something."

"No, I was about to come," she mumbled drowsily.

"Excuse me?"

Suddenly she was wide awake. Her hands flew to cover her face that burned with mortification. "Oh God."

Aidan chuckled beside her. "Em, you naughty girl. Were you moaning because you were having a sex dream?"

Ignoring him, she rolled over to her side. She fluffed the pillow and flopped back down.

"Wait a minute. When you said, 'Be gentle with me Aidan', that wasn't about me waking you, was it?"

"I'm going back to sleep now."

He nudged her shoulder playfully. "Oh come on, Emma. Admit it. You were dreaming about having sex with me." His voice vibrated with pleasure. "I must've been good if you were about to come."

She snorted exasperatedly. "I'm surprised you're even asking about how good you were. Don't you always think you're amazing?"

His hand snaked around her shoulder, rolling her back over. With one arm on the other side of her head, she was pinned beneath him and forced to face him. "You're the only woman in the world I want to be amazing in bed for or to give mind-blowing, multiple orgasms to." He shook his head. "No one else, I swear."

Staring into his eyes, she brushed the back of her hand over the stubble on his cheek. "You need to shave," she murmured.

Aidan arched his eyebrows. "You don't want me to grow it out? Maybe have a goatee or a beard?"

"No, I like it just the way it is."

"Then I'll shave. For you."

Overwhelmed by her burning feelings for him and still reeling from her sex dream, Emma leaned up and brought her lips to his. Aidan immediately froze, and she felt like she was kissing a marble statue. When her mouth opened to slide her tongue against his lips, he slowly started to thaw. Her hand that had been caressing his cheek slipped into his hair. She ran her fingers through the silky strands, tugging and pulling as she went just like her teeth did to his bottom lip.

Aidan gave a low moan in the back of his throat as he thrust his tongue into her mouth. God, she had missed the feel of his mouth on hers—his tongue dancing tantalizingly along hers. Desire pooled below her waist, and she knew she wanted him more than ever before.

He moved his hand from her shoulder to her breast, kneading and cupping the sensitive flesh through her nightgown. She widened her legs, allowing his hips to dip between them.

But when he started to lift the hem of her nightgown, Emma's eyes flew open as reality, rather than a dream, crashed over her. "Wait, Aidan no!"

He pulled his head from her neck to stare at her with eyes hazy and drunk with desire. "Please tell me this isn't because you don't want to do this, but it's because we've both just realized the doctor said not to?"

She nodded. "I'm not even supposed to have an orgasm because it can cause contractions."

He smirked at her. "Then it was a good thing I woke you from the sex dream, huh?"

Blushing, she gave a half-laugh. "I guess so." As he pulled himself off of her, she said, "I'm sorry."

"Don't be. We both got carried away." He smiled as he snuggled against her. "Besides, it may not be as physically gratifying just to hold you all night, but there's nothing I'd rather do."

Emma groaned. "Why do you have to say things like that?"

"What?"

She lowered her gaze. "You keep saying and doing all these amazing things. It confuses me."

"You want me to be an asshole or something?"

"No, of course not."

"Oh I get it. You want me to be the old, self-centered Aidan, so it's easier for you not to feel what you do."

"I didn't say that."

"But don't you want me to change?"

"I fell in love with the old Aidan, remember?"

He growled in frustration. "But don't you want me to be a better man for you and for Noah?"

"Of course I do."

"Then let me say and do what I want."

"Fine."

They lay in silence a few moments. "You're really never going to forgive me, are you?" Aidan asked.

"Wait, where did that come from?"

He rose up into a sitting position. "Everything I've done for you in the past eight days, everything I've said, all the apologies, trying to make it right…it hasn't meant shit to you, has it?"

"That's not true," Emma argued.

"Obviously it is. If you were totally sold on us getting back together, you wouldn't let Pesh come over, even in a medical capacity. You would have already said you wanted to be with me."

"I said if it bothered you so much, I wouldn't let Pesh come over, and you were more than welcome to have stayed here—it's your house for goodness sake. You could have stayed and seen for yourself that nothing romantic happened between Pesh and me. But you chose to leave."

"So now you're trying to act like I left so that must mean I didn't really care if Pesh tried to make a move?"

"No, that's not it at all."

"Once again, everything is all my fault, right?"

[230]

Emma rubbed her temples. "Can we please not argue about this? I'm tired."

"Yeah, well, so am I." He flung the covers back and stomped from the bed. Emma didn't bother asking where he was going. The pounding of his feet on the stairs told her everything she needed to know.

Using her fists, she ground the tears from her eyes. Dammit, why didn't she know what was the right thing to do? Why couldn't it be clear that she needed to be with Aidan, or she needed to tell him good-bye? Why did she constantly feel like her emotions were yo-yoing back and forth?

At her weeping, Beau appeared and jumped into the bed with her. "Oh Beau," she sobbed, wrapping her arms around him. He lay stock still, letting her get all of her emotions out. Finally, she fell into an exhausted sleep.

CHAPTER THIRTEEN

The atmosphere between Emma and Aidan was strained for the last few days of her bed-rest. Although Aidan brought her everything she needed, catered to her every whim, it wasn't the same as before. He no longer stayed and watched movies with her. And even with Beau beside her, the bed was cold and empty without him at night.

Aidan was forcing her hand. He felt he had done everything humanly possible to make her forgive him, and now he was done going the extra mile. Whatever happened between them was now up to her. And she was completely clueless on how to proceed.

When she went to see her OB, Dr. Middleton, she was satisfied that everything looked great, and Emma could come off bed-rest and return to work the following week. Although she should have been happier, uncertainty still remained heavy. Did she leave that afternoon and go back to her house? Did she stay and try to work things out with Aidan? Or did she prepare to move to Ellijay to be with Grammy and Granddaddy like she had originally planned?

After she and Aidan got into the car, a tense silence hung around them. Finally after what felt like an eternity, Aidan sighed. "Listen, Em, you're probably not going to like what I'm about to say, but I feel like I need to."

"Okay," she replied hesitantly.

"I know you're officially off bed-rest, but I don't think you need to be doing anything really strenuous to start with. So if you're willing, I'd prefer if you kept staying at my house…at least a little while longer."

When she turned to stare at Aidan, she saw his jaw clenching and unclenching. He was trying to keep his emotions in check. She knew that meant he really wanted her to stay. That thought made her heart beat a little faster. "Are you sure you wouldn't mind?"

Aidan tore his glance away from the road to pin her with his stare. "Of course I wouldn't. Stay a couple more days or weeks." Then under his breath he murmured, "Stay forever."

Her breath hitched at his allusion to commitment, but she decided not to press it. "If you're really sure, then I'd love to stay."

She gave him a bright smile, which caused a smirk to curve on his lips. "Good. I'm glad to hear it. Now why don't we celebrate by letting me buy you dinner?"

[233]

"No, no, this one needs to be my treat. You've already done enough."

"Hmm, I don't think I've ever let a woman pay for dinner," Aidan mused.

"Good. You can learn that there's a first time for everything."

Aidan chuckled. "All right, Em. Since dinner is on you, let me find the most expensive place possible!"

***

The following night Emma prepared for her non-date to the opera with Pesh. After putting the final touches on her hair, she stood back from the bathroom mirror and took in her image. With its empire waist and wide spaghetti straps, the violet colored cocktail dress came just below her knees. Her nose wrinkled a little at how her straining pregnancy cleavage wanted to spill out of the top. It seemed like she had gone up a cup size in the last few days. She would be sure when she wasn't wearing her coat to wear her drape.

She hadn't been dressed up in so long, and she had originally bought the dress to wear to Casey and Nate's rehearsal dinner since it promised to be a swanky affair. But she was glad to get more wear out of it to the opera.

At the sound of the front door slamming, she cringed. "Em?" Aidan's voice called.

"I'm in the bathroom." Like a true coward, she had yet to mention her plans of going out with Pesh. She knew it would cause unnecessary trouble. She had hoped to be able to sneak out before Aidan got home. Leaving behind a note or text that she would be out would have been so much easier than having to face him. But Aidan couldn't seem to get it through his head that there was nothing between her and Pesh, and at the same time, he had yet to tell her the magic three words she had been longing to hear.

While in her mind she told herself that her opera plans were innocent, her heart raged in fury at her. Deep down, she knew she was hurting Aidan, and that regardless of what he had done to her, that made her a horrible person. She should have told Pesh no the first time he broached the subject of attending the opera, but instead, she gone against her better judgment and agreed.

She was snapped out of her thoughts at the sound of Aidan shuffling down the hall. "I picked up some Chinese on my way in. I thought if you were feeling up to it, we might go to Percy's swim meet tonight. He really wants us to come. I swear, he's called me like five times."

Emma winced at the fact she would not only be disappointing Percy but Aidan as well. He appeared in the bathroom door with a half-eaten egg roll in his hand. He took one look at her, and his mouth gaped open. "I think you're going to be a little overdressed for the YMCA."

Warmth flooded her cheeks. "Actually, I'm going to the opera tonight."

Aidan's face fell. "With Pesh?"

She gnawed her bottom lip before responding. "He asked me last week because he had an extra ticket. Another couple will be there, so it's not like we'll be all alone. It's a way of celebrating me being off bed-rest." At the hurt radiating in Aidan's eyes, she quickly added, "It's just downtown at the Fox. I won't be out late, and I promise to stay off my feet as much as I can."

His silence caused her chest to cave in. She knew she had to get away from him. As she started to brush past him out the door, she noticed a crumb of eggroll on his face. Raising up, she ran her thumb over the corner of his lip, catching it.

He grabbed her arm, his blue eyes flashing with desperation. "Em, don't go. Please."

She hoped he didn't noticed how she had started trembling. "Aidan, I've already told Pesh I would, and I'm dressed. Besides, it's not a date. I promise."

[236]

He scowled at her. "Of course, it's a date. You may think it's just as friends, but I'm sure he doesn't. Or he at least wants you to believe that lie while he's moving in for the kill!"

Emma stared down at the bathroom tile. "Yes, it's true that Pesh would like us to be more, but I told him I didn't know what I wanted."

"That's not true. You want us. I know you do." When she refused to look at him, Aidan's hand gripped her chin, forcing her to look at him. "Why do you keep fighting this? Fighting us?"

She tried pulling away, but he tightened his arms around her. "I'm not fighting us. There isn't really an *us* anymore, is there? You made damn sure of that when you couldn't tell me you loved me and tried to screw another woman!"

He narrowed his eyes at her. "Oh hell yes there is! There was before, and there still is."

Emma shook her head as tears burned her eyes. "Will you ever get it? You broke my heart, Aidan! You shattered me into jagged pieces from which I'm not sure I can ever be whole again with you or any another man."

His face contorted with agony. "And I said I was sorry. I've begged and pleaded with you to forgive me. I've even tried to show you in every way how very sorry I was. Because of the last ten days, what we have is even stronger now, but dammit, you keep railing against it because you're afraid I'm going to fuck up again!"

Emma cheeks warmed from her anger. "And how do I know you won't? You said you wanted more with me last time and look where it lead us. How do I know that you won't put a ring on my finger and then freak out and screw around on me?!" she demanded.

"Because I won't. I swear to God and everything that is holy that I *won't!*"

"You can't make a promise like that. You can't be sure what you'll do tomorrow or five years down the road."

"I *am* sure! I know in my heart that I've never felt for anyone like I've felt for you. All I want is you."

"Aidan—"

His response was to crush his lips to hers. That familiar electricity popped and crackled around her. Physical need, along with love, pulsed through her, and she thought she would die if she didn't get closer to him. She wanted to touch and taste every inch of him.

Aidan gave an agonized groan when her tongue brushed against his lips. He widened his mouth, accepting her tongue and teasing it with his. Almost instinctively, she wrapped her arms around his neck as his went around her waist. They moved frantically against each other.

When he started to pull away, she gave a cry of protest. "Feel us, Emma. It's right here, and all you have to do is accept it," he murmured against her lips.

Her eyes opened, and she gazed up at him. "Emma, I l—"

The sound of the doorbell cut him off and snapped her out of his spell. "Oh God," she moaned. Her hands dropped from his neck to push against his chest. "Let me go." When he still held her tight, she brought her panicked gaze to his agonized one. "Please, Aidan."

His arms dropped limply from her as his shoulders drooped in defeat. "Fine. Go to him. I hope he can give you what you obviously don't want from me. But don't think for one minute that you're not doing the same thing I did. You're running away from happiness and trying to calm your fears with someone else."

He then turned and left her alone in the bathroom. Feeling lightheaded, she gripped the countertop. Tears pooled in her eyes, but she fought to keep her composure. She heard Aidan open the front door and ask Pesh inside. She glanced in the mirror and grimaced. Her kiss with Aidan had smeared her lipstick. "Just a second!" she called.

"Take your time," Pesh replied good-naturedly. Emma was sure he was just being polite considering the fact Aidan was there.

Once she finished adjusting her make-up, she grabbed her purse and hurried down the hallway. Pesh stood in the foyer with his back to her. His hands were thrust into his pockets nervously playing with his keys while Aidan was nowhere in sight. She cleared her throat. "I'm so sorry I was late."

He whirled around and then drank in her appearance. A bright smile curved on his face. "You look so absolutely gorgeous that any man would be a fool not to instantly forgive you."

"Thank you," she replied. She couldn't help noticing how handsome he looked in his dress coat that hid the suit and tie he was wearing underneath. A cream colored scarf was draped around his neck. "You look very nice yourself."

"Thank you. I appreciate that." He glanced around the foyer. "Where's your coat?"

"Oh, just one second." She started for the closet by the kitchen when Aidan appeared, clutching her formal dress coat in his hands. "You don't want to forget this. It's supposed to be down in the 40's tonight. I don't want you or Noah catching a chill," he said.

She started to reach for it, but he held it out to put it on her. Turning her back to him, she faced Pesh. His jaw clenched as she

[240]

watched Aidan slide the coat up over her arms and onto her shoulders. "Thank you."

"You're welcome." Aidan's fingers lingered on her until she finally stepped away from him.

"I guess we better go. We don't want to miss our dinner reservations," Emma said to Pesh.

"Good seeing you again, Aidan. Tell your father I hope he's taking good care of himself."

"Yeah, same to you. I'll tell Pop you said hello."

Emma couldn't believe that Aidan was practically being cordial. But when they reached the front door, he called, "Take care of my girl."

Pesh's hand froze on the doorknob. "Um, I will," he muttered before he jerked the door open for Emma. Once it closed behind him, Pesh exhaled noisily.

"I'm so sorry for that," Emma began as they started down the stairs.

"It's okay. I would probably have reacted the same way."

"Seriously?"

Pesh nodded as he held open the door of his Jaguar. "If someone was trying to encroach on the woman I loved, I'd probably be less than civil."

"But you're not encroaching. He knows we're just friends." Emma couldn't help noticing that Pesh flinched at the word *friend.* "We are still friends, aren't we, Pesh?"

A smile forced its way to his lips. "Of course we are."

Uneasiness crept into the pit of her stomach. Her expression must've alerted Pesh to her feelings because he said, "Emma, if you don't feel comfortable about tonight or leaving Aidan, we don't have to do this. I would never, ever want to do anything that makes you uncomfortable."

The sincerity in his voice made Emma shake her head. "No, I'm fine. Let's go." But the truth was she was far from fine. Her emotions buzzed and hummed like a swarm of locusts ready to overtake her at any moment.

He nodded, and after she had eased down into the seat, he closed the door for her.

Once he made his way around the car, he slid inside and cranked up the engine. He turned to her and smiled. "I'm glad you've consented to come with me tonight. My sister and brother-in-law will be joining us."

"Oh," she murmured at the insinuation of a double date.

"But Shevta is aware we're not committed to one another, so you don't have to worry about it being strange."

Yeah, I'm sure she thinks there's a lot more between us than you're letting on—just like Becky did! Emma thought, but she pinched her lips tight. Her fingers went to the hem of her coat, and she twisted it with nervousness.

Pesh tried filling the uncomfortable silence with conversation about his sister and brother-in-law. Emma could tell he was very fond of Shevta, and she sounded like an amazing woman.

"Where are we eating?"

"An Indian restaurant close to the Fox."

Emma's stomach churned at the prospect, but before she could try to put on a poker face, Pesh burst out laughing. "I'm only teasing you."

A nervous giggle escaped her lips. "Really?"

He momentarily tore his eyes away from the road to give her a beaming smile. "I made reservations at The Livingston, so we would be right across the street and have plenty of time to eat and relax."

"Oh, I've always wanted to eat there. It's in such a beautiful, old building with the Georgian Terrace Hotel."

"I'm glad I made a good choice."

Emma smiled. "I think one day when I'm not pregnant, I'll get up the courage to try Indian food again."

"Do you really think so?" When she bobbed her head, Pesh said, "Now that is what I call courage."

"Actually, you don't know the entire story and how true that statement is!"

"Oh, what happened?"

She winced before relating the story of throwing up on Aidan. Of course, she did manage to leave out a lot of details about what went on between them that night.

Pesh's expression turned serious. "I hate to hear you got so sick. I should have realized mixing all those spices wouldn't be good for you—especially if you had such a sensitive palate."

"It's okay. Things like that happen," Emma said as they eased into the parking lot across from The Livingston.

After turning off the car, Pesh turned to her. "So we'll be on the lookout for the blandest food possible tonight to ensure you

[244]

don't have to make a run for the bathroom or throw up in the orchestra pit?"

Emma laughed. "I'm not that sensitive."

"Phew, good to hear." He then came around not only to open the car door for her, but he took her hand to help her up out of the car.

She cocked her head at him. "You know, I'm not so enormous yet that I'm having mobility issues."

He winked. "I know. I just used it as a ploy to get to hold your hand."

Emma couldn't help laughing at the impish grin that formed on his cheeks. "May I keep it to escort you into the restaurant?"

"I suppose so."

"Didn't want you to think I was getting too forward."

"I'll make sure to let you know if that happens."

When the crosswalk sign turned, they hustled across the street and into the restaurant. Once they reached the hostess stand, Pesh dropped her hand. "Reservation for Nadeen," he said.

The hostess glanced down at her book. "Yes, two of your party is already here. Please follow me."

Pesh motioned for Emma to go first, and she fell in step behind the hostess. When they stopped in front of the table where an attractive Indian couple sat, Emma drew in a deep breath.

"Shevta, Sanjay, this is my friend, Emma Harrison," Pesh introduced.

Emma thrust out her hand to Shevta. "Nice to meet you."

Shevta rewarded her with a broad smile as she pumped Emma's hand. "The pleasure is all mine, Ms. Harrison. Please sit down."

Emma shook Sanjay's hand before eyeing an empty seat. After helping her off with her coat, Pesh pulled out her chair and then eased her up to the table.

Once they had given their drink orders, Shevta turned to Emma. "So I understand you're a big fan of the opera?"

"Oh yes. My mother used to bring me to the Fox when I was younger. I was only thirteen when I first saw *Aida*."

"Sanjay and I have had season tickets since we got married. With his crazy schedule, we haven't been able to include Alpesh as much as he would like," Shevta said.

"I'm so very grateful you allowed me to tag along this evening."

With a sly smile, Shevta said, "Oh no, we're thrilled to have you."

Emma shifted in her seat and tried focusing her attention on her menu and not the growing tension at the table about what she and Pesh were or weren't.

***

The rest of dinner went smoothly, and she actually enjoyed being out with Shevta and Sanjay. Of course, Pesh was his usual charming self, and she couldn't help feeling a tiny fluttering in her chest each time she caught him looking at her or whenever he winked playfully.

Once they finished their meal, they walked across the street under the flashing lights of the illuminated Fox Theater sign. When the usher led them to the third row in the orchestra, Emma turned back to Pesh with widened eyes. "These seats are amazing!"

He smiled as he took her coat. "I'm glad you like them."

"Like them? I don't think I've ever been this close. I'll feel like I'm back on the stage. Well, not like I was ever on a stage like this."

"You were involved in the theater?" Pesh asked as they eased down into the plush velvet seats.

"Oh yes." Emma then spent the remaining time before the lights dimmed regaling Pesh about her musical roles.

From the time the curtain rose, Emma sat mesmerized in her seat. The costumes, the score, the performances—they were breathtaking and so much better than she remembered. When the cast came out for their curtain calls, she clapped until her palms stung and turned red.

As they started up the aisle, Emma felt Pesh's hand on her lower back, guiding her from being knocked about in the crowd. Blustering cold air met them as they pushed through the lobby doors and under the awning.

"It was very nice meeting you," Sanjay said.

"Same to you," Emma replied, shaking his hand again.

Shevta leaned over to whisper in Emma's ear. "We hope to see you again soon. I haven't seen Pesh so happy in a long time."

At the insinuation, Emma's chest caved, and she found it hard to breathe. How could she explain to Shevta that she didn't reciprocate Pesh's feelings, and that no matter how hard she tried not to, she was only going to hurt him in the end? Or was she only lying to herself by ignoring the tiny flickering building within her whenever Pesh smiled at her or did something sweet or thoughtful? With Pesh, she would never have to worry about unfaithfulness or not being able to say how he felt. He wore his heart on his sleeve, and he was so old-fashioned, he would never think of cheating.

Finally, she murmured, "Thank you."

As they waved good-bye to Sanjay and Shevta, Pesh linked his arm through hers. "So did you enjoy *Aida* again?"

"Oh I adored it! It's such a beautiful love story, even the sad parts."

"You had me worried with all the sniffling."

Emma grinned. "I couldn't help it. It's a mixture of me being a hormonal ball of mush as well as the fact I always cry in emotional parts of movies, books or the theater."

They were about to round the corner to the parking lot when Pesh stopped. "What's wrong?" Emma asked.

Pesh motioned to the horse drawn carriage at the curb. "How about a ride?"

Emma widened her eyes at both the romantic sentiment and the prospect of getting into the carriage. "I would love to, but..."

"You're afraid you can't get up there?"

She furrowed her brows. "How did you...?"

He laughed. "Lucky guess. But have no fear. I'm pretty sure we can manage it." He took her hand and put it on the carriage side. "Now put your foot in the stirrup." His hands went to her waist and tenderly hoisted her up. She pulled her other leg up and then pitched forward onto the seat. "Oomph," she muttered, as she tried rearranging her dress.

"Are you okay?"

"I'm fine."

"Okay, we're ready," Pesh called to the driver.

"Yes, Mr. Nadeen." With a crack of the reins, the carriage lurched forward, sending Emma collapsing back against Pesh's chest.

As she pushed herself off of him, Emma asked, "How does he know your name?"

"If you want a carriage ride after ten, you have to hire one."

"You hired a carriage ride for us?" Emma questioned incredulously.

"Yes, well, at the time, it seemed like a good idea—another way for me to woo you. Of course, that was before I picked you up and experienced the whole scene with Aidan."

Emma ducked her head. "I'm so sorry."

[250]

Pesh's fingers tenderly cupped her chin, forcing her to look at him. "Please don't apologize. I'm just happy to have had this lovely evening with you."

At his earnest expression, Emma smiled. "So am I. And thank you for being so understanding."

"It's my pleasure."

They took in the sights and landmarks while the traffic and people bustled around them. To combat the cold, she snuggled closer to Pesh. He momentarily tensed before wrapping her in his arms. Although she hated herself for it, she couldn't help noticing how he felt entirely different than Aidan. He was taller, more muscular. She felt almost tiny wrapped in his embrace, even with her ever expanding belly.

"Emma," he whispered.

She jerked her head off his chest to stare up at him. The intense longing burning in his eyes took her off guard and sent the tiny flickering within her to start crackling and building. Before she could stop herself, she leaned forward, giving Pesh the invitation he sought.

His warm lips brushed tentatively against hers. When Emma didn't pull away, he pressed them harder. Ever the gentleman, he didn't try to deepen the kiss by seeking entrance for his tongue.

Instead, he pulled away to stare into her eyes. The flickering had sent flames shooting below her waist, and she brought her lips back to his. This time she slid her tongue along his lips. Pesh gave a moan low in his throat before darting his tongue against hers.

In that instant, Emma couldn't get close enough to him or get enough of him. Her hands were in his hair while she shifted to almost sit on his lap. She whimpered in frustration when Pesh's hands came to her shoulders to push her back. "Emma, no."

"What?" she muttered through her haze.

He shook his head. "This isn't you. It's your hormones."

"Wait, no. That's not it at all." She gazed up at him. "Trust me when I say, you're a really, really good kisser."

Pesh chuckled. "And in five minutes, you're going to hate yourself and me, just like I do right now."

"Why?"

"Because I feel like a giant jackass for even putting the moves on you considering you've just come off bed rest, we barely know each other, and your emotions are with someone else."

She blinked a few times, taking in his words. Then her hands flew to cover her face. "Oh God, I just acted like a complete and total slut, didn't I?" Emma moaned.

[252]

"No, you didn't." When she peeked at him, Pesh gave her a sheepish grin. "Besides, you have your pregnancy hormones to blame. I should have known better."

She reached out to take his hand in hers. "It's not just the hormones that make me want you, Pesh. You're an amazing man—handsome, strong, compassionate, giving of yourself and your heart. Any woman in my place would be willing to drop her panties for you, even if they usually had morality."

He laughed. "All this time and who knew I was such a panty melter."

Emma grinned. "You need to get out of the ER more."

"If I had more evenings to look forward to like this, then maybe I would."

At his insinuation, Emma stared down at her lap. A frustrated noise came from the back of Pesh's throat. Unwrapping himself from her, he scooted over to the other seat and tapped the driver. "Ed, I think it's about time you backtracked and took us back. It's a little too cold for Emma to be out this long."

"Yes, sir."

For the remainder of their ride, he sat across from her, and they talked of Atlanta, not what was happening or not happening between them. Emma felt frozen solid by the time they got back to the car. She thrust her hands in front of the heater while shifting to enjoy the heated leather seats.

"I'm sorry you got so cold. I should have realized the weather wasn't cooperating for a carriage ride."

Rubbing her hands together, she turned to smile at him. "No, I enjoyed it. Everything about tonight has been so wonderful."

"Hmm, should I take that for a real compliment considering you've been cooped up for two weeks?"

Emma laughed. "Yes, you should. Although you probably could have taken me to something I hate like a sporting event, and I would have enjoyed it."

"Not much on sports, huh?"

Wrinkling her nose, Emma said, "My heart is with the theater and the arts."

Pesh smiled. "I'll have to remember that."

They had barely gotten on the interstate when exhaustion set in. The toasty warm car and the fact she hadn't done so much in weeks kept her fighting to keep her eyes open. It wasn't long before she nodded off.

The car coming to a stop jolted her awake. Her eye-lids fluttered open to take in Aidan's driveway. Yawning, she turned to Pesh. "I'm pretty rude company, aren't I?"

He shook his head. "I'm surprised you made it as long as you did. It's been a big day."

"Yes, it has."

"Here, let me walk you to the door."

As Pesh started around the car, Emma grabbed her purse. The house was dark as they started up the front walk-way. Aidan hadn't left the porch light on for her. She drew in a shaky breath at the thought of facing him again.

When they got on the porch, Emma turned to Pesh. "I want to thank you again for the lovely evening."

Pesh smiled. "It was my pleasure. I hope it's something we can do again."

Emma nodded. "Me too." She leaned over to kiss Pesh chastely on the cheek. When she started to pull away, Pesh quickly pecked her on the lips. And then before she knew it, his lips were moving against hers. Within a second of them being joined, his tongue plunged into her mouth, and Emma knew it was all over.

He wrapped his arms around her, drawing her flush against him. She brought her arms against his chest, but instead of pushing him away, she slid her hands up to his neck and curled her fingers into his hair.

At her actions, a growl reverberated deep in Pesh's chest. Without warning, he pushed her back against the brick wall. As he pressed himself into her, she could feel the fabric of her dress, along with her thigh highs, snagging against the rough foundation. But she didn't care. She couldn't get enough of him being close to her. His smell, the way his body molded against hers, the way his tongue set her on fire as it darted in and out of her mouth.

All thoughts of any propriety flew out of her head. The very fact she was making out with another man on Aidan's front porch should have immediately doused any desire she felt. But instead, her chest rose and fell in rapid breaths.

Pesh tore his lips from hers and started kissing down her neck. Throwing her head back, she murmured, "Mmm, oh Aidan."

Her eyes flew open as Pesh stilled his lips. A strangled cry erupted from her throat as she pushed away from him. Oh God, she had said *his* name. In a moment of pure and electric passion with Pesh, she had called out *Aidan*. Embarrassed tears stung her eyes as she turned to flee.

Pesh grabbed her arm. "Wait, Emma."

"Oh God, I'm sorry! I'm so, so sorry!" she cried, as tears streaked down her cheeks. She tried pulling away from him to escape because she couldn't bear to look at his face.

"Stop it, and look at me!" Pesh commanded.

Emma dragged her gaze off the tiled porch floor and up to Pesh's face. "Please, just let me go. There's nothing you can say that would make me hate myself any more than I already do."

Surprise flooded her when he drew her into his strong embrace. "I don't hate you, so you sure better not hate yourself."

She jerked her head back to stare incredulously at him. "I just called out the man who broke my heart's name while I was making out with you!"

Pesh's expression saddened. "And when I pressed you back against that wall, all I saw in my mind was Jade, and all I wanted to feel was her."

Instead of being angry, Emma's heart ached for Pesh. "I'm so, so sorry."

"I think she confirms what I've feared for a long time. We're just two broken people who aren't ready for someone else, no matter how hard we try to force it." He pushed a strand out of her face. "We're both still desperately in love with other people."

[257]

"I want to love Aidan…I mean, I do love him, desperately at times, but I'm afraid to let myself feel what I do. Your wife was always true to you. She would have never left you."

"I'll admit that what Aidan did still infuriates me to where I want to inflict bodily harm on him. But he loves you, Emma. He's been working his ass off the past two weeks to try to get you to see that."

"But he can't even say the words. Every time he tries, he gets interrupted and then he never makes an effort again!"

Pesh took her chin in his fingers and forced her to look him in the eye. "I want you to think about this for a minute? What would you rather have? Words that can be spoken lightly and then taken back so easily, or would you rather actions?"

A reel of images of Aidan's behavior over the last weeks flickered through her mind. He had risked his job to take care of her. Not to mention, he had cooked everything and anything she wanted, made midnight runs for bacon and ice cream, massaged her feet while watching chick flick movies he hated and held her when she had felt despair.

He smiled. "I don't know why he can't say the words, but I know without a doubt he loves you. For most of his life, Aidan probably loved himself more than anyone else in the world. And now he loves you more." His hand briefly touched her belly. "And he loves his son."

A sob tore through her chest, and she didn't fight the tears that came. She threw her arms around Pesh and squeezed tight. "Why do you have to be so wonderful? You should be mad as hell and turning over furniture, calling me a tease or something!"

Pesh laughed. "The last thing I am is a hypocrite. I know exactly how you feel."

"You're going to make someone a wonderful husband." She pulled away to cup his face in her hands. "I want a wife and family for you more than you can ever imagine."

"It's just not time, yet, Emma."

She kissed his cheek tenderly. "I'm going to pray for your heart to open to someone. Jade would want you to be happy."

Pesh clenched and unclenched his jaw, and Emma knew he was fighting his emotions. "I know she would," he whispered.

"Then make two women who adore you proud and find yourself a wife."

His mouth fell open as he stared at her. Emma smiled and nodded. "I do care for you, Pesh. I realize now the feelings I had for you weren't entirely romantic, despite my behavior in the carriage or here on the porch. Regardless of the fact I love Aidan, I can't help but care for you deeply."

"I care for you, too. And I want you to be happy more than anything in the world." He leaned over and whispered in her ear, "And I think that happiness is right inside that door."

Tears stung Emma's eyes. Unable to speak, she bobbed her head in agreement. When Pesh pulled back, he winked at her. "Hurry on in and make Aidan's night."

She gave him a final kiss on the cheek before digging the keys out of her coat pocket. "Thanks again for everything."

"You're welcome." He then waved good-bye before hurrying down the porch steps to his car.

Emma's fingers trembled as she unlocked the door. Tentatively, she stepped inside the house. Darkness enveloped her as she made her way through the living room. She was surprised not to find Aidan awake. Her nose wrinkled as she eyed the beer cans littering the coffee table.

As she took off her coat, something warm and furry brushed against her leg. "Aw, boy, were you waiting for me to come home?"

Beau whined and nudged her belly. "We're home now. You don't have to worry anymore." She reached over to scratch his ears. "Where's Daddy, boy?"

He yipped and then started for the stairs. With the way they had left things, she wasn't too surprised that he wanted to be apart from her so he hadn't slept in his bedroom. Taking the stairs one at a time, she then crept down the hall to the guest room. Beau's claws clacked behind her. When she reached the door, she turned back to him. "Stay boy."

He reluctantly slid down on his paws to lie outside the bedroom. She smiled at him. "Good Beau."

Her shaky hand worked hard to turn the doorknob. Aidan's soft snores met her as she stepped inside the darkened bedroom. Since he hated sleeping in the dark, the nightlight next to the bed lit her way across the floor. She eased down on the bed beside him. Lying on his back, the sheet was bunched around his waist while one arm was thrown lazily over his head.

As she gazed down at him, she wondered how she had ever thought she could want anyone else. Mortification caused her to shudder when she thought of how she had kissed Pesh when all along she had only wanted it to be *Aidan's* lips and *Aidan's* hands on her. Just like Aidan had fought his feelings for her by taking home a stranger, she had tried to do the same thing with Pesh. And like him, nothing she could have ever done with Pesh would have driven away her true feelings for Aidan.

In the end, there would only be two loves in her life—Travis and Aidan. She rubbed the back of her hand along his cheek. It brought a smile to her lips because she realized how he was keeping a close shave because he knew she liked it.

When he didn't wake at her touch, she leaned over and kissed his lips. She pulled away and stared into his sleeping face. "I love you, Aidan Fitzgerald. I always have, and I always will. I'm sorry for hurting you," she whispered.

He grimaced in his sleep, his hands fisting the sheet. "Em...Em please...I...I love you."

Emma's heart jolted and then restarted. Her hand flew to her chest and rubbed where the slow, aching burn filled her. He was calling out to her. Somehow, somewhere in his subconscious he really did want her, and he had said the words she had longed to hear. At that moment, she wanted nothing more than to make love to him and truly cement their feelings for each other.

With another kiss, Aidan still slept soundly. Biting her lip, Emma knew the one way she was going to have to wake him up to ensure he would be ready and willing. Leaning over she began kissing a moist trail down his bare chest. When she reached the waistband of his underwear, he still hadn't stirred. Easing it down, she took his cock in her hand. Working her fingers over him, his length began to swell. Aidan shifted in the bed, but his breathing didn't change.

When she slid him into her mouth, his hips bucked. Then a low groan rumbled through his chest. "Emma," he murmured, and she paused. Her heart stilled when she realized he was still asleep and calling out for her.

CHAPTER FOURTEEN

Aidan tried shaking himself out of his dream. Once again, his nights were filled with Emma. His days were consumed by the growing ache of his feelings and now he was even tormented in his dreams. Tonight was physically painful as he could actually feel her lips on him, moving him in and out of her warm mouth.

He groaned. "Emma," he murmured. God, he wanted her. He wanted to wrap his arms around her and bury himself deep inside. He wanted to hear her cry out his name again like she had before. "Emma, I need you."

"I'm here, baby, and I want nothing more than to make love to you."

His eyes flew open. He realized he wasn't alone in the bed. This was no dream Emma. She was real and was straddling him while she worked her lips and tongue over his erection. "No, wait," he croaked. When she licked and then sucked one of his balls into her mouth, he threw his head back against the pillow. Fuck, it had been so long. His hips moved involuntarily, bucking his length farther into her mouth.

No, no, no. He couldn't do this. Their relationship started on sex, and he wasn't about to let it restart that way. It was about love this time—pure and beautiful love. He pushed himself into a sitting position. "No, Emma, don't," he said.

Her eyes glanced from his cock up to his eyes in surprise. He shook his head. "I don't want you to do this."

She pulled away so violently he winced as her teeth scraped along his length. He tried to grab her shoulders, but she stumbled off him so fast that he couldn't. She ran into the bathroom and slammed the door.

He rolled his eyes up to the ceiling. Why did he seem to have a gift for completely and totally fucking things up every single time he was around her? He threw back the sheet and hurried over to the bathroom. He could hear her crying. When he reached for the doorknob, he found it locked. "Em, I'm sorry. You misunderstood me, I swear."

At his words, she cried harder. Aidan banged his fist so hard into the wood his hand screamed in agony. "Dammit, Emma, would you please open the door and let me explain?"

"How could I possibly misunderstand you? You said you didn't want to sleep with me!" she screeched in between the sobs that drove spikes into Aidan's heart.

Growling with frustration, Aidan kicked the door. "Em, has there ever been a time in our relationship when I didn't want you? You've always kept me at half-mast just being in the same room."

Her crying grew louder, and he could hear her fumbling under the counter for what he assumed was more toilet paper. He was correct when he heard her blow her nose loudly.

Raking his hands through his disheveled bed hair, he shook his head maniacally. He knew he had to do something and do it fast. He was losing her to Pesh, and in her fragile physical and mental condition, this was enough to drive her over the edge. He sighed. "So are you really going to make me do it this way—in my boxers with a hard-on from your delicious mouth while you're crying in the bathroom?"

"Please…just leave me alone."

"No, I will NOT leave you alone. I want to be with you, Em. I want to be with you every fucking moment of every fucking day!" As his heart began beating rapidly, he took in a few ragged breaths. This was it. Now or never.

"And you know why? Because I love you! Did you hear that? I *love* you, Emma Harrison! I love you with everything in me. If I was honest with myself, I've probably loved you since that first night at O'Malley's. I just couldn't say it until now."

Silence echoed back at him. "Trust me. It's not that I didn't want you to keep sucking me off. It's that I didn't want us to do anything else sexual until I told you how I felt about you. Even though the doctors say we can, I don't want to fuck you or have sex with you. I want to make *love* to you, Em." He stared at the closed door. Why wasn't she saying anything? Why hadn't she thrown the door open and rushed into his arms? Wasn't he saying what she wanted to hear?

Aidan didn't know what else to do, so he just kept speaking from his heart. "Everything has been so crazy with Pop and you and that damned Alpesh trying to steal you away and making me crazy with jealousy. I'm so fucking sorry I didn't tell you I loved you that day on the dock. Even before you told me, I knew how I felt, and it scared the shit out of me. I felt more for you in that instant than I did for Amy in the four years we were together."

When she still didn't say anything, his throat burned as tears flooded his eyes. Dammit, he never wanted to cry in front of her. He rested his forehead against the door. "Please, Em. I love you so much it hurts. I ache for you in my soul. Please…I can't live without you. I want to be with you every minute of every day. I want to marry you and make a life with you. I want to raise Noah and be a family together. Please…please say you want to be with me forever."

[267]

When the door flew open, Aidan had to brace his arms against the frame not to fall forward. Emma stood before him, wide-eyed, open mouthed, and with mascara blackened tears streaming down her cheeks. She took a tentative step toward him. "Say it again," she finally whispered.

A sob choked off in his throat. "I love you."

"Oh, Aidan," Emma replied. She cupped his face in her hands, brushing away the tears that had fallen down his cheeks with her thumbs. She brought her lips to his and gave him a tender kiss. When she pulled away, her expression was a mixture of happiness and regret. "I'm so sorry for tonight and for hurting you with Pesh. Deep down, I never, ever stopped loving you, and you were right when you said our feelings had grown in the last two weeks. It was just...I was angry and bitter and broken hearted over what you did. But even though I wanted to hate you, I never could. And once again you were right because I thought I could make my feelings for you go away by trying to start something up with Pesh, but I couldn't." She gripped the sides of his face in her hands. "I swear to you that my heart will always belong to you."

He shook his head with disgust. "You never should have had to wait, Em. Part of me wanted you and Pesh to end up together. I knew he could give you everything I should have without question, and his love wouldn't be tainted by cheating."

Emma brought her finger to his lips to quiet him. "Stop beating yourself up. You made a mistake, and now it's forgiven."

Aidan sucked in a breath. "Really?"

"Oh yes." She gave him a lingering kiss before pulling away. "And I should have never gone out with Pesh tonight or had him over. Not only was it disrespectful and hurtful to you, it was stupid of me to try to tempt fate. Besides, he could never give me what you have. You made my dreams come true by giving me Noah. The fact that I fell in love with you exceeded anything I could have ever imagined. And now that I know you love me back—" A sob cut off her voice.

Aidan tenderly swept the tears from her cheeks. He couldn't bear seeing her cry, especially since everything was finally right between them. "I'm serious about marrying you, Em. But I want to propose to you the right way—not half-naked and sporting wood. I want to ask Earl for his permission, and I want to get down on one knee and put a ring on your finger. You deserve that, and I want you to have it."

Her green eyes widened. "Really?"

He bobbed his head. "I swear."

"Oh God, you make me so, so happy!" she cried, throwing her arms around his neck. Rocking her back and forth, he squeezed her tight. "I love you, I love you, I love," she murmured into his ear.

"I love you, too," he replied.

She squirmed against him, and when he eased up on his embrace, she stared up at him with a combative mixture of both love and lust in her eyes. "Make love me to Aidan," she pleaded.

"Is that what you want? Because there's nothing else in the world I would rather do."

Grinding her pelvis against his, she said, "I want you more than anything in the world."

Aidan's hand went to the zipper on her back. He slid it down agonizingly slow. Emma wiggled, trying to hurry out of the dress. "Why are you taking so long?"

He chuckled. "I didn't realize you wanted to be naked so much."

Her green eyes blazed up at him. "I want to be as close to you as I can. I need to feel your skin on mine. Then I'll know this is all real...we'll be full circle to where we started from."

With a groan, Aidan jerked the straps of her dress off, letting it puddle to the floor. He unhooked her bra and whisked it away. As his hungry gaze took in her breasts, he licked his lips in anticipation. "Is it just me or—"

She rolled her eyes. "Way to ruin a moment."

Aidan chuckled. "Sorry, but I couldn't help noticing that they're…bigger."

"Yes, and they'll probably grow even more. Don't you remember I told you they would?"

"It must've slipped my mind." With a smirk, he said, "Trust me, I'm not complaining."

She grinned. "I didn't think you would."

He kissed along her cheek and nibbled her neck as his hands cupped and kneaded her ample breasts. His lips came back to hers as he caressed her flesh until her heaving breaths came harsh against his lips. He broke their kiss to suckle one of her nipples. She tugged the strands of his hair as he swirled his tongue over the sensitive bud. When he grazed it with his teeth, she cried out, arching into his mouth.

Once he had worked one nipple into a hardened peak, he kissed his way over to the other. All the while, Emma began to grind herself against his erection. "I want you now, Aidan. Please," she panted.

[271]

"It's been too long, hasn't it?" he murmured against her breast.

"Oh, yes," she cried, thrusting her hips against his hand as it dipped below her waist.

His thumbs slid inside the waistband of her panties and then pulled them down her thighs. When they dangled at her knees, she kicked them off. Her fingers then went to his boxer shorts to slide them off his hips.

Standing naked together, they gazed into each other's eyes. "I think we can skip most of the foreplay, don't you?"

"Mmm, hmm," Emma murmured sliding her hands up Aidan's bare chest.

He eased himself down on the side of the bed. Taking Emma's hand, he tugged her to him. She kept her eyes locked on his as she rose up to straddle him. When the warmth between her legs covered his cock, he moaned. "Wrap your legs around me tight, Babe."

Emma quickly obliged, and then Aidan pushed them back to the center of the bed. Then his hand delved between her legs, causing her to whimper. As he thrust a finger into her core, he felt her walls clench around him. "I just wanted to make sure you were ready for me."

"I'm always ready for you, my love," she whispered.

He brought both of his hands to her waist and gently raised her up. He then guided his erection between her wet folds. As Emma slowly slid down on him, Aidan feathered tender kisses along her collarbone. After he was all the way in, he shuddered with pleasure. "Oh God, I've missed the feel of you."

When he lifted his head, she smiled down at him. "I've missed every glorious inch of you, too."

He laughed. "There you go stroking my ego."

"I think we fit together perfectly." She gazed down to her expanding belly. "Well, except for that getting in the way."

Aidan pushed the long strands of auburn hair out of her face. "Don't ever think Noah's in the way. He will always be the string that ties us together. He's our love growing inside you. He may not be the reason why I fell in love with you, but he's the reason why I got another chance at life." He gave her a deep, lingering kiss. "You saved me, Emma."

Tears sparkled in her green eyes, and her chest rose and fell in harsh breaths like she was trying to keep her emotions from spiraling out-of-control. "Oh Aidan." She cupped his face in her hands. "I love you so much," she murmured against his lips.

Pressed chest to chest, Emma began to lift her hips as Aidan raised his. She panted in his ear as the slow, languid strokes took him deeper and deeper. Wrapped together, they kept their eyes on each other. They were a tangle of arms and legs—but they were one.

CHAPTER FIFTEEN

Two Weeks Later

The shrill ringing of her cell phone roused Emma from a deep sleep. Fumbling her hand along the nightstand, she finally gripped it in her hand. Almost robotically she slid her thumb across the answer key and brought it to her ear. "Hello?" she croaked.

"Em!" Casey shrieked before dissolving in sobs.

Emma jolted awake like she had downed several cups of coffee. "Case, what's wrong?"

In between hiccupping sobs, Emma could decipher only a few words. "Jason. Groomsman. Alcohol poisoning after the Bachelor's Party. Hospitalized. Short one of the bridal party. Wedding ruined."

Emma pulled herself into a sitting position. "Casey, take a few deep breaths and calm down, okay? The wedding is not ruined just because some asshat groomsman drank himself into the hospital."

"But we rehearsed everything with seven groomsmen. The pictures will be all screwed up!"

"Isn't there another one of Nate's friends or relatives that could fill in and wear Jason's tux?"

"I don't know! Besides who the hell is going to fit into a 6'4 bodybuilder's tux anyway?!!?"

Emma glanced over her shoulder at Aidan sleeping soundly, and an idea popped into her head. "Um, well, Aidan has a tux." There was a long pause on the other end of the line. "Are you still there?"

"Why am I not surprised James Bond has his own tux?" came Casey's biting reply.

"It was for work purposes, Case." Emma sighed. "Look, I get that he's still not one of your favorite people, but—"

"No, no, you're right. We don't have many options, and Nate actually likes him."

"Well, I'm glad at least one of you likes the father of my child."

Casey groaned. "You know I like him…I'm just not back in *love* with him like you are."

"So you want me to tell him to be suited up and ready to roll at noon with the rest of the bridal party?"

"Yes, I would be thrilled and honored if he would be there."

Emma laughed. "Yeah, you sounded really convinced on that one."

Casey snickered. "I'll work on it by the time I see him, okay?"

"Okay then. I'll see you later."

"Bye."

After Emma hung up the phone, she slid back under the covers. Snuggling up to Aidan's warm body she leaned over and kissed his lips. "Wake up, baby."

He grimaced while his eyes remained closed. She kissed him again. "Em?" he murmured against her lips.

She nuzzled her forehead against his neck, her thigh draping over his. Mistaking it for an invitation, Aidan snaked his arms around her waist and pulled her up to straddle him. Emma shook her head. "Whoa, cowboy, just what do you think you're doing?"

He grinned lazily up at her. "I'd think you were more the cowgirl in that position."

Emma laughed. "Yeah, well, this cowgirl isn't ready to ride today." When Aidan made a face, she added, "Well, at least not right now. I need to ask you something."

Aidan cocked his eyebrows at her. "What is it?"

Emma then related everything she had talked to Casey about. When she finished, Aidan exhaled noisily. "You mean she actually wants me in the wedding?"

"Sure, she does."

Aidan gave her a skeptical look. "Seriously?" When she bobbed her head enthusiastically, Aidan smirked at her. "Emma Katherine Harrison, you are the worst liar in the world."

"Look, Nate really likes you, and Casey always did. She's just having a hard time forgiving you." Her response elicited a grunt from Aidan. "So does that mean you'll do it?"

"Of course I will."

"Thank you, thank you, thank you," she replied, kissing his cheeks and then his lips. "You're really going to make Casey so happy doing this. She thought her perfect day was ruined. No woman wants the slightest thing to go wrong on her wedding day. I mean, it's supposed to be the happiest day of your life, right?"

A far-away look clouded Aidan's eyes. "Maybe I should call and tell her I'll do it. You know, really try to smooth things over."

"That would be awesome."

He brought his lips to hers, kissing her tenderly, while running his hands up her back. "You go on and get in the shower. I'll come join you in a minute."

"Why do I have the feeling the cowboy is going to expect to ride off into the sunset during our shower?"

He threw his head back and laughed. "Go on and let me talk to Casey."

"Fine, fine," she muttered as she climbed off of him.

Whatever Aidan had to say, it took him awhile to do it. Emma was getting out of the shower when he came in the bathroom. "Everything go okay?" she asked, sweeping her hair back in a towel. When he didn't respond, she caught his reflection in the bathroom mirror. He was brushing his teeth, but his lips were fixed in a wide, almost goofy grin.

"Aidan, did you hear me?"

He spat out a mouth-full of toothpaste. "Huh?"

"I asked you how the call went."

Once again, a wide grin curved on his lips. "It went really, really well."

She eyed him suspiciously as she dried off. "Well, good. I'm glad to hear it. Having you and Casey back on friendly terms would be the answer to a prayer."

Aidan turned off the water. "Em, I'm not the one who hasn't been accepting. I mean, I got nailed in the balls for Christ's sake!"

"I know you haven't." She kissed his bare shoulder. "That's why I'm so proud of you for being the bigger person by trying to make things right."

He cocked his brows at her. "You're proud of me?"

"Mmm, hmm." At his grin, she smacked his ass. "Now get a move on, mister. Casey's emotions today are like treading on thin ice. Being late is the last thing we need."

"I thought you had to go get beautified with her?"

"I do." Emma eyed her phone on the counter. "Shit. I better throw something on. I'm supposed to be at the spa in thirty minutes. Will you be a real sweetheart and bring my dress to the church?"

"Of course I will." When he leaned over to kiss her, his mouth tasted of mint.

"Thanks," she murmured against his lips.

"I love you," Aidan said as he pulled away.

"I love you more," she argued with a grin.

***

After a luxurious morning at the spa having facials and massages, the entire bridal party's hair and makeup were done. Emma couldn't help giggling at how comical Casey looked in a tracksuit coupled with her full make-up and intricate veil and sparkling tiara.

Casey stared down at herself. "What? You don't think there's something wrong with this look, do you? I bet I could walk in Wal-Mart like this, and no one would say anything."

Emma grabbed her purse. "Hmm, high praise indeed from the Wal-Mart shoppers."

Casey laughed. "Come on. We gotta haul ass to the church."

Rolling her eyes, Emma said, "Only you would say ass and church in the same sentence."

"You know you love my potty mouth."

"I love everything about you, bestie."

Casey held up her hand. "No more emotional landmine comments like that, Em. I can't risk my make-up."

Emma laughed. "Fine. I'll be a total hard ass the rest of the morning. Happy?"

"Thrilled. Now come on."

Emma and Casey, along with the rest of the bridal party, headed to Christ the King Cathedral. It had been Nate's church since childhood, and Emma thought it made a beautiful venue for a wedding.

Once locked into a preparation room, they got busy getting Casey into her mammoth dress. Emma stood back, gazing at Casey. Her earlier promise was forgotten when tears filled her eyes. "You look amazing!"

Casey pointed a finger. "Em, you promised!"

"I can't help it. It's the hormones making me even more emotionally crazy!"

"Ugh, you seriously have to quit the waterworks or you'll have me crying, and this waterproof stuff only works so much."

"Fine, I'll go put on my dress."

"Good. And while you're at it, think of disgusting things, people who piss you off—anything not to be crying."

Emma swept a hand to her hip. "Don't you think people will wonder why you're very pregnant bridesmaid has such a 'screw you' look on her face?"

Casey laughed. "As long as you're not crying, we're good."

"You're impossible," Emma grumbled as she slipped into the dressing room. The maroon dress hung in its bag on the hook where Aidan had delivered it. She slipped into it, and then after trying to wrestle with the zipper, she headed back into the main room for help. Carlee, Casey's sixteen year old sister, happily obliged.

Emma eyed her reflection in the mirror as a knock came at the door. "It's Aidan," a voice called. Carlee giggled as she ran to open the door.

When Aidan stepped inside, his gaze flickered over the room for her. The moment he saw her, he beamed. "You look beautiful!"

Emma grinned. "Thank you." Staring down at her dress, she shook her head. "Frankly, I feel like an Oompa Loompa at the moment!"

"Trust me, babe, you don't look like one." When she gave him a skeptical look, Aidan winked at her. "Then I must have a Willy Wonka fetish because I'd like to devour you right this instant."

[283]

Emma smacked his arm playfully as Casey asked, "And what about me? No compliments for the bride?"

Without missing a beat, Aidan said, "You're an exquisite vision of perfection in white who will take Nate's breath away the moment he sees you."

Casey grinned. "Smooth Big Papa, very smooth."

He leaned in and pecked her check. "It's the truth."

"I'll take it then," she replied.

"I'm so glad to get to be a part of your happy day."

"So am I," Casey replied, with a wink.

Emma's mouth gaped at their exchange, especially when Casey kissed Aidan's cheek as well. What happened to her hating him? Was the very fact he had been willing to stand in and save the day enough to make Casey forgive Aidan for all he had done wrong?

"Did you need something?" she asked.

"I just wanted to check on you, see how you're feeling, but most of all, I wanted to bask in your rapturous beauty."

"OMG, that's so sweet!" Carlee exclaimed while one of the other bridesmaids bobbed her head.

Aidan's lips curled into a cocky grin at their appreciation of his sentiments while

Emma rolled her eyes. "Seriously?"

He laughed. "Actually, it's time to take the bridal party photographs."

"I thought as much."

Aidan placed his hand on her shoulders, his expression waxing concern. "I may have been joking, but I did want to check on you."

Her heart warmed at the seriousness his tone had taken. "I'm fine."

His lips tightened into a hard line. "Try to stay off your feet as much as you can today."

"Aidan," she protested.

"I'm serious."

"I was cleared to return to work and all normal activity two weeks ago, remember?"

"That still doesn't mean you should be going full throttle all the time. It was one thing going back to work, but between the rehearsal dinner and bachelorette party this week, you've been pushing yourself."

As much as she hated to admit it, she was exhausted. "Okay, okay, Mr. Bossy. When we finish with the pictures, I'll sit down and put my feet up until the ceremony."

A pleased smile filled his lips. "Good." He brushed one of the curly tendrils out of her face. "But save me at least one dance at the reception."

Her stomach clenched at the very mention of the reception. Not only was she singing at the ceremony, but Casey had asked her to sing during hers and Nate's first dance. Aidan must've noticed her apprehension because he drew her to him. "Getting stage fright?"

She gulped down the rising bile in her throat. "A little."

"You'll sound amazing. You always do."

"I hope so," she croaked.

He pulled away to cup her face in his hands. "Well, I know so." He brought his lips to hers. Both a calming and pleasing tingle spread from the top of her head down to her toes.

"No, no, no! Don't you two start! You'll ruin Emma's make-up before the pictures!" Casey protested.

Aidan groaned against her lips before Emma broke apart from him. "You are such a bridezilla," he kidded.

Casey laughed. "Watch it, Big Papa. I might find another purse to nail you with."

With a shake of his head, Aidan only chuckled at her jibe. "Don't think I haven't warned Nate to steer clear of you when you're pissed and wielding a purse. It's a dangerous weapon!"

Emma continued to be so shocked by their friendly banter that she merely followed dumbly behind them as they walked into the sanctuary. After taking a million pictures, first with Casey, and then after she disappeared, with Nate, Emma began to feel her face was frozen in a smile, and she might be blinded from all the flashbulbs.

All too soon it was time for the ceremony to start. Emma took her place in front of Carlee and gazed out at the massive crowd in attendance. Glancing over her shoulder, she watched as Casey took her father's arm. He leaned over and kissed her cheek. "You'll always be my little girl," he said.

A pang of sadness washed over Emma that her own father would never walk her down the aisle. At the same time, she knew that if she and Aidan ever married, Granddaddy would be more than happy to do the honors. She turned away from her feelings of sadness and regret. Instead she embraced the ones of pure and complete happiness at the future ahead for both herself and Casey.

She didn't have to force a beaming smile to her face when she met Aidan at the altar door. As she slipped her arm through his to take their walk down the aisle, Noah gave a gentle kick. She couldn't help feeling like the most blessed woman on earth.

CHAPTER SIXTEEN

Emma sat with the bridal party at the head table under multiple glittering chandeliers. She couldn't believe how beautiful everything looked from the overflowing floral arrangements to the ice sculptures. Casey and Nate's families had gone all out for the reception.

After devouring his plate, Aidan cut his eyes over to survey how she was playing with her food. "Noah's going to get feisty if you don't eat," he cautioned, wiping his mouth with his linen napkin.

"I'll eat when I finish singing. The last thing I want to do is puke from nerves on Casey and Nate's big day." At his skeptical look, she replied, "I promise as soon as I'm done, I'll shovel it in, including several pieces of the bride *and* groom's cakes!"

Aidan took a sip of champagne before nodding in agreement. "When are you up?"

"After the speeches."

"That's not long."

"Looks like it's sooner than I thought," she replied, motioning to where Nate's brother and best man stood with a microphone in his hand.

While Anthony spoke, Emma noticed it was Aidan, not herself, who had begun squirming in his seat. His hand shifted from his thigh to his coat pocket several times. When she shot him a questioning look, he mouthed, "Sorry."

Once Anthony finished his speech to a round of applause, Carlee took the microphone with a shaky hand. Already teary, she lost it as soon as she began speaking about her sister. It wasn't long before everyone was crying, Emma included.

When the bandleader took the microphone from Carlee, Emma felt the butterflies in her stomach turn to boulders. Once again, Aidan became shifty in his seat. "Don't tell me you're nervous for me?" she whispered in his ear.

"Oh, um…yeah, I think I caught your nerves or something," he finally mumbled.

"And now it's time for the bride and groom to take the floor for their first dance as man and wife."

Emma winced. "That's my cue."

Aidan grinned. "Break a leg, babe."

"Thanks a lot," she mumbled.

Without anyone else seeing, he reached out and smacked her ass. His playfulness melted her nervousness.

The first time Casey ever heard her sing at an open mic night at one of their favorite coffee shops, she swore Emma sounded just like one of her personal favorites, Patty Griffin. So there had never been any question that Casey wanted Emma to perform *Heavenly Day* for her first dance with Nate. It was also one of Emma's favorite songs to sing.

She gripped the microphone confidently and stared out into the packed ballroom. "Seven years ago my late fiancée said, 'Hey, I think you're going to love my roommate's girlfriend. She's really sweet, but more than that, she's crazy and funny as hell too!'"

Emma smiled at the guest's laughter. "I knew the first time I met Casey that Travis had been right, and we were going to be best friends. I also came to love Nate as well. I've been blessed to call her my best friend for all these years, and that she and Nate have been a part of my life in both the good times and the bad." Emma saw the tears sparkling in Casey's eyes. "There aren't words to express how happy and thrilled I am for them as they start this new journey of their life together as man and wife. I wish them all the blessings in the world and pray that God showers them with many, many heavenly days."

The band struck up the first few notes of the song, and then Emma found herself wrapped in the zone. She poured her heart and soul into the words, and when she finished carrying out the last note, she knew she had hit it out of the park.

Thunderous applause sounded all around Emma, bringing her out of the high she received from performing and back onto the stage. She smiled at the reaction. "Thank you very much."

When she handed the microphone back to the bandleader, he cried, "Wasn't that amazing?"

Applause continued ringing through the ball room, causing Emma's cheeks to redden even further. She hurriedly plopped down into her seat next to Aidan.

"How many of you would like to hear Emma sing something else?"

Whistles and cat calls erupted at the prospect. "Looks like they want an encore, babe," Aidan said, with a grin.

Emma shook her head. "I've already sang twice. They're going to think I'm some attention whore or something," she protested.

"Not when people are requesting you do it."

The band leader's voice interrupted them. "Aidan, why don't you come up here and see if you can't convince Emma to sing something else for us?"

When he started to get up, Emma grabbed his shirt sleeve and hung on for dear life. "No!" she screeched.

He smiled reassuringly down at her. "I'll never understand how one minute you can be the most self-possessed, professional singer, and the next scared to death to perform."

"It's just part of my sweet neurotic side," she replied.

"Look, just take a deep breath. I'll go make up some excuse that you're too exhausted to sing again in your delicate condition."

"Thanks a lot," she grumbled.

Aidan stepped over to the stage and took the microphone from the band leader. He gazed out at the audience. "Well, I'm supposed to be up here to either beg Em to sing for you again or to make her apologies." He glanced back at Emma. "But I must admit that the real reason I'm standing before you has nothing to do with either one."

A whisper of conversation cut through the crowd. "I'm standing before you today as one of the happiest men in the world. I have the love of a beautiful woman and a healthy son on the way. But even that isn't enough. Witnessing the commitment today at the

[293]

ceremony, I can't help but want what Casey and Nate have." A chorus of 'aw's" rang throughout the room. "So there's just one question I want to ask Emma right now."

As he strode over to her, Emma couldn't help feeling absolute and total disbelief. He sat the microphone down on the table to a loud squeal. Reaching into his suit pocket, he took out a black, velvet box. Emma widened her eyes when it opened it to reveal a sparkling diamond.

Once he had it in his fingers, he knelt down on one knee before her. "Emma Katherine Harrison, angel of mercy and forgiveness, love of my life and mother of my son, will you make me the happiest man in the world and say you'll marry me?"

"Oh my God," Emma murmured. She couldn't stop the tears from pooling in her green eyes as her hands flew to cover her mouth. "Oh my God," she repeated.

"That's not exactly the response I was hoping for," Aidan teased.

Tears of elation streamed down her cheeks as she threw her arms around his neck. "YES! Yes, I will marry you!"

The room erupted again with applause. Emma brought her lips to Aidan's. Just when he started to deepen their kiss, she pulled away to feather kisses over his cheeks, his nose, and his forehead. Finally, she brought her lips back to his.

He pulled from their embrace to take her left hand in his. His thumb tenderly ran over her knuckles before he slid the ring on. "There. Now we're officially engaged."

She giggled before grabbing him by his shirt and jerking him to her again. As she kissed him passionately, he laughed against her lips. "Em, you do remember we're in a room full of people, right?"

She squealed and then pulled away. Laughter echoed around them. "That's a mighty fine yes, don't you all agree?" he called the crowd.

"Hell yeah!" Connor called from his table.

Emma covered her face in embarrassment. Fortunately, the band leader came over and took the microphone back. "How about a song for the newlyweds and the newly engaged couple?" he asked.

"No! I don't want to take away anything from Casey's day," Emma protested.

"Babe, she and Nate knew all about this. That's what I called to ask her about."

"Really?" Emma then glanced past Aidan to where Casey stood with a broad grin on the dance floor. When Emma raised her brows questioningly, Casey nodded and then blew her a kiss. Looking for Nate's approval, he smiled and gave her a thumbs up.

"Okay then. Let's dance."

Aidan then led her out onto the floor. As she brought her arms around his neck, she couldn't help but stare in wonderment at her ring. From time to time as they swayed to the music, she would momentarily forget about it until the light caught the diamond, and it sparkled back at her. She felt the urge to pinch herself to make sure it hadn't all been some wonderful dream.

"You like it?"

"It's beautiful."

Aidan beamed. "I wasn't sure what you'd like, so Connor helped me pick it out."

"Really?"

He nodded. "He has damn good taste." A grin cut across his face. "Of course, each time I tried to go for a cheaper ring, he liked to remind me of things from our past."

Emma laughed. "I don't think I even want to know what all he said to induce you into buying such a large diamond."

"He should think of a side career for the CIA. His powers of persuasion are intense."

The song then came to a close. "All right everyone. It's time to cut the cake. Does anyone wanna put good money on the fact that Nate will be drenched in icing in about two seconds?" the bandleader questioned to a chorus of laughter and catcalls.

After the cake was cut and everyone stuffed themselves on the sugary, decadent deliciousness, Emma once again returned to the dance floor with Aidan. As they swayed to the music, Aidan smiled down at her. "So future Mrs. Fitzgerald, when are we going to tie the knot?"

Emma tilted her head to the right, lost in thought. "As much as I'd like to not be pregnant in a wedding gown, I want us to do it before Noah's born."

"Ah, legitimize the Little Man and all, huh?"

She giggled. "Exactly."

"Do you want something like this?" he asked, motioning around the swanky ballroom.

Emma wrinkled her nose. "I had something like this planned many years ago." Aidan tensed at her alluding to her wedding with Travis. "I want something simple with just our closest family and friends." She glanced up at him. "We could get married at my church and have the reception at the barn."

[297]

Aidan inhaled sharply. "Pop's gonna shit a brick when I don't get married in the Catholic church."

"Then we can think of something else."

"What about the meadow that overlooks the pond?"

"You don't think it'll be too cold?"

"We'll keep the ceremony short and sweet," Aidan joked.

Emma grinned. "Okay, that sounds good. Then we can have the reception in the barn. Will that suit you better?"

"All I care about is the part where you say 'I do' and become my wife." Aidan brought his lips to hers. When she darted her tongue in his mouth and pressed herself against him, Aidan pulled away in surprise. "Are you trying to start something with me, Ms. Harrison?"

Not taking her eyes off of his, she bobbed her head. "Take me upstairs."

"You're joking?"

"Do you want me to beg?"

"Emma," he growled.

"Aidan," she began sweetly, "Will you please take me upstairs to our big rented suite and make love to me until I pass out from exhaustion?"

His eyes widened like she had lost her mind. "I can't believe you just said that."

"Would you rather me be dirty and say please take me upstairs and fuck me until I pass out from exhaustion?" she teased.

"You're killing me, Em. Absolutely and completely killing me."

"Then do something about it."

"Aren't we supposed to stay until Casey and Nate leave?"

"Nate's family is Italian. They're going to be drinking and partying until two in the morning."

Aidan's blonde brows furrowed. "Like Mafia Italian?"

Emma giggled. "I don't think so." She nudged him playfully. "Just go on over and make them an offer they can't refuse on taking your fiancée upstairs to consummate your engagement."

He scowled at her. "You're supposed to consummate a marriage, not an engagement."

[299]

"Fine. I'll do it." Emma took his hand and led him off the dance floor.

"At least the crowd is thinning out," Aidan noted.

"What are you so worried about?"

"I just don't want to piss Casey and Nate off. They've already been forgiving and generous enough to agree to share their day with my proposal."

When they walked over, Casey was licking the icing off Nate's cheek where she had previously smashed him with it. Emma leaned over and whispered something in her ear. Casey grinned broadly and nodded her head. Aidan shot Nate a helpless look to which Nate winked. "I gotcha man," he mouthed.

Emma tugged on Aidan's hand. "All right, Big Daddy, you can take me upstairs and ravish me now."

He chuckled. "If I had known putting a rock on your hand would have made you this playful, I would have done it a helluva lot sooner."

CHAPTER SEVETEEN

As they stepped onto the empty elevator, Emma took Aidan off guard by shoving him against the wall. "Em, what—"

She cut him off by crushing her lips to his. Taking his hands in hers, she jerked them above his head and pinned them against the wall. Her tongue thrust into his mouth, greedily seeking out his own and rubbing tantalizingly over it. A low groan erupted deep in his throat. Clasping both of his hands in her one, Emma trailed her other hand down his chest and below his waist to cup his growing erection.

He tore his lips away from hers. Panting, he stared into her emerald greens eyes that burned with desire. "Emma Harrison, are you trying to rape me in this elevator?"

Squeezing his cock, she raised her eyebrows at him. "I didn't think you could rape the willing?"

He chuckled. "Good point." As she worked his length over his pants, her lips went to kiss a warm trail up his neck. He shivered as she licked along his jaw-line. "Let me guess. This extremely horny moment was made possible by pregnancy hormones?"

Her giggle vibrated against his cheek. "Yes, it was. Ugh, they're insane." She released his member and pulled away. "I think I'm starting to understand what it's like to be you."

Throwing his head back, Aidan roared with laugher. "You mean what it feels like to be a horndog?"

Wide-eyed, she replied, "Uh-huh."

"Then why did you pull away?"

"Well, because—"

"That wasn't me complaining, babe."

She grinned as she ran her hands up the front of his tux. "So you don't mind being molested in a public elevator?"

"Nope. In fact, I was enjoying it a lot."

The elevator dinged, and the doors opened on their floor. "Guess we'll have to continue this in our suite," Emma said.

Aidan slipped off his tux jacket and brought it in front of his waist to hide his condition. Although he enjoyed the hell out of Emma being so aggressive in the elevator, it somewhat wrecked his plans for the evening. There would be no slow seduction scene as an engaged couple considering he was at half mast.

Emma took the keycard from him and unlocked the door. He held his breath as she stepped inside. "Oh my God," she murmured.

He craned his neck to watch as her heels tapped across the rose petals littering the floor. On the table, there was a bucket of champagne and strawberries. Even though he couldn't see her face, he knew her gaze was taking in the bedroom where candles waited to be lit, and a pink wrapped package sat on the bed.

She whirled around to stare at him in the doorway. "It's just like…"

He smiled. "Our first time."

Tears shimmered in her eyes as she closed the gap between them. This time when she kissed him it was with love, not passion. "I love you so, so much, Aidan," she murmured against his lips.

"I love you too."

Pulling away, she cocked her head at him. "I'm not even going to ask what's in that box because I can't believe you found lingerie to fit me."

He rolled his eyes. "You act like you're some wide load. All you have to show for being pregnant is your bump." He brought his hand to her stomach. "You're the sexiest, most beautiful pregnant woman I've ever seen."

"Aw, baby, you're so sweet." She leaned up to nip his bottom lip with her teeth. "But you don't have to keep complimenting me because you're so getting laid tonight."

He grunted. "You and that mouth."

She grinned. "Well, you're stuck with it, so you better enjoy it."

"Oh, I'll enjoy it, and so will many parts of my body."

"Naughty, naughty boy," she murmured before kissing him again.

Aidan kicked the door shut while Emma nudged him toward the bedroom. When they passed the table with the strawberries and champagne flutes, he stopped. Desperately wanting to savor the moment, he said, "Wait, a minute babe."

"What is it?"

"Why don't I pop open some bubbly and celebrate our engagement?" he asked.

Emma's auburn brows furrowed. "But I can't—"

Aidan turned the bottle around to reveal it was only sparkling cider, sending a beaming smile on Emma's face. "Oh, I love it. You thought of everything."

He started unwrapping the bottle, but Emma took it away from him. "Let's save it for later." Her fingers then went to the buttons on his shirt.

"You don't want some cider first?" he questioned, amusement vibrating in his voice.

She stared up at him—a mixture of love and lust radiating in her eyes. "No. I just want to make love to my fiancée."

"I like the sound of that," he replied as she pushed his shirt over his shoulders and down his arms. "I'll like it even better when you're Mrs. Aidan Fitzgerald."

"Hmm…my feminist sensibilities should get riled at that insinuation, but I do like the sound."

As he took off his pants, Aidan asked, "You don't want to do something crazy like Emma Harrison-Fitzgerald, do you?"

"No, Mr. Neanderthal, I don't." She grinned up at him. "I just want to be your wife."

"And as soon as possible right?"

"Of course."

"Think we could throw something together in a few weeks."

Emma sucked in a breath. "Wow, I didn't know you were in such a rush."

His knuckles tenderly grazed her abdomen. "We don't have that much time before Little Man's arrival."

"That's true, but wedding planning isn't easy—even for a small one like we're considering."

He poked his lip out. "I just wanna be your husband."

She laughed. "And you will be, Mr. Impatient. I'm not going anywhere, and if you try to make a run for it, I'll lasso and hogtie you."

"Mmm, there's my naughty cowgirl."

"You're impossible." Raking her fingers through his hair, she shook her head. "We may not be bonded together in holy matrimony, but our relationship was cemented the moment Noah was conceived."

As Aidan's lips met hers, his fingers went to the zipper on her dress. With a flick of his wrist, the dress fell open, and he pushed it off her shoulders. His brows furrowed before his lips quirked up at the sight of her granny panties. "Ooh, Em, can you get a few more pairs of these?"

Emma's face turned the color of the fuchsia dress pooled at her feet. "I had to wear these, thank you very much." She crossed her arms over her bare breasts in a huff. When he chuckled, she shot him a death glare. "It's not a laughing matter, Aidan. I mean, I've always been a curvy girl, but you better prepare yourself for a lot more of me to love."

"I already told you that you're nothing but a belly...but any fat that wants to set up shop here," he paused to cup her breast while his other hand went to her ass cheek, "Or here, is fine with me!"

She rolled her eyes. "Once again, you're completely and totally impossible."

"And you're so sexy when you're pissed off." He kissed her before she could back talk him. Her mouth tightened with her resistance, so he slid his tongue against her lips. When she refused to budge, a low growl came from the back of his throat. "Quit being so damn stubborn, Em," he muttered against her lips.

His hand snaked between them to cup between her thighs. He stroked and caressed her over her alleged granny panties, causing Emma to tense. When he slipped a finger between the elastic and into her warmth, she gasped. He took the opportunity to thrust his tongue in her mouth. Her hands that had been hanging limply at her side went to his hair, and as she threaded her fingers through the strands, Aidan knew she had surrendered. "There's my girl," he said as he feathered kisses across her cheek. When he got to her ear, he plunged another finger inside of her as he whispered, "My beautiful, sexy girl who takes my breath away no matter what size she is or what underwear she has on."

A breathy moan turned into a laugh. "You're smooth, Big Papa. Very, very smooth," she replied, repeating Casey's line from earlier that day.

With his fingers still working their magic, he eased her down onto the bed. He curled up beside her. Her eyes pinched shut as she writhed against his hand, bucking her hips against him as he sped up his pace. "Mmm, please," she murmured, her breath hot against his cheek.

"Please what, babe?"

"Make me come, Aidan." The moment his thumb brushed against her clit, her fingers gripped the edges of the blanket as she cried out.

Not wasting anytime, he slid his fingers out of her still clenching walls and discarded her panties. He wrangled out of his boxers and rose up on his knees. With her expanding belly, it was always interesting finding a position. Spreading her legs, he thrust himself inside her.

Emma wrapped her legs tight around his waist, and he gripped her behind the knees. As he pounded into her, she raised her arms above her head and fisted the sheets. When she bit down on her lip to keep her passionate cries quiet, Aidan stilled his movements. "Don't be bashful, Em. Let me hear you," he urged.

Her cheeks tinged pink. "What if someone else does?"

"Who cares? *I* want to hear you. I want to know what I do to you."

She trembled at his words. "Okay," she murmured.

He grinned down at her. "Good." When he plunged back inside her, he was rewarded with a low moan from Emma. Bringing his hand between them to stroke her while he moved in and out caused her to shriek and then scream. He closed his eyes and threw his head back as Emma's cries were music to his ears. It wasn't long before she went over the edge, calling out his name over and over again. He continued thrusting in and out of her as her walls convulsed around him. He wasn't ready yet. He wanted to prolong his pleasure as long as possible. But when he felt Emma tightening herself around him, his eyes snapped open. She smiled triumphantly at him as he started to let himself go. Now it was his turn to emit deep, throaty cries and groan.

Once he finished shuddering inside of her, Aidan rolled over on his back, collapsing beside Emma on the bed. His chest heaved, and he fought to catch his breath.

She snuggled up to him and kissed his cheek. "I love you, Aidan."

"I know," he panted. The loud smack of her hand coming down on his thigh echoed through the room along with his deep chuckle. He turned to catch her outraged expression. "And I fucking *love* you too, Emma."

CHAPTER EIGHTEEN

Three Weeks Later

Emma surveyed her reflection in Grammy's full length mirror. Turning left and right, she let the poofy layers of her bridal gown twirl around her. In her mind, the dress had been the most beautiful thing she had ever seen with its empire waist flowing into yards of satin along with the intricate pearl and sequined encrusted beading of the bodice. She never imagined finding such a beautiful maternity bridal gown, especially on short notice.

But now that the big day had arrived, she wasn't so sure. "Ugh, I think it's safe to say I look like the Stay Puff Marshmallow Man," she moaned.

"Oh hell no, you do not!" Casey argued, adjusting the glittering tiara at the top of Emma's head.

Emma's cousin, Stacy, nodded as she helped to fluff out the long veil. "Don't be silly, Em. You're absolutely gorgeous."

"If I were straight, I'd totally want my bride to look just like you," Connor said, with a wicked grin.

"Oh God, you're starting to sound too much like Aidan," Emma replied.

[312]

"Now you listen to them, sugar. You look stunning!" Grammy cried from behind Emma. She hadn't even looked up from digging around in her jewelry box for one of Emma's "borrowed" items. The blue lace interwoven into her garter counted for her something "blue" while the dress and veil completed the "new". Carefully concealed under the yards of fabric was her "old" in the form of a pair of cowboy boots. Today she was going for comfort as well as shoes that fit on her swollen feet and wouldn't make her trip and fall.

Emma sighed. "I appreciate you guys trying to make me feel better, but seriously, it's a toss up between the Stay Puff dude and The Michelin Tire guy."

Casey snorted. "Stop fishing for compliments." Grasping Emma's shoulders, she turned her around. "You are the most beautiful bride I have ever seen in my entire life, and I'm including myself in that figure! It doesn't matter if you're seven months pregnant. The moment you start down that altar, you're going to take Aidan's breath away."

Tears welled in Emma's eyes at Casey's compliment. "Oh shit, don't start the waterworks now and mess up your makeup!" She waved her hands frantically in front of Emma's face.

Emma pushed them away. "Okay, okay, I won't cry."

"Good."

With a strand of pearls in her hand, Grammy stepped over to them. "Can you all give us a moment?"

Casey smiled. "Sure. We'll go get the bouquets out of the fridge."

"Don't even think I'm letting you put on my boutonnière."

"And just why not?"

"Because you always end up stabbing me!" Connor cried. They continued bickering as they went out the door.

Once they were alone, Emma arched her brows expectantly. Grammy's expression was so serious it made Emma uneasy. Trying to lighten the mood, she joked, "You know you don't have to have the sex talk with me, right?"

Grammy waved her empty hand dismissively. "I should hope not. Of course, I assume that ship sailed back with Travis."

Emma's face warmed as she nodded. Without another word, Grammy moved to stand behind Emma. She brought her hands over Emma's head and then slipped the strand of pearls around her neck. They rested a little past Emma's collarbone.

After she fastened the clasp, Grammy gripped Emma's shoulders and then caught her gaze in the mirror. "All my life, I wanted a strand of real pearls. For our third wedding anniversary, your granddaddy worked two extra jobs to buy these pearls for me after he did something much like Aidan did."

Emma gasped in horror. "Oh Grammy, I can't believe Granddaddy would ever do something like that!"

"He thought he could run from marriage and commitment, but when he did, he realized his mistake. It's something I've never told anyone, not even your mama." Grammy smiled. "Of course, our making up after his affair was the whole reason why she was here in the first place. I guess I got these pearls and your mama out of the deal."

"So you forgave him?"

"I'm still with him, aren't I?"

Emma fingered the pearls while thinking of all the happy years her grandparents had together. Never once had she ever seen a crack in the façade. They were what she aspired to be when it came to a married couple.

Grammy patted Emma's back. "I wanted to tell you this today so you would understand that no marriage is perfect. There's going to be good times and bad times and heartache and joy. Don't ever think that because of what happened before that your love isn't as strong or as beautiful as anyone else's. It's the love that goes through the hardest trials and survives that is worth having."

[315]

"Thank you, Grammy." She leaned over and kissed Grammy's wrinkled cheek. "Do you think Aidan and I will be as happy as you and Granddaddy have been?"

Grammy smiled. "I think you will."

"I hope so."

"Time flies so fast when you're happy and in love. One minute you'll be young, and the next minute you'll be standing in front of your granddaughter, who looks so much like her mama did on her wedding day."

At the mention of her mother, Emma's eyes misted over again. She would have given anything for her mother to be standing beside her, adjusting her veil, and telling her she made the most beautiful bride.

When she met Grammy's eyes again, Grammy shook her head. "The last thing on earth your mama would want is for you to be sad today. She would want you to be happy and to embrace the wonderful future ahead of you with Aidan and with Noah."

"I know she would. It's just hard."

Grammy stepped around to touch Emma's cheek. "I know, baby girl. She was my only daughter, and I'd give anything to have her here. But she's never very far away. She's always right here." Grammy placed her hand over Emma's heart. "She'll be there with you today, and when that sweet baby boy comes into this world and is put into your arms for the first time, she'll be right there too."

Emma bit down on her lip to stifle her emotions before throwing her arms around Grammy. "Thank you for being here with me today."

"It's my pleasure honey."

Granddaddy cleared his throat in the doorway. "All right, that weddin' plannin' woman said to tell y'all it's time."

Emma pulled out of Grammy's arms. For a flickering second, she saw Granddaddy in a different light for the mistakes of his past, but then she thought of Aidan and of forgiveness, and a smile curved on her lips.

She walked over to him and kissed his cheek. When she pulled away, she grabbed the lapels of his suit and smiled. "Look how handsome you are."

Granddaddy beamed. "It's my best suit. I hoped it would do."

"I'll be honored to be on your arm."

As they started out the door, he stopped her. "Virginia told you about the pearls, didn't she?"

Emma's mouth gaped open. "How did you know?"

"The look on your face when I walked in."

"I'm sorry."

"Don't be, Emmie Lou. I'm just surprised that Aidan didn't tell you."

Her eyes widened in disbelief. "You told him? When?"

"The time he came up here to get the food while you were on bed-rest."

"But why?"

Granddaddy grimaced. "I wanted him to understand that I knew where he was coming from, but at the same time, I wanted him to fight like hell to get you back."

"You like him that much?"

"I do." Granddaddy grinned. "I think I might even love him."

Emma jerked her head up to stare at him in surprise. "Seriously?"

"I'm happy for you, Emmie Lou. I think ol' Aidan's gonna make you a mighty fine husband."

"Oh Granddaddy," she murmured, her eyes filling with tears.

"Don't cry now."

"They're happy tears, I promise."

"Yeah, but you'll get me in trouble with all the hens around here if you mess up your make-up."

She giggled. "All right then. I wouldn't want to get you in trouble."

"Good then." Eying Emma's dress, he scratched his head. "Let's see how we're gonna get you out of here in that thing."

She giggled as she turned to the side and slid out of the bedroom doorway. As she swept out into the living room, she found the wedding planner organizing the bridal party. "How do I look Aunt Emma?" Georgie asked, spinning around in his tiny tux.

She grinned. "You look so handsome and so grown up."

He thrust out his pillow. "I thought today I would get the real rings."

"I'm sorry, sweetheart, but Casey and your Papa Patrick are in charge of the rings."

Georgie cocked his head. "Then why the hell am I the ring-bearer?"

Emma's eyes widened while Casey tried to hide her laughter behind her bouquet. "George Byron Parker! Don't you dare say a naughty word like that!" Emma chastised.

"Is hell a naughty word?"

"Yes, it is."

Georgie shrugged. "Oh, I just heard John and Uncle Aidan using it."

"Well, let them be in trouble, not you." She patted his back. "You have a very important job as the ring bearer, even without the real rings. You're part of our wedding party, and that makes you very special."

"Really?"

"Yes."

Georgie seemed momentarily appeased. Then his face clouded over again. "Do I really have to walk with her?" he jerked his chin over to Emma's cousin, Sarah, the flower girl.

"What's wrong with Sarah?"

Georgie rolled his eyes in exasperation. "She's a *girl!*"

Emma bit her lip to keep from grinning. "I promise she's a very nice girl, and you won't have to hold her hand or anything."

"Good!"

Marie, the wedding planner, clapped her hands. "Okay then. It's time. Georgie, Sarah, you'll go out first. Then I need Connor, Stacy, and Casey...oh my, that rhymed," Marie giggled.

Casey rolled her eyes as she handed Emma her enormous bouquet. "This chick has seriously got to go."

Emma welcomed the laugh that bubbled from her lips. It helped to ease the nerves she felt. Drawing in a few deep breaths, she tried to calm herself down. After all these years, it was finally happening. She was getting married. As she felt Noah kick beneath her yards of fabric, she shook her head and smiled. God had certainly blessed the broken road of heartache and loss to get to this point of extreme joy.

As they stepped onto the front porch, Emma glanced up at the sky. It was like God had smiled down on their special day by blessing them with not only a beautiful cloudless sky, but one of Georgia's unseasonably warm days for late January. She leaned on Granddaddy's arm as they took the path around the house. Memories flashed through her mind of taking the same turn with Aidan as they snuck away for their midnight skinny dipping escapade.

The grassy aisle leading up to the altar was covered with intertwining red, pink, and yellow rose petals. Emma's heart warmed as it was a special touch, not just to liven up the dying winter grass, but it was a reminder of happy times with rose petals in the hotel room on their first baby-making venture as well as their engagement. It brought a beaming smile to her face. But her smile grew even wider at the sight of Aidan standing at the front of the altar. He peered down the aisle, trying desperately to catch a glimpse of her.

The string quartet finished playing *Canon in D* and then changed over to the first strains of the *Bridal March*. "It's show time, Emmie Lou," Granddaddy said, a mixture of amusement and regret vibrating in his voice.

She drew in a deep breath and stepped forward into the aisle. As everyone rose out of their chairs for her entrance, her gaze honed in on Aidan's as he finally took her in.

His mouth gaped open while his blue eyes widened. Her breath caught at his reaction. Instead of the cocky grin she expected at her appearance, surprise filled her when Aidan's eyes shimmered with tears. Her heart shuddered and then restarted. In that moment, all she wanted was to power-walk up the aisle so she could get to him and throw her arms around him. She couldn't imagine ever loving him more than she did in that moment.

An eternity seemed to pass before she reached his side. Aidan swept the tears from his eyes with the back of his hand.

Although a shaky smile flashed on his face, emotion raged in his blue eyes. Without thinking, she let go of Granddaddy's arm and wrapped her arms around him. "Oh Aidan," she murmured, squeezing him tight.

"Emma, I'm almost speechless. I mean, you're like nothing I ever could have imagined." He sucked in a ragged breath and shuddered in her arms. "You're like a fucking vision."

Once again, a flashback filled her mind of the night she met him for their first baby-making session. He had crossed the crowded hotel lobby, kissed her, and then told her those words. "God, Em, I love you so much it hurts," came his pained whisper in her ear.

"I know. I love you so much, too."

The minister cleared his throat. "I don't believe we've gotten to that part yet."

Remembering where she was and how she was totally blowing the carefully scripted plan, she jerked away. "Oops," she replied, a warm flush filling her cheeks.

Laughter rang through the crowd. Stepping back, she slipped her arm once again through Granddaddy's. "I'm supposed to give you away, Emmie Lou, not have you run away as fast as you can," he quipped.

She smiled at him through her tears. "You're never giving me away, and you know that."

"I wouldn't have it any other way, Baby Girl. Especially not with you carrying that fine, strapping great-grandson of mine. He's gonna need a man to teach him a few things."

"Granddaddy!" Emma hissed as Earl winked at Aidan.

The minister once again cleared his throat. "Dearly beloved we're gathered here today in the sight of God to join together Aidan Patrick Fitzgerald and Emma Katherine Harrison in the bonds of holy matrimony." Emma began to tune the minister out and drown herself in the smiling image of Aidan before her.

She barely noticed when Granddaddy officially gave her away and left her side to go sit with Grammy. She even had a hard time focusing on her cousin, Dave, as he sang a twangy rendition of John Lennon's *Grow Old Along With Me.* There was no one for her in that moment but Aidan—the man who had made all of her dreams come true.

Emma jolted back into reality when the minister called her name, and she then repeated her vows as he prompted her. "I, Emma Katherine Harrison, take you, Aidan Patrick Fitzgerald, to be my lawfully wedded husband. To have and to hold, from this day forward, for better or for worse, in sickness and in health, for richer or for poorer until death us do part."

In a booming voice, Aidan repeated his vows with complete and total assurance, which made Emma's heart flutter. He then took her wedding band from Patrick, his best man, and slid it onto her finger. "With this ring, I thee wed."

When she glanced up at him, he winked at her, and she couldn't help grinning at the glimmer of his cocky side rearing its head. She took his ring from Casey and slipped it on his finger and repeated the words.

They then turned to the minister who smiled. "By the power vested in me by God almighty and the fine state of Georgia, I now pronounce you husband and wife." He gave Aidan a pointed look. "You may *now* kiss your bride."

"About time," Aidan replied before bringing his hands to cup her face. His lips met hers in a chaste, yet passionate kiss. Thunderous applause echoed around them as Aidan pulled away.

Linking her arm through his, they started down the aisle and down the hill to the barn to celebrate.

***

As Dave and her cousins' band perfectly harmonized the lyrics to her first dance song, Emma swayed in Aidan's arms. Glancing up at the canopy of twinkling lights, she couldn't believe how Marie and her team had transformed the barn into a winter wonderland. It was utterly breathtaking, and she couldn't help sighing with contentment at how perfect everything had turned out.

Working on their tight schedule hadn't been easy, but Grammy, along with her aunts and cousins, had whipped up a meal better than any catering company. Just the thought of the delicious BBQ she had consumed sent a small burp escaping from her lips.

With his blue eyes twinkling with amusement, Aidan gazed down at her. "Excuse me," she peeped.

"Eat a little too much?"

"Maybe."

"Damn, it was good."

"It was, wasn't it?"

"Yes. Everything has been good. Well, this song could be a little better." Aidan wrinkled his nose. "How in the hell did I let you talk me into John Denver for our first dance as man and wife?"

"*For You* is a beautiful song. Did you even bother listening to the lyrics? It's about how the rest of my life is for you and you alone!"

Aidan grinned at her outrage. "You're right. It is a beautiful song. And Dave is knocking it out of the park. But still…"

"And just what would you have preferred?" Emma asked as the last chords of the song finished.

Before she could press him again, Dave interrupted her thoughts. "Our next song was especially picked out by Aidan. He wanted Emma to know how much the lyrics mean to him and their relationship. So Em, here's *You Save Me*."

Emma gasped as she jerked her gaze from Dave to Aidan. His signature cocky smirk curved on his lips. "You really did that?" she asked as Dave began singing the Kenny Chesney classic.

"Yes, I did."

As she stilled in his arms, she let the familiar lyrics echo through her mind. She felt Aidan's breath warming her cheek. "And it's the truth, Em. You do save me. I would still be lost if you hadn't come into my life, and I thank God everyday that you gave me another chance to show you how much my soul cries out for you. There will never be anyone else for me in the world."

Tears welled in her eyes as he tilted her chin to look at him. His jaw was hard-set with determination. "I mean it, Em."

"You saved me too," she whispered.

He kissed her tenderly before pressing his face to her cheek. "If you would have told me this time last year I would be a married man with a kid on the way, I would've laughed my ass off and

[327]

called you crazy," he mused. When she tensed, he pulled away and smiled. "Boy, I was a crazy bastard then."

She returned his smile. "I would have done the same thing if someone had told me I would not only be married but carrying the child of the creep who hit on me at the Christmas Party."

Aidan laughed. "Fate has a funny way of working things out, doesn't it?"

"Yes, it does."

He tightened his arms around her as the song came to a close. "So why don't we hurry up and cut the cake, so we can get the hell out of here and start our honeymoon?"

Emma rolled her eyes. "Are you really that impatient?"

He grunted. "You cut me off ten days ago. I'm going to explode."

"I wanted our first night as man and wife to be special," she countered.

A smirk twitched on his lips. "Then let's make it special sooner."

"Patience is a virtue, Mr. Fitzgerald. I'm not going to miss out on dancing the night away with you because of your libido. Besides, I want to dance with Granddaddy and your father, and I want you to dance with Grammy. We're only going to have a wedding reception once."

"Okay, okay," he grumbled.

Leaning in, she whispered in his ear, "I promise I'll make it worth your while."

Aidan chuckled. "You don't have to promise me anything, babe. I'm so crazy in love with you I'll do anything you ask—including waiting to get laid."

Wrapping her arms around his neck, she said, "Oh, who needs poetry when I have you to say romantic lines like that?"

He grinned. "You know I'm one hell of man, babe!"

CHAPTER NINETEEN

As sparklers lit the way through the dark, Emma and Aidan ran to their car while being pelted with birdseed. Emma only gave the shaving cream covered and condom decorated Mercedes a fleeting glance before throwing open the door and collapsing onto the seat. She swiped off the pieces of birdseed stuck to her hair and dress.

Aidan grinned as he cranked up the car. "Sure hope we don't get attacked by a flock of militant birds with all this shit on us."

Emma laughed. "So how far is it to your buddy's cabin?"

"About twenty minutes from here in Blue Ridge."

With Emma in her last trimester, Aidan had put his foot down about them flying anywhere for their honeymoon. He had been able to get a week at a secluded cabin that belonged to one of his work buddies.

"I'm sorry it's not somewhere exotic like the Caribbean or romantic like Venice," Aidan said as they pulled onto the highway.

"After Noah is born, I'm holding you to that Italy promise."

"It's a deal. And since I know you won't get on a plane without him, we'll make the Little Man an international traveler before he's a year old."

"Aw, I love it." Reaching over, Emma took Aidan's hand in hers. "It doesn't matter where we go as long as I'm with you."

He brought her hand to his lips and kissed her knuckles. "I feel the same way babe."

After taking a turn off the interstate, they drove along the dark and curvy mountain roads. Glancing at the directions on his phone, Aidan made a final turn. "Greg had maintenance come out this afternoon and get things set up for us."

"Like sex up the place?" Emma asked with a grin.

Aidan grinned. "Maybe. They delivered some food as well. We'll go out to dinner a couple of times too if you want."

"With us out here in the middle of nowhere, how do I know you won't hold me hostage as your sex slave?"

Aidan threw his head back and roared with laughter. "No babe, you're my wife, never my sex slave."

"Pity," she murmured. When he jerked his wide-eyed gaze from the road to meet hers, she giggled. "Just kidding."

[331]

He exhaled a noisy breath as they turned into the driveway. Floodlights momentarily blinded her. When Emma stepped out of the car, she fought to keep her mouth dropping to the ground in disbelief. She glanced at Aidan and shook her head. "What?" he asked.

"You said your buddy was letting us have his cabin. That," she motioned to the giant mansion, "is *not* a cabin. It's a lodge at least. I bet it has eight or ten bedrooms."

"And we can christen every one of them while we're here," Aidan remarked.

She laughed. "Yeah, we'll just have to see about that one."

"Come on. If you think this is amazing, wait until you see inside." Taking her hand, Aidan pulled her up the front walk-way and up the porch steps. Once Aidan unlocked the door, he glanced back at her with a mischievous twinkle in his eyes.

"Whatever you're thinking, I can without a doubt say the answer is no!"

Aidan chuckled. "Come on. I just wanted to carry my bride over the threshold."

She couldn't help rolling her eyes. "Your bride is seven months pregnant. Besides, you're supposed to do that at your home, not your honeymoon destination."

Ignoring her, Aidan swept his arm underneath her knees while the other went around her back. She shrieked when he swept her off her feet before kicking open the front door. "Oomph," he muttered as he staggered across the threshold.

Emma burst into laugher at both his determined expression and his purple coloring. "Don't go incapacitating yourself before we can get the honeymoon started, babe," she teased.

"Yeah, yeah," he replied as he gently set her on her feet in the foyer.

"Aw, my hero," she said, leaning up to kiss him.

He grinned at her. "Go on and explore the ca—"

"Lodge," Emma corrected.

"Whatever. I'm going to go get our luggage."

"Be careful. I wouldn't want a city boy like you taken off by a bear or a coyote."

He shook his head. "Always that mouth of yours."

Once Aidan headed out the door, Emma turned her attention to the living room. It was outfitted with large, overstuffed couches and chairs. A floor to ceiling stone fireplace sat in the middle of the room, and after picking up the remote on one of the tables, a press of a button sent it roaring to life. Tilting her head, Emma took in the high ceilings with their crisscrossing wooden beams. As she walked around the room, she saw the large circular staircase leading to the next floor.

Aidan came huffing inside with three of their bags. "Need some help?" she asked.

"No, I got it," came his muffled reply from behind the luggage.

When he started down the hallway, she followed him. At the end of the hall was the master bedroom. Her eyes widened when Aidan flipped on the light switch. Not only did it boast a huge four poster bed, a sitting area with a couch, loveseat and chair, but its own fireplace with a furry rug in front of it.

"Is that...?" she asked, pointing down at the floor.

Aidan grinned. "No, it's fake bearskin or some other politically correct fake fur."

"Good to know."

"I bet it feels soft against your skin though," he murmured, his breath hovering over her cheek.

"I bet it does." She leaned in and gave him a lingering kiss. When she pulled away, her gaze fell to the bags at their feet. "Wait, that's not everything."

Aidan scowled. "Isn't it enough to get us started?"

She shook her head. "You didn't bring in my treat case."

His brows shot up. "You're what?"

A sly grin stretched on her lips. "You heard me. It has all the treats that I got at my lingerie shower. Handcuffs, massage oil, some edible underwear—"

Aidan held up his hand. "No need to explain anymore. You had me at handcuffs," he replied before hurrying out of the bedroom and down the hall.

Shaking her head, Emma then turned her attention to the far wall of the bedroom. It had floor to ceiling windows with glass doors that opened onto a balcony. Emma gasped as she stared out of the window at the magnificent view. Even with just the glow of the porch light, she could see the mountains for miles and miles. She couldn't imagine how breathtaking it would be when the sun came up.

The sound of more luggage dropping to the floor alerted her of Aidan's presence again. His arm snaked around her waist, pulling her back against him, while another hand slid up to caress her breast. "Isn't the view amazing?"

"Yes, it is," he murmured into her neck as his erection dug into her backside.

[335]

"Would you stop being a horndog for just a minute and look out there?" She gestured to the wide expanse of pine trees.

"Five seconds ago the words massage oil and edible underwear were coming off your delectable lips. I don't want to look at anything but your body until I've had you at least twice." When she started to squirm out of his hold, his breath scorched against her earlobe. "You.Naked.Hot tub.Now."

She glanced over her shoulder at him and rolled her eyes. "You sound like a caveman!"

He chuckled. "I feel like one too. Making me go almost two weeks without sex is torture, Em."

"Actually, it's good practice. After Noah's born, it'll be at least five or six weeks before I'm operational down there again."

Aidan groaned. "Oh God, don't remind me." Taking the hem of her dress, he pulled it over her head. "Take your shoes off," he instructed. Gladly, she stepped out of the low heels that were already causing her feet to swell.

Taking her hand, he started to lead her out into the hallway. "But I'm not supposed to get in a hot-tub when I'm pregnant," Emma protested.

"I've got it all taken care of, babe. I made sure they took all the necessary precautions to lower the water temperature. It'll be about the same as lukewarm bathwater."

"Really?"

He nodded and pulled her closer to him. "Besides, I figure with you riding me, you won't be totally submerged in the water anyway."

Emma shook her head. "You always have a devious little sex plan, don't you?"

"Yep."

She laughed as Aidan opened the door to the room across from the master bedroom. With just a flick of a switch, dimmed candlelight illuminated the room. "Electric votive candles? Who is your friend? The Ladies Man or something?"

Aidan laughed as he started unbuttoning his shirt. "Actually, he's married with five kids."

"Guess he likes to keep the romance alive, huh?"

The hot-tub sat bubbling in the corner of the room against more floor to ceiling windows. In the daytime, she imagined the view would be almost as impressive as the one in the bedroom.

After ripping off his shirt, Aidan started for his pants. Emma took the cue and started helping him. Once she slid off his belt, she doubled it over in her hands. While Aidan bent over to slide his pants and boxers down, she took the opportunity to smack his bare ass with the belt. The cracked echoed through the room.

Aidan whipped up in surprise while rubbing his ass cheek. "Emma, what the hell was that about?"

She giggled. "You don't like a little spank every now and then?"

The corners of his lips curved up in a smirk. "Now I didn't say that."

Without taking her eyes off of his, she smacked his other cheek. She shivered when his blue eyes burned dark with desire. "Why are you spanking me?"

"Because you've been a naughty boy."

His blonde brows arched up. "Have I now?"

"Mmm, hmm. All you've cared about since we got here is getting *your* pleasure." She brought her hand to her chest. "What about *mine*?"

"Ah, so I should attend to your pleasure first?"

"Yes, please."

"And what would you have me to do?"

Emma's sassiness began to waver, and suddenly she didn't think she could say the words. "Um, well…I want us in the hot-tub."

"And?" Aidan prompted as he reached around to unhook her bra with quick, expert precision.

"I want your mouth on me."

"You do?" He whisked her panties away, leaving her feeling very vulnerable under his hungry gaze. He brought his thumb to her mouth and traced her bottom lip. "You want my mouth here?"

"No," she murmured.

His fingers trailed down over her chin and down her neck to cup her breast. "You want my mouth here?" he repeated.

She shook her head. Releasing her breast, he slid his hand down her hip to cup the mound between her legs. "Do want my mouth here?"

"Yes. Please," she whimpered as his hand began to work her into a frenzy.

"Then come here."

Emma cried out in frustration when Aidan took his hand away. He backed up toward the hot tub. She watched as his deliciously naked form climbed inside. He crooked his finger at her. Still clutching the belt, she let it fall from her fingers to clatter to the floor. When she stepped into the hot tub, Aidan was still standing. Gently, he pushed her to have a seat on the side. Kneeling down before her, his hands went to her knees to widen her legs.

Glancing up at her, Aidan feathered his fingertips back and forth over her outer thighs, causing her to shiver. Emma bit down on her lip to keep from arching her hips toward him. Leaning over, he began tediously kissing and nibbling his way up the inside of her thigh. Just when his warm breath hovered over her mound, he turned and began to give her other thigh the same attention. "Aidan…"

"What babe?"

"Stop being a tease," she murmured.

His laugh vibrated against the sensitive skin of her inner thigh. He raised his head. "I'm sorry. You did tell me where you wanted my mouth, right?"

"Yes."

Dipping his head back between her legs, Aidan licked a slow trail up her moistened slit. His fingers came to spread her warmth before he thrust his tongue inside. As he plunged in and out of her, Emma bit down on her lip to keep her vocal cries silent, but a deep moan rumbled through her chest. With one hand, she grasped the side of the hot-tub while the other went to the strands of Aidan's hair.

After he removed his tongue from inside her and began circling and suckling her clit, he thrust one finger and then two into her. Mimicking the crooking he had done before with his finger, he hit her g-spot, and Emma threw her head back and screamed. As he continued to assault her with his fingers and tongue, she cried out his name. Her hand abandoned his hair and both went to grip the sides of the hot-tub. Her hips moved against his mouth and fingers, forcing him deeper, as she lifted her ass on and off the side of the hot-tub. Just when she thought she couldn't stand anymore, she tensed as she came hard and fast.

"Aidan! Oh yes! YES!" she cried.

Although she was still clenching around his fingers, Aidan used his other arm to pull her off the side of the hot-tub to straddle him. Instead of having her face him, he turned her to ride him the opposite way. He replaced his fingers with his pulsing erection. He groaned against her back when he slid deep inside. Gripping Emma's hips, he worked her on and off his cock.

Emma leaned back so she could turn her head to kiss him. Her arm curved around to wrap her fingers in his tousled hair. As his tongue plunged into her mouth, his hands left her waist to cup her aching breasts. He kneaded the flesh and twisted her nipples into hardened peaks, causing her to gasp with pleasure into his mouth.

"Can you take it harder, babe?" he panted against her cheek.

"Yes."

His hands left her breasts, and he once again gripped her waist. He raised his hips to thrust harder as he pushed her on and off his cock. Emma glanced over her shoulder at him before clenching her walls tight around him. "Oh fuck, Em," he muttered before throwing his head back against the hot tub wall.

Bracing her hands on her thighs, she rode him faster and faster until they were both grunting and groaning with pleasure as the sound of smacking skin and thrashing water echoed through the room. After awhile, Aidan asked in a ragged breath, "Are you close?"

"Maybe," she replied.

His response was to take one of his hands and bring it between her legs. The moment his fingers rubbed against her clit, she came undone. She cried out his name again as she collapsed back against him, resting her head against his shoulder. He gave a few more hard thrusts before spilling himself inside her.

Once Aidan finished convulsing, he wrapped his arms tightly around her before kissing a moist trail up her neck. "Damn, that was worth the wait."

Since she could barely move, Emma murmured, "You think?"

"Oh yes."

"I'm glad you think so. I wanted our first time making love as man and wife to be special." Glancing at him, she grinned. "I'm not sure what we just did qualified as making love, but I'll take it."

Her body rose and fell with his laugher. "No, it wasn't. I'll make it up to you. Next time it'll be slow and gentle—real lovemaking for my wife." When he sucked on her earlobe, she shivered.

"Mmm, that sounds good." Their moment was interrupted by Emma's stomach rumbling.

"Guess you worked up an appetite, huh?" Aidan mused.

"I'm always hungry lately. Or I guess I should say *Noah* is always hungry lately."

"Go on and raid the pantry."

[343]

"You sure?"

With a cocky grin, he asked, "What kind of sex-obsessed asshole would I be to deny you sustenance?"

"Hmm, your usual self?" she teased.

"Not funny." He grunted before easing out of her and gently pushing her to her feet. When she wobbled a bit, his hands grabbed her waist. "Easy now. Let me help you out." After he climbed out of the hot-tub, he took both of her hands in his to make sure she didn't slip.

She rewarded his efforts with a kiss. "Thank you, my love."

"You're welcome."

Two terry cloth robes hung behind the door, and after toweling off, Emma gladly threw on one. She padded down the hallway into the kitchen. Flinging open the massive stainless steel refrigerator door, she eyed the contents. Aidan must've placed quite an order for them because there was a huge vegetable tray, one of all kind of sandwich meats and cheeses, and a bowl of fresh fruit.

After grabbing the vegetable and fruit, her eyes landed on a can of whipped cream. Glancing back at the bedroom, she nibbled her lip and wondered if she had the sassiness to actually suggest it. Turning around, she placed the items on the counter before taking a deep breath and grabbing it. As she started munching on some carrots and celery, she knew what she really wanted. "Babe?" she called.

"Yeah?"

"Did you bring in that box of food that Grammy sent with the BBQ leftovers?"

"Hang on. I think it's in here."

While she heard him fumbling around in the mountain of suitcases, she opened the fruit bowl. She was half-way through it when he finally appeared. "Grammy's to-go boxes look like luggage," he mused.

"She's serious about the Tupperware and containers." Motioning to the floral bag, Emma said, "I bought her that from the Americus Mart in Atlanta." Then something else caught her eye, and she gulped. "You found my handcuffs?"

A mischievous grin curved on his lips. "While looking for the leftovers, I found your treat bag."

Her cheeks warmed at the thoughts of some of the items. "Most of what was in there were joke gifts from my lingerie shower. Not real stuff for us to use."

"Then why did you bring them?"

She shrugged. "I was in a hurry, so I just threw it all in the bag."

Aidan twirled the furry green handcuffs on his finger. "You don't want to try these?"

Nibbling on her lip, she said, "I will if you will."

"What's that supposed to mean?"

Slowly she walked around the side of the counter. Aidan hadn't even bothered putting on a robe or any clothes. She snatched the handcuffs off his finger with one hand while she brought her other to his chest. Pushing him, she directed him over to one of the kitchen chairs. "Sit," she instructed.

"Yes, ma'am," he replied, a curious gleam in his eye.

Opening up one of the cuffs, she took his hand. Without protesting, Aidan let her snap it around his wrist. Walking behind him, she pulled his other hand back and then cuffed him. Aidan tugged against the binding, but it didn't give. "Hmm, am I your prisoner now?"

"Maybe."

Glancing over her shoulder, the can of whipped cream caught her eye. When she started over to get it, Aidan shimmied around in the chair. "Where are you going?"

She grinned back at him. "You'll see." She grabbed the can then made her way back over to him.

He gazed at the can and then cocked his brows at her. "And just what do you plan to do with that?"

"Why eat it of course." She shook it up and then popped off the top. Leaning over, she squirted a zigzagging line from his chestbone down to his belly button. Aidan jerked at the cold liquid hitting his skin. Straddling him, she eased down on his lap. When she licked her lips in anticipation, Aidan's growing erection bucked between them. She stared down at it and grinned. "Down boy. You'll get your turn."

Aidan groaned at the insinuation and let his head fall back. She brought her mouth to his chest and started licking and sucking off the whipped cream. Aidan's breath hitched as she went further down, nibbling and tasting his skin. Just when she got to his erection, she started her way back up his chest. He let out a frustrated gasp of air and bucked his hips. Once she had licked his chest clean, she climbed off his lap.

"Stand up."

"Wait-what?" Aidan frantically asked.

Emma rolled her eyes. "Do you honestly think I'm getting on my knees on this hardwood?" She made a tsking noise. "You gotta work with me Big Papa."

A relieved look flashed on his face. "Thank God."

She brought her lips to his, giving him a long, lingering kiss. Aidan swept his tongue around her mouth and over her lips, searching out the sweetness of the whipped cream. Sliding her hand between them, she worked her fingers over his hardness.

Aidan moaned against her lips. She released him and then broke their kiss to ease down in the chair. His hands fought against the cuffs. "Take off your robe," he commanded.

She glanced up at him and shook her head. "Please?" he croaked.

"You really want me naked?"

"Mmm, you know I always want to see you. Your breasts, your legs, your pussy."

"Aidan!" she squealed dropping the whipped cream.

"What?"

"I can't believe you said that word!"

"Which one?" he teased.

[348]

Knowing he wouldn't let up until she said it, she whispered, "Pussy."

He chuckled. "What would you rather me say? Your cu—"

Her hand flew over his mouth to silence him, and she shook her head wildly. "No, no! That one is even worse."

When she took her hand away, a smirk curved on his lips. "Emma, did you not enjoy me stroking and licking your *pussy* tonight?"

"Please stop saying that!" She bent over to pick up the whipped cream can.

"When I get out of these handcuffs, I'm going to finger your—"

She shot him a warning look. "I mean it, Aidan."

A wicked grin flashed on his face. "You're going to beg me to fuck your...*down there*."

Fighting not to smile, she said, "If you don't stop, I'm going to use the sash of this robe to gag you so I don't have to hear you anymore."

Aidan chuckled. "At least that means you'd be naked."

"You're impossible."

"Come on, babe. I just saw every inch of you fifteen minutes ago."

"Fine, fine. If it'll shut you up," she huffed. She untied the sash, and the bulky robe fell from her body.

Aidan gave her an appreciative wink. "Thank you, beautiful."

She glanced shyly up at him. "You're welcome."

Cocking his head, he then asked, "Now will you please suck me off?"

Emma busted out laughing. "When you ask nicely like that, of course I will," she teased. She waved the can of whipped cream at him. "But let's sweeten the pot, okay?"

"Mmm, okay."

After squirting a considerable about of whipped cream into the palm of her hand, she started slathering Aidan's cock. He shuddered and closed his eyes. When she leaned over to flick her tongue across the tip, he groaned. She slid her tongue from the root back to the tip, nipping and licking off the sweetness. Then she gripped him in one hand and swept him into her mouth. Hollowing her cheeks, she suctioned him hard.

He bucked his hips while his arms flexed against the binding of the cuffs. She knew he wanted to be free to wrap his fingers in her hair. When she let him fall free of her mouth, his body trembled. "Em, please."

Ignoring him, she went about licking off the remaining whipped cream while making long strokes with her hand. Her fingers were almost stuck together, so she sped up the pace. Taking only the tip back in her mouth, she swirled her tongue around and around the shaft, alternating between suctioning it and teasingly flicking it. Aidan's chest heaved, and his breath came in raspy pants.

When she took him deeper in her mouth, a groan rumbled through his chest. She could feel him tensing and tightening for release. She jerked him harder and faster in her hand while her mouth worked over him. "Yes...uh...oh God, Em!" A shudder ran through his body as he came into her mouth. "Fuck yes!" His hips jerked and bucked through his release.

He gazed down at her with a thoroughly fucked gleam in his eyes. "Please tell me you have a key for these?"

Rising out of the chair, she then crooked her finger for him to follow her down the hall, and he happily obliged.

CHAPTER TWENTY

One Month Later

Aidan trudged through the garage door, exhausted at the prospect of boarding a plane for Charlotte in just a few hours. At least he'd gotten to leave work a little early. After he dropped his briefcase on the kitchen table, he called, "Em?"

"I'm in the nursery," she replied, her voice muffled from above.

He smiled as he started up the stairs. Her voice raised in song trilled back to him. When he got to the nursery doorway, he saw her bustling around, putting away some blue blankets in the chest of drawers. "Hey baby."

She whirled around. "Hey. I was just finishing up in here, and then I was going to pack your bag."

With a grimace, he said, "I'm still not so sure about leaving you."

She crossed the room to him. "It's going to be fine. You'll barely be gone for two days."

"I still don't like it."

Emma wrapped her arms around his neck. "My due date isn't for another three and a half weeks. First babies rarely come early, so it's going to be fine."

"You're still having Casey come spend the night with you, right?"

She grinned. "Yes, worry-wart. In fact, she and Connor are taking me to dinner, and then we're having a slumber party."

Aidan laughed. "That should be an interesting evening."

"Jealous that you'll miss the make-overs and gossip?"

"No, I think I'll pass."

"Suit yourself."

He gazed around the light blue nursery walls. At first, he was skeptical about Emma's idea of doing a Noah's Ark theme to play on Noah's name. Through her work contacts, she had found an artist to draw a rainbow and animal themed mural along the walls. He couldn't believe how amazing it had turned out. The last piece of furniture had been delivered the week before, so the room was now outfitted with a bed, changing table, chest of drawers, and glider and ottoman. Now all it needed was Noah himself to complete the picture. "Looks like you've got everything just about ready for Little Man's arrival."

She nodded while rubbing her belly. "Just a few more stuffed animals…the full-sized giraffe and elephant are still on backorder."

"More stuffed animals? You already have enough animals in here to make a zoo."

She grinned. "No, it's an Ark we're going for, babe."

"Whatever."

She grabbed his hand. "Come on. You can shower and shave while I get you packed."

"Are you insinuating I stink?"

She giggled as they started down the stairs. "No, but considering you overslept this morning and ran out the door without shaving, least of all showering, I'm thinking you should have one before your business dinner tonight."

"I thought you liked it when I had a little stubble?"

She smiled and rubbed his cheek. "I do, baby."

His reached out to caress her backside as they started into the bedroom. "You usually like it most when it's rubbing against your thighs as I'm going down on you."

"Aidan Fitzgerald!" she squealed smacking his hand away.

He laughed. "You know it's the truth."

She wagged a finger at him. "Go get in the shower, dirty boy."

Wrapping his arms around her waist, he pulled her to him. "I could be a lot dirtier if we were to have a quickie—a nice send-off before I have to leave."

She squirmed out of his arms. "You need to clean up, and then you have a flight to catch, mister. So get busy."

Aidan groaned. "You're such a party pooper lately. No loving for your man. I thought the sex ban wasn't supposed to happen until *after* Noah was born."

He knew he was in serious trouble when her green eyes narrowed at him. "Yeah, well, I'm *so* sorry that I'm exhausted from working full-time, keeping up this house, and most of all, carrying your son whose Fitzgerald stubbornness knows no bounds when he wants to kick and move all night when he should be sleeping," she countered.

Raking his hand through his hair, he gave a defeated sigh. "I'm sorry. I just miss you—I miss us. That's all," he said before he trudged into the bathroom.

He showered and shaved in record time. Wrapping a towel around his waist, Aidan opened the bathroom door. He took one step into the bedroom and froze. His mouth gaped open in shock.

Emma lounged on the bed, propped up on her elbows in the green negligee he had bought for their engagement night that she never got to wear. What truly made his cock twitch was the fact she was wearing her cowboy boots and a cowboy hat.

His mouth ran dry. "What are you doing?"

"Well, since I've been so tired lately and haven't been in the mood, I felt bad about denying you a quickie. You really have been kind and understanding, and a horndog like you does have his breaking point."

Aidan chuckled. "Thanks...I think."

"So, I thought I'd make it up to you by giving you the going away present wanted," she replied with a coy smile. She patted the bed beside her. "So giddy-up, Cowboy. I'm finally ready for a ride."

Aidan cocked his head and grinned. "Well, yippee ki-yay, mother fucker!"

She giggled as he closed the gap between them. "I can't believe you just made a *Die Hard* reference."

"Yeah, well, I can't believe you told me to giddy-up like I'm some horse."

"You were my stud horse once upon a time, remember?"

"*Were*. I'm your husband now, so the whole giddy-up thing is a little ridiculous."

"Roll-playing, babe." Sweeping her hat off her head, she placed it on his. When he started to take it off, she said, "Uh-huh. I like it."

"You can't be serious?"

She bit her lip before reaching over to snap the towel from his waist. She drank in his appearance and then grinned up at him. "Mmm, yes, I like the sight of you naked in a cowboy hat very, *very* much."

"Em, you naughty girl," he murmured, as he leaned over to kiss her. He made quick work of whisking the negligee over her head. The sight of her voluptuous, naked form sent his erection bobbing against his stomach. He cupped her full breasts as his tongue plunged into her mouth. He worked the nipples until they were erect buds, causing Emma to moan and nibble his bottom lip between her teeth.

She then brought her hands around his neck and stroked and tugged the hair at the base of his neck. He groaned into her mouth as his fingers trailed from her breast down to the apex of her thighs. "No underwear? You were pretty confident your little stunt would ensure I was a sure thing, huh?"

She laughed. "And when are you *not* a sure thing?"

"Never. Because I never get enough of you."

Emma's amused expression faded. "Aw, baby, that's so sweet," she said, her eyes shining with love for him. She brought her lips to his and kissed him passionately, letting her emotions flow out through her kisses. "I love you, Aidan," she murmured against his lips.

"I love you, too." Easing her on her back, he gripped her hips and slid her bottom to the edge of the bed. Opening her legs wide, he positioned himself between them as he stayed on his feet. "You okay with not taking me for a ride?"

"You can take me anyway you want, Cowboy."

He gave her a wicked grin as his fingers found her center, which was already dripping with need. "You really were ready for me, huh?"

"It's the hat," she panted as he worked his fingers in and out of her.

He rolled his eyes. "Seriously?"

She scowled at him. "You fantasize about me in green lingerie—I wanted you in a cowboy hat."

"Then I'm glad I can make your fantasies come true." He found her sweet spot, and she gripped the sides of the bed.

"Oh yes, yes, right there, Aidan. Oh God! Please!" she cried, bucking her hips into his hand. When he sent her over the edge, her head writhed back and forth as she came.

He slid his fingers out of her and then positioned himself at her entrance. With one thrust, he filled her, causing them both to moan. "Mmm, wrap your legs around me tight, babe. I want those delicious cowboy boots digging in my ass."

She obliged him, and he gasped with pleasure. Gripping the sides of the mattress, he began thrusting in and out of her. Emma's legs remained tight around him, and when he slowed his pace, she dug her boot heels into his flesh, indicating she wanted him to speed up.

Staring down at her, he cocked his brows. "Are you sure?"

She licked her lips. "Mmm, hmm," she murmured.

Obeying her command, Aidan pounded into her. The more frantic his movements became the more sweat began to trickle down his body. He would almost need another shower when he was finished with her. He knew they didn't have long so when her walls clenched around him, signifying she had gone over the edge, he gripped her hips and thrust faster and harder until he cried out her name as he came inside her.

Panting, he leaned over to plant a kiss on her lips. "Thank you, babe. That was a helluva send off."

She giggled. "And thank you for indulging my cowboy fantasy."

"You're welcome, ma'am." Aidan replied, while tipping his hat back. "Now after you unwrap your delicious legs from me, might you oblige me with a ride to the airport?"

"I'd be happy, too."

"Just give me a second to drown myself in some cologne to mask this heady sex smell. Don't want to make my business associates jealous that I got some."

"Aidan!" Emma squealed, shoving him off of her.

He chuckled. "There's nothing I love more than teasing you, Em. Especially when you react like that."

She grinned. "And I love that you have to tease me so mercilessly."

His thumb came to caress her cheek. "And I love you."

CHAPTER TWENTY-ONE

After dropping Aidan off at the airport, Emma hurried back home. She had just enough time to get ready before the doorbell rang, announcing Casey's arrival.

Beau trailed down the hallway behind her as she went to answer the door. On the second ring, Emma cried, "Would you give me a break? I'm moving slow."

She heard Casey's laughter out on the porch before the doorbell began to go on and off at lighting speed. "Don't be a twatwaffle, Case!" Emma said, as she threw open the door.

Casey wiped her eyes from her amusement. "I had to tease you." She then took in Emma's appearance. "Aw, Em, you look beautiful," she squealed, kissing her cheek.

"Thanks. I feel like I threw myself together."

"What do you mean? You had all afternoon to get ready before you took Aidan to the airport, didn't you?"

Emma ducked her head, a flush creeping across her cheeks. "Well, I might've given Aidan a going away present."

Casey once again roared with laughter. "Em, you naughty girl."

"I can't help it. Even though I'm exhausted, stupid pregnancy hormones have me horny all the time!"

"Hmm, I'm horny all the time, and I don't even have the benefit of being pregnant," Casey mused.

"Then you'll kill poor Nate when you're pregnant. It's insane. Trust me."

Wrinkling her nose, Casey said, "Well, that's something I'll have to worry about in the far distant future. It sure as hell ain't happening now."

Emma grabbed her purse. "Ready to go?"

"Yep. Let's go get Connor."

Fifteen minutes later, Casey swung into Connor's driveway. He was insistent on driving them in his brand new Lexus 350 SUV. "Sweet ride, buddy," Emma said as she climbed into the backseat.

"Thanks. Jeff and I really like it."

"Everything still going well with you two?" she asked.

Connor glanced back at her and grinned. "Yep. In fact, we're talking about getting married."

"Really? That's wonderful."

"Yeah, obviously we won't be able to do it around here, but we're all about making the commitment.

"That's awesome," Casey said, buckling her seatbelt.

"I'm going to expect you two to be my bridesmaids…or groomsmen…hell, something in the bridal party."

Emma and Casey laughed. "It would be our pleasure," Casey replied.

"As long as it's after I've had enough time to get some baby weight off," Emma teased.

Connor eased up to the red-light. "Oh please. Like you'll have that much to lose."

Emma groaned. "Trust me. It's more than you think." Leaning forward in the seat, she waved her swollen fingers at Connor. "See some of the lovely fluid retention."

"Ew, that's disgusting."

"You should see my feet."

Casey shook her head. "Oh please, Em. You're weight gain is basically only tits and belly."

Emma wrinkled her nose as Connor snickered. "And you've had a bodacious set of ta-ta's since 7th grade."

[363]

"Connor!" she cried before smacking his arm.

"Please, you know that from the time you turned twelve, every guy was talking to your boobs and not your face."

Emma rolled her eyes. "Okay, okay. That's enough talk about my breasts for one evening. I think it's time for a conversation change!"

"Fine," Casey and Connor murmured in unison.

"So where are we off to eat?" Casey asked.

"There's two new restaurant openings downtown tonight. Might be some celebrity sightings, too," Connor said. He glanced back at Emma to gage her response.

She wrinkled her nose. "Can't we do something more familiar with less of a crowd?"

"Jesus, you already sound like an old-fart married woman," Connor moaned.

"I can't help that being pregnant makes me tired."

"Oh no. Don't be blaming it on the pregnancy. It's your fault for giving Aidan a sexy send-off complete with cowboy boots," Casey said with a wicked grin.

Emma flushed as Connor groaned. "Oh God, I could have lived a life-time without that one." He shook his head like he was trying to shake himself of the thought. "Okay, so no high-end, glitzy places for Miss Banging Boots back there."

"Ugh, I can't believe you two sometimes," Emma grumbled as Casey snickered.

"Well, it's your night, love, so you can pick," Casey said.

"How about the Cheesecake Factory?" Emma suggested.

"Fine, we'll go to the uber not happening Perimeter location," Connor joked.

"Good. I'm excited," Emma said with a grin.

When they got to the restaurant, they had to fight their way through the teeming crowd. "Doesn't look so uber not happening to me!" Emma shouted over the noise.

"It's Friday night. It's going to be crazy anywhere."

Thirty minutes later when they finally got a table, Emma's feet were screaming in agony. As she flopped down in the booth, pain shot up her lower back. "Ow!" she yelped.

"Are you okay?"

She giggled. "Yeah, I was expecting a little more cushioning—not that I don't have enough padding back there." When Connor started to open his mouth, she wagged a finger at him. "I don't need any comments about how I've always had junk in my trunk either, thank you very much."

"You're such a prude," he replied with a wink.

By the time they finished their meal and Emma had gorged herself on her favorite Reese's Peanut Butter Cup Cheesecake, she was exhausted. She wanted nothing more than to go home, get into her pajamas, and curl up on the couch. She just hoped that Casey and Connor didn't have anymore big plans for the evening.

As they got up, Emma winced as her hand flew to rub her back. What had been a dull throbbing during dinner was now pulsing. She hobbled out of the restaurant and tried desperately to keep up with Connor and Casey.

"Guys, we're not running the Peachtree Road Race. Would you slow down!" she called.

"God, Em, just when I thought you couldn't be any slower," Casey remarked, walking back to her.

"My back is killing me."

Casey snorted. "Do you have a sex sprain?"

Emma narrowed her eyes. "It isn't a sex sprain. It started back in the booth."

Thankfully, they made it to the car. When she got up into the SUV, a strange feeling rippled through her back and belly before a deluge of water swept down her thighs. At first, mortification filled her that she was experiencing pregnancy incontinence. But then the revelation hit her. She had gone to the bathroom before their meal arrived…and before dessert. "Oh God," she murmured.

"What's wrong?" Casey asked, checking her reflection in the mirror and applying more lip stick.

Emma drew in a ragged breath. "Um, I think my water just broke."

Both Casey and Connor whirled around in their seats, shock and horror etched across their faces. "What?" Casey demanded.

"Yeah, I'm pretty sure. It's all over me."

"Oh shit, Em, don't tell me you just ruined my new leather seats?" Connor moaned.

Casey smacked his arm hard. "It's not like she can help it."

Embarrassment warmed Emma's cheeks. "I'm so, so sorry, Connor. I promise I'll pay to have it professionally cleaned." The moment the words left her lips raging pain crisscrossed its way through her abdomen, causing her to cry out. She pinched her eyes shut and breathed in deep, trying to ride it out.

"Em?" Casey questioned.

Once the pain passed, she opened her eyes. Both Casey and Connor stared expectantly at her. "Yeah, um, I think we're going to have to cancel our sleepover. I need to get to the hospital. *Now*."

CHAPTER TWENTY-TWO

"Goodnight!" Aidan called as he left his business dinner. Rolling his shoulders, he fought the fatigue that filled him. He wanted nothing more than to get back to the hotel and call it a night. When Emma's familiar ring tone came on, he dug his phone out of his pocket. "Miss me already, sweetheart?" he joked.

"You have no idea," she replied, her voice strained.

He froze on the sidewalk. "Em, is there something wrong?"

"Um, well, don't freak out—"

"Too late."

"My water broke, and I just got admitted to the hospital."

Aidan's eyes closed in agony. "You can't be serious."

"Trust me, I wish I was joking."

"But you're not due for three more weeks. I would have never, ever left."

"Listen, it's okay. You just need to get to the airport."

"Em, there's not a single flight out of Charlotte back to Atlanta tonight."

"I know. That's why I have Plan B."

"And just what does that entail?"

"Pesh is on his way up to get you in his plane."

"You have got to be kidding me." When she didn't respond for a minute, he said, "Em, are you there?"

He heard her draw in a ragged breath. "Having.a.really.bad.pain."

He winced. "Oh shit. I'm sorry. I want to be there so bad to hold your hand...to help you."

It took her a few seconds to respond. "Good. Then you'll meet Pesh at the airport—"

"Em, you know I have a thing about small planes."

"Aidan," she growled before huffing and puffing.

When she groaned in agony, he knew he was in trouble. "Let me guess, at the moment, you don't give a shit about my fears or what I want or don't want to do, right?"

"Exactly!" she snapped.

"Okay, okay. I'll get to the airport, and I'll be there as soon as I can."

"Good."

"I love you, Em."

"I love you, too."

With fear and trepidation rocketing through him, Aidan raised a shaky hand to flag down a cab. Screw his bags back at the hotel. Noah was on the way, and he desperately needed to get to Emma. He had just slid across the cab's leather seat when his cell phone rang again. Even though it was an unknown number, he had an idea who it was.

"Hello, this is Pesh Nadeen," the familiar voice echoed on the other line.

"Um, hey."

"Listen. When you get to the airport, have them bring you to the small planes hanger, rather than the main gates. I'll be waiting for you."

"Okay. And uh, thanks again for doing this for Emma...I mean, for me. For us."

"No problem. It's my pleasure."

Aidan rolled his eyes as he hung up the phone. Of course, it was his pleasure. Pesh was just the kind of standup guy that even when nothing could be gained romantically with Emma, he would still do the right thing. Pesh's kindness shouldn't have irritated Aidan so much, but for some reason, he just couldn't let go of what had almost happened between Emma and Pesh.

Aidan wrung his hands the entire trip to the airport. When he got out, he glanced around the hanger. His eyes widened and a shudder ran over him at the sight of what he imagined was Pesh's plane already on the small runway.

He stuck his head in the door, eyeing all the other death traps contained within. "Um, hello?"

Pesh came out of a side door with a clipboard. "Hey, Aidan. I was just logging our flight plan with the tower. But we're good to go now."

"Oh, okay."

As they started out of the hanger and onto the tarmac, Aidan skidded to a stop. When Pesh realized he was no longer walking beside him, he turned around. "What's wrong?"

"Emma didn't mention what I thought about small planes?"

"No, but she seemed to be a little preoccupied with getting you to Atlanta when I talked to her."

Aidan winced. "It's just I sorta have this aversion…or fear about anything smaller than a 747."

[372]

Pesh's dark brows furrowed. "But this is a Cessna 270—one of the safest small planes around."

Gesturing at the aircraft, Aidan asked, "That isn't the kind that JFK Jr. crashed, is it?"

Pesh shook his head. "That was a Piper Saratoga." He opened the side door for Aidan. "Go on, hop in. We need to get on our way." At Aidan's continued hesitation, the corners of Pesh's lips quirked up. "You're really afraid, aren't you?"

Aidan narrowed his eyes. "Yeah, I am. Call me a pussy or whatever you want to, but these things are death traps!"

Without another word, Pesh dug into the bag at his side. He took out a bottle of pills and tossed it at Aidan. "What the hell is this?" Aidan demanded.

"Valium. It'll help you relax during the flight."

Aidan smirked at Pesh. "Isn't that kinda illegal for doctors to just have drugs lying around to push off on people?"

"I'm not a pill pusher," Pesh snapped. Pain washed over his face. "The pills belonged to my late wife. She always got nervous flying commercially or in my plane. They're expired, so they won't be as potent, but it should be enough to calm you down."

Aidan opened his mouth, but Pesh started around the plane. "Fuck," he muttered under his breath. He had just been a major dick to a guy who was just trying to help him get back home to see his child be born. Popping open the bottle, he threw back two of the pills since they were expired. He swallowed them down and then shuddered at the remaining taste in his mouth.

Putting one foot in front of the other, he walked over to the plane and climbed inside. Pesh already had a head-set on and was flipping switches. "Hey," Aidan said. When Pesh didn't reply, Aidan reached over and touched his arm. "I'm sorry. That was a real asshole thing for me to say to you. I mean, you were only trying to help me—in more ways than one."

Pesh shrugged. "It's all right. You're just stressed."

"That's no excuse for me to act like such a dick, especially about your late wife." Aidan drew in a ragged breath. "Emma never told me you were a widower. I'm very sorry for your loss."

"Thank you," Pesh replied. He gave Aidan a genuine smile before turning back to the cockpit and controls. When they lurched forward to start their descent down the runaway, Aidan gripped the side of his seat.

Pesh handed him a set of headphones. "Here, this will help with the cabin noise."

Aidan reluctantly put them on. He heard a voice ringing in his ear. "Flight 33, you are now ready for take-off."

"Roger that," Pesh replied.

Aidan closed his eyes tight, hoping the expired Valium would start taking effect. He focused his thoughts on Emma, wondering how she was doing. He hoped and prayed that Noah would wait to come until he could be there. Aidan wanted nothing more than to see his first born take his first breath.

The next time he opened his eyes they were climbing altitude. Darkness enveloped the plane as they careened through the wispy strands of clouds. Once they had leveled off, Pesh reached for his phone.

"Dude, what the hell are you doing?"

"I need to make a quick call."

Aidan shook his head wildly back and forth. "Uh-huh. Watch the skies or something. You don't need to be distracted and make us crash!"

Pesh chuckled. "Calm down. I've got this covered."

Aidan grumbled under his breath. He would have given anything if he had his rosary with him. Of course, he would probably have to dig through several of his drawers to find where it was. *God, I will totally and completely go to Mass every day…well, at least every week, if you will get me safely out of this death trap and safe and sound to Emma's side.*

Pesh's voice snapped Aidan out of his thoughts. "This is Dr. Alpesh Nadeen. I'm requesting to be kept in constant contact on the condition of Emma Harrison, 4th Floor Maternity. Anything and everything on delivery status should be called in." After a beat, Pesh nodded. "Thank you." He turned his phone off and handed it to Aidan. "Now you'll know everything that's going on."

Aidan arched his eyebrows at Pesh. "Wow, thank you."

"No problem. I can't imagine how hard this must be for you."

With a snort Aidan replied, "Whatever emotional hell it might be on me, I don't even want to think about what Emma's going through."

"You can rest assured she's getting the best physical care."

Aidan grimaced. "Shit, I don't even want to think about the physical part…especially the pain she might be in. I wanted to be there for her through all that."

"If there's one certainty about Emma, she's as strong as nails emotionally and physically. She'll make it through."

[376]

"You think?"

Pesh turned to him and grinned. "After the epidural takes effect, I'm sure of it."

They were interrupted by the ringing of Aidan's cell phone. He snapped it out of his suit pocket. "Hello? Em?"

"No, it's Casey. Emma wanted me to call and make sure you were okay and in flight."

Aidan's heart melted at the thought that even in her condition, Emma was still her usual compassionate self and worrying about him. "Tell her I'm fine, and to not give one more thought of me."

Casey started to relay the message and then Aidan heard a shriek. "Damn, Emmie Lou, lighten up with the squeezing! I'd like to be able to have feeling in my hand again," Connor screeched.

"Um, so how are things going?" he asked hesitantly.

"You don't want to know."

"Well, Pesh has the hospital keeping us posted on her condition too."

"Good because right now she's giving me the evil eye for being on the phone."

"Hey, Em, we could put you and Aidan on Skype if you'd like?" Connor suggested.

"I do not want my vagina Skyping! I just want Aidan here, okay?" Emma shouted with a rage that Aidan hadn't experienced very many times.

"See what I mean?" Casey asked.

"Shit, that's intense."

"Oh thank God. The anesthesiologist just walked in. Be careful okay?"

"I will. Give Emma my love."

"Will do."

Aidan hung up the phone and squirmed in his seat. "Things are pretty rough at the moment, huh?" Pesh asked.

"Yeah," he murmured.

"It's going to be fine, Aidan."

He turned to see Pesh's reassuring smile. "She'll still love you after this, too. You've made all her dreams come true. The moment she holds Noah in her arms for the first time any of the pain and suffering she experienced will just evaporate in an instant. And *you* will be the one who gave that to her."

"Damn, you really are a decent guy, aren't you?"

Pesh chuckled. "I guess I am."

The cockpit seemed to start spinning around, and Aidan had to close his eyes from the dizziness. "Is that you doing that or the drugs?"

"It's safe to say that it's the drugs."

The next thing Aidan knew he was being shaken awake. "Come on, sleepy head. We gotta get in the car."

"It's over? We didn't crash?" Aidan asked as he rubbed his eyes.

"Nope. We're safe and sound here at McCollum."

The mention of the airport snapped Aidan into action. He fumbled out of his seat belt and then fell out the door Pesh had opened for him. "We're only ten minutes from the hospital, right?"

"Yep. Last call came through shortly before we landed. Noah's still not here, and Emma's only dilated to seven."

Aidan's brows furrowed. All the pregnancy knowledge seemed to have flown out the window. "Wait, so that means…?"

"No pushing until ten. We've got time."

"Thank God."

[379]

They slid into Pesh's waiting Jaguar. At Pesh's lead foot, Aidan raised his brows. "Not worried about cops?"

"Being a doctor is like having a Get Out of Jail free pass. All I have to say is there's an emergency."

Aidan grinned. "I'm liking you more and more every minute."

Pesh laughed. "I knew I would grow on you."

"I'm not sure about that one."

They pealed up to the entrance of Labor and Delivery. Aidan threw open the car door. When he went to close it, he met Pesh's gaze. "I can never, ever thank you enough for this. I'm serious."

"I was happy to do it. For Emma…and for you." Pesh smiled. "Now go meet your son."

"I will. And thanks again!" Aidan sprinted from the curb and through the mechanized sliding doors. He hopped onto the first available elevator. Once he got to the floor, he raced down the hallway to Emma's room.

He skidded in the door. At the sight of a nurse between Emma's legs, he had an odd feeling of Deju vu from when he brought her to the emergency room. Bending over, he propped his elbows on his knees and tried to catch his breath.

"Hello there, Big Papa! You're just in time," Connor said, with a grin.

"Really?" he panted.

The nurse smiled. "Yes, she's just dilated to ten, and we're going to start pushing."

"Aidan, come here," Emma said, her voice a little hoarse.

He stumbled forward to reach her side. He cupped her face in his hands before kissing her on the lips. He then kissed both her cheeks and her forehead. "I'm sorry, Em. I'm so, so sorry I wasn't here for you."

"It's all right. You couldn't help it."

"I know but—"

Emma gave him a weak smile. "I'll let you make it up to me some other time, okay?"

He gave a playful groan. "Ah, so this will be the ammunition you use against me for years to come, huh?"

"Maybe."

He brushed the sweat slick strands of silky auburn hair out of her face. "Has it been bad?"

"The pain?" When he nodded, she made a face. "It was pretty horrible until the epidural kicked in."

"The bruises on my arms will vouch for that one," Connor quipped.

"So you're not hurting now?"

"Nope. In fact, they have to tell me I'm having a contraction."

Aidan glanced over his shoulder at Casey. "Guess you guys got to have all the fun without me, huh?"

Casey grinned. "From the brief glimpse you got on the phone with me, I'm not sure how you can categorize it as fun." She shook her head. "When Em's in pain, she's scarier than Reagan in *The Exorcist.*"

Aidan laughed while Emma blushed. "Was I really that bad?"

"Yeah, but I still love you," Casey replied. She leaned over and kissed Emma's cheek.

The kind, middle aged nurse thrust her hand out to Aidan. "I'm Annie. I assume you're the proud father-to-be?"

Aidan bobbed his head. "Yes, I am."

"I'm so glad you made it in time to see your son come in to the world."

"So am I." His gaze went to Emma's. "I never thought I would say this, but thank God for Pesh."

She smiled. "We do owe him a lot."

Aidan held up his hand. "Let's not get carried away now."

The door pushed open, and a female doctor not much older than Emma entered the room. She looked familiar, and Aidan remembered that he had met her once before when they were doing a Round Robin with all the OB doctors in the practice. The name on her white coat read Dr. Karen Middleton.

She smiled at them. "So Baby Noah has decided to make his entrance into the world?"

Annie nodded her head. "Yes, he has."

Slipping on a pair of rubber gloves, she glanced between Aidan and Emma. "Then let's get the show on the road. Shall we?"

CHAPTER TWENTY-THREE

Emma drew in a deep breath. This was it. When it came down to pushing, it was the real deal.

"Okay, Emma, if you're ready," Annie said.

She nodded, and using her hands, she pushed herself up in the bed.

"If you don't object, we're going to put up a mirror, so you can watch Noah be born. Is that okay?" Annie asked.

"Sure. I want to see him."

"Um, where can I stand to ensure I won't be seeing Em's vagina?" Connor asked. Emma shot him a look, and he held up his hands. "I love you, darlin', but I've made it eighteen years without seeing your vajayjay, and I'd like to keep it that way."

Annie chuckled. "Stand there behind the bed, and you won't catch a glimpse or a reflection," she instructed.

"Thank you so much!"

Annie then motioned at Aidan. "If you'll take one of her legs and," she paused to look between Casey and Connor. Immediately Connor shook his head. "Like I said, I'll be back here in the corner."

Casey laughed. "I would love to help."

Aidan took Emma's left leg while Casey took her right. "Okay, Emma, breathe normally, grab the backs of your legs, and push down while we count," Dr. Middleton instructed.

Emma sucked in a deep breath and then started pushing as hard as she could. She barely heard Dr. Middleton and Annie counting to ten. "Good. Stop." Emma had just caught her breath when Dr. Middleton said, "Okay, again."

Pinching her eyes shut in concentration, she went through three more exhausting rounds when Annie exclaimed, "Open your eyes, honey. He's crowned."

Emma's eyelids flew open, and her expectant gaze honed in on the mirror, peering in wonder at Noah's tiny head. "Aw, Em, it looks like he's got strawberry blonde hair!" Casey commented.

Aidan grinned. "Nah, I think it's redder, and he's more of a Ginger."

She gritted her teeth at him. "Don't you dare call our son a Ginger!"

Connor and Casey laughed while Aidan leaned in and kissed her cheek. "I'm only teasing you, babe. I just hope it will darken up and be as beautiful as yours."

Emma opened her mouth to thank him, but Dr. Middleton interrupted her by saying, "Okay, now another big push." When Annie got to ten and Emma started to relax, Dr. Middleton shook her head. "Keep going, keep going." Just when Emma thought she couldn't go anymore, Dr. Middleton said, "Okay, stop."

Emma's head fell back against the pillow from the exertion. She didn't know if she had any strength left within her to push again. Closing her eyes, she drew in a few deep breaths to dry to dispel the exhaustion.

"Just one more big push, Emma," Dr. Middleton said.

Gripping her hands tight into the backs of her thighs, she put everything she had left and then some into the push. Dr. Middleton's voice echoed over the loud groan emitting from Emma's lips.

"And here he is!" she exclaimed, holding a wailing and bloody Noah up for both Emma and Aidan to see.

The world around Emma shuddered to a stop, and all she could focus on was Noah's strong cries. It was as if every molecule, every cell, and every fiber of her being hummed and buzzed with the new life in front of her. Noah—flesh of her flesh and bone of her bone—was the most beautiful thing she had ever seen or heard for that matter. Tears stung her wide eyes.

"My, my, he's still a big boy for being three weeks early," Dr. Middleton remarked with a smile.

Unable to speak, Emma reached out her arms for Noah, desperate to hold him. He wouldn't feel real until she could put her hands on him. "Hang on, Mama. Let's get him cleaned up a bit," Annie said.

A towel was placed on Emma's belly, and then Noah was laid in it. He continued to scream as Annie toweled him off. Once he was cleaner, she wrapped him in a blanket. An eternity seemed to pass before she handed Noah into Emma's waiting arms.

After kissing the crown of his head, Emma gathered him against her chest. His wailing immediately ceased. His eyes, once pinched shut in anger, popped open, and he stared up at her. The moment their eyes met, Emma's heart stilled and then restarted. Her emotions spiraled out of control, and she wasn't sure if she could keep them in check. "Hey my little angel. I've been waiting for you for so, so long," she murmured.

When Aidan leaned over the side of the bed to rub his thumb over Noah's cheek, Noah kept his gaze on Emma. "Looks like he only has eyes for you," Aidan mused.

She didn't bother wiping the tears streaming down her cheeks. Glancing up at Aidan, she asked, "He's beautiful, isn't he?"

Aidan smiled. "He's the most amazing and beautiful thing I've ever seen in my entire life," he replied, his voice choking off with emotion.

"Daddy, are you ready to cut the cord?" Dr. Middleton asked passing Aidan a pair of surgical scissors.

Emma watched with amusement as Aidan's shaky hands took them from her. "Um…where should I…?"

Annie motioned to an area, and Aidan hesitantly cut Noah from Emma. "Good job."

"Okay, Mama, I hate to take him away, but we need to weigh him and get his PKU done. Then you can have him back for awhile."

After kissing each of his cheeks and his tiny button nose, Emma reluctantly handed Noah over to Annie. Craning her neck, she watched as they set him down on the scales. "He's seven pounds, seven and a half ounces."

"Imagine if he would have stayed in cooking for another three weeks or longer," Aidan said.

Emma shuddered. "Don't even joke about how big he could have been. He was plenty big enough!"

With a chuckle, he kissed her. "Speaking of amazing and beautiful, can I just say how proud I am of you?"

She grinned up at him. "Really?"

He bobbed his head. "I just saw life come out of you. It's…well, it's fucking intense!"

"You know, some men have a hard time ever looking at their wives or girlfriends the same way again after experiencing birth," Dr. Middleton said, finishing up with Emma's post delivery care.

"I can see why," Connor murmured from his corner perch.

Aidan shook his head. "She might be a mother now, but she'll always be my Em," Aidan replied.

"Damn, Big Papa, that was sweet," Casey remarked, swiping the tears from her eyes. She leaned over to brush the hair out of Emma's face. "That was both exhilarating and terrifying. But I wouldn't have missed it for the world."

Emma kissed Casey's cheek. "I'm so glad you were here with me." Glancing over her shoulder, she smiled at Connor. "And you too."

"I'm just glad I got to see it all without having to really see *it* all…if you know what I mean," Connor replied, with a wink.

[389]

Emma and Aidan laughed while Casey shook her head. "I can't believe you're so scared of a vagina."

"I'm intimate enough with Emma without having to get up close and personal with her vagina!" Connor countered.

Emma turned her attention away from Casey and Connor's bickering and back to Noah. She watched as he had his footprints taken, screamed as he was stuck for the PKU, and then finally was swaddled into a blanket and a cap placed on his head. "Ready to hold him, Daddy?" Annie asked with a smile.

Emma's heart melted a little when Aidan glanced back at her for her approval. She grinned and bobbed her head at him.

"You don't want him back first?"

Although she wanted nothing more than to have Noah in her arms again, she wanted Aidan to have his first moment as a father. "No go ahead. It's time you held your son."

"Okay," he said.

As Annie passed Noah into Aidan's waiting arms, tears welled in Emma's eyes at the look of absolute and total wonder that came over Aidan's face. He stared down at Noah, unblinking and unmoving. Finally, he shook his head. "He kinda looks like a glowworm all bundled up like this."

"Keeping him swaddled makes him feel like he's back in the womb," Emma replied.

Aidan continued staring down at Noah. One tiny fist escaped his tight bindings, and he thrust it up at Aidan almost defiantly. It caused Aidan to smile broadly. "Ah, there's that Fighting Fitzgerald spirit coming through. No one ties you down, right Noah?"

Emma shook her head. "You'll be changing your tune about that defiant spirit when he gets to be a teenager."

"Nah, I like him tough and feisty." Noah's response was to stick his tongue out, which made Aidan chuckle. "Yep, see, already a cocky little thing like his Old Man."

Casey took a hesitant step towards Aidan. "So we know he's got his daddy's douchenozzle personality—"

Aidan arched his brows. "Hey now."

Casey grinned and patted his back. "Just teasing you, Big Papa. My question is who does he look like?"

"He looks just like you, Em," Aidan noted as he took in Noah's tiny features.

"Hmm, let me see," Casey said, peering over Aidan's shoulder. She squealed and clapped her hand to her chest. "Oh my God, that face! He's so handsome and adorable!"

Emma beamed from ear to ear at Casey's compliment. Connor walked over to them. "Between Aidan and Emma it was a given he'd be good-looking. But is he really Emma's mini-me?" Connor questioned.

Casey cocked her head. "No, he's got a lot of Big Papa in him, too."

Aidan threw a glance over his shoulder at Casey. "Really?"

She nodded. "His definitely got Em's hair and mouth, but he's got your nose and eyes.

Aidan grinned at Emma. "He got some mighty fine genes that's for sure."

She laughed and rolled her eyes. "Uh-oh," Aidan murmured as Noah's face clouded over, and he appeared ready to cut lose with a giant scream.

"Looks like right now might be a good time to see if he wants to latch on," Annie suggested.

"He's already hungry?" Aidan asked incredulously.

"Some come out of the womb ready to eat, others it takes hours," Annie replied.

"If he's hungry, I want to try," Emma said, holding her arms out for Noah.

"Yeah, um, on that note, I think I'll head out," Connor said, starting for the door.

Casey laughed. "Why don't we go out and tell the rest of the waiting crowd that Noah's here."

"There's a crowd?" Emma asked in surprise.

Casey nodded. "Nate texted me that the waiting room is full with yours and Aidan's families. Patrick's out there, and Grammy and Granddaddy just walked in. He said Becky's boys made her promise to bring them even if it was the middle of the night. "I'm sure they will all want to get a peek at Mr. Handsome.""

Emma felt slightly overwhelmed at the prospect of all the visitors, especially with her post-delivery exhaustion setting in. But a sense of renewal filled her at the thought of all the people waiting to see and love Noah. It made her feel very grateful and very loved. "Okay, that sounds good."

Once Casey and Connor left, Emma slid her hospital gown down on one side and took Noah from Aidan. As she brought him to her breast, apprehension filled her that she might not be able to do this. What if her milk wasn't strong enough, or they had to seek out a Lactation Consultant? She had heard from her friends as well as reading in books how breastfeeding was tricky business.

But miraculously after rooting around for a few seconds, Noah latched on to her nipple and began to nurse heartily.

"Oh you're so very lucky," Annie noted.

With tears filling her eyes, Emma glanced lovingly from her son back up to Aidan. A smile filled her cheeks. "Oh, you have no idea."

Epilogue

Aidan rubbed his blurring eyes before stretching his arms over his head. A glance at the clock on the computer screen told him it was clearly past time to call it a night. His phone buzzing in his jacket pocket also reminded him to get his ass moving. So he grabbed his jacket off the back of the chair along with his briefcase and headed out the door.

When the elevator doors dinged opened, a loud commotion drew his attention. Instead of barreling forward ready to save the day once again, he only smiled. He knew that the cause of the commotion was an eight month old angel with his father's blue eyes and a lighter version of his mother's fiery auburn hair.

Turning the corner, he saw Emma standing beside a stroller, flushed with all the attention Noah was receiving from a gaggle of female admirers. Even though they had almost been married a year, she still took his breath away each and every time he saw her. Most days he didn't get to see her all dressed up like she was now. Outfitted in black stilettos, a short black skirt, and a slinky green top that showed off her fabulous cleavage, she made heat stir below Aidan's waist.

Lately since becoming a stay-at-home mom, Emma spent her time in yoga pants or jeans. But to him, she could look amazingly beautiful and sexy in a ragged t-shirt and his boxers. While she lamented the alleged ten pounds of baby weight she still needed to lose, he loved the fact it seemed to reside in her breasts and ass just as he had teased her about.

In the end, quitting work had been a tough decision for Emma. At first, she had tried working part-time, but most days she still ended up in tears at the prospect of leaving Noah. Because Aidan wanted her to be happy, he suggested she quit. So when Noah was three months old, Emma left the company.

That's why this particular evening she had wanted to meet him at the office so the women she used to work with could see how much Noah had grown. He noticed that not only were several of the women those she worked with, but some of them were from his floor as well, including his secretary Marilyn. They all stood around, smiling and cooing at Noah. He perched in his stroller like a King with his court. Peeking up at them though his long eyelashes, he flashed his two new bottom teeth when he grinned.

Aidan shook his head at his son. He was already a terrible flirt and knew exactly how to work the ladies or anyone for that matter. He was truly a chip off the old shoulder when it came to attracting the attention of females. Of course, anytime Aidan made that comment, Emma liked to smack his arm and roll her eyes.

He strode over to the group of women. "Well hello there."

Noah's gaze jerked from his admirers and over to Aidan's. "Dada!" he cried holding his arms up.

Aidan's heart melted at the sight. No matter how many times he heard Noah call for him, he always had the same reaction. Pure love tingled from the top of his head down to his toes. "Hey Little Man," he said, picking Noah up out of the stroller.

"Give Daddy a kiss," Emma prompted.

Noah immediately leaned over to bestow a wet, slobbery smooch on Aidan's cheek. A chorus of "aw's" rang around him.

"I can't believe how much he looks like you, Aidan," Marilyn said.

"He does, doesn't he?" he replied with a grin directed at Emma.

She rolled her eyes while another woman shook her head. "I see some of Emma in him too—especially that sweet smile of his."

Emma laughed. "That's only when he's not giving the cocky Fitzgerald grin that he does most of the time."

Noah began to squirm in Aidan's arms. "You getting hungry, Little Man?"

Reaching in her bag, Emma took out a pacifier and popped it in Noah's open and ready to scream mouth.

Marilyn smiled. "Well, we better let you two get going."

It took a couple of minutes for them to say their good-byes and for each one to give Noah a kiss on the cheek. While he may have been fussy before, he reveled in their attention and waved happily good-bye before taking out his pacifier to blow kisses.

Aidan set Noah back into the stroller. "I'll get him, babe. You take a breather."

As Emma held open the door for Aidan, she shook her head and grinned. "What?" he asked.

"I'm sure that most people in this building would do a double take at the sight of Mr. Manwhore Fitzgerald pushing a stroller."

He scowled at her. "That's former Mr. Manwhore, thank you."

She giggled. "That's right. You're *my* Mr. Manwhore now." She gave him a playful smack on the behind as they started down the sidewalk.

"Mrs. Fitzgerald, I will kindly ask that you not maul my ass in public."

"Oh really?"

[398]

A sexy smirk curved on his lips. "Save it for when we get home."

Emma giggled. "Okay, then I will."

When the crosswalk sign flashed for them to go, Aidan pushed the stroller onto the street. "Are you sure we should be taking Noah to O'Malley's?"

Emma shot him an exasperated look. "We've brought him here at least five times. Jenny has been blowing up my phone with texts about when we're coming back."

"Yeah, but he was smaller then. And there's all that smoke."

"We sit in the non-smoking section, Aidan." Once they made it to the other side of the street, she gazed up at him. "Besides, he's part Irish. Shouldn't he be growing up around booze?"

He rolled his eyes. "Har fucking har."

She grinned and then linked her arm through his. "I love you, babe."

"Right back atcha," he replied, before leaning over to kiss her.

When Emma reached to open the door, Jenny burst through it. "Oh my God! I thought you guys had decided not to come!" She barely gave a fleeting glance at Aidan and Emma before she reached out to Noah. "There's my big, beautiful boy!" After spitting out his pacifier, he grinned and waved his arms to let Jenny pick him up.

"I see we rank pretty low these days, huh?" Aidan said with a smile.

"Exactly. At least it's consistent. I mean, everywhere we go from your dad's to Grammy and Granddaddy's it's the same," Emma replied.

As Jenny bounced Noah in her arms, they followed her inside. "Can we get a booth as far away from the smoking section as possible?" Aidan asked.

He watched as Emma and Jenny exchanged a glance before Jenny nodded. "Sure. Nikki, can you take them to booth fifteen, please?"

Nikki nodded and started trailing through the bar. When Emma reached for Noah, Jenny shook her head. "No, no, no. I haven't gotten my fill of him yet."

Emma laughed. "When he gets fussy like he wants to eat, just bring him over."

"I will. You two can have some privacy. Like a date night," Jenny said, with a grin.

"Right. I don't even remember what those were like," Aidan mused.

"Yes, you do. Remember how Megan kept Noah for us two months ago so we could go back to the lodge in the mountains?"

Aidan's mind immediately flashed to dropping Noah off at his niece, Megan's, apartment before they went back to the lodge where they spent their honeymoon. While Noah had been happy to go to Megan and excited to get to play with his cousin, Mason, Emma had wept the entire ride to the mountains. Thinking of her behavior, he shook his head. "You mean the night you spent texting Megan every five minutes to make sure Noah was all right?" Aidan countered.

Emma grinned. "Yes, that's the one."

"Whatever," he replied as they hurried to catch up with Nikki. She was standing in front of the booth in the farthest corner.

When Emma slid in beside him rather than across the booth, Aidan's brows furrowed. At the sight of the dreamy expression on her face, he asked, "What are you all moony about?"

"Don't you remember?"

"Remember what?"

She sighed. "This is the same booth we sat in the night you came home from India."

"Really?"

She bobbed her head before leaning in to give him a lingering kiss. Her tongue had just brushed against his when someone cleared her throat, ending their brief make-out session. Nikki gave an apologetic smile as Emma snapped back from Aidan like a rubber band. "So what can I get you two to drink this evening?"

"Just a Coke for me," Emma replied.

Aidan grinned. "You should have a drink. I mean, you aren't breastfeeding anymore, and we're allegedly on a date night."

A flush crept across her face, and Aidan knew he had embarrassed Emma by mentioning breastfeeding. Finally, she shrugged. "Nah, I'm good."

"Come on. Have a margarita, Em. You deserve to celebrate and cut loose a little. I'll even be the DD tonight," Aidan urged.

She shook her head at him and then glanced up at Nikki. "Just a Coke."

Aidan grunted. "Fine. Be a killjoy. I'll have a Heineken on tap."

"I'll be back to get your food orders in just a minute."

Aidan nodded at Nikki before she walked away. Then he turned his attention back to Emma. "Why didn't you want to have a drink? Were you afraid I was plying you with alcohol to get you drunk, so I could take advantage of you?"

She grinned. "Since when do I have to have alcohol in me to get your libido kicking?"

He threw his head back and laughed. "Never."

A squeal drew their attention to where Jenny was bouncing Noah on her hip. He was reaching for one of the balloons that the bartender was blowing up for him. Aidan couldn't help smiling at the look on Noah's face as he kicked his legs excitedly.

Emma cleared her throat, and Aidan glanced over at her. "I'm sorry, babe. Now I'm the one not doing a good job at date night."

"Well, speaking of your libido…" Aidan watched as she shifted her menu and chewed her bottom lip.

"Em, what's the matter? You look a little pale. Are you all right?"

"I need to tell you something."

[403]

Out of the corner of his eye, Aidan saw Jenny with three bobbing balloons walking Noah over to a group of admirers. He held up a finger. "Just a second, Em." He rose up from the booth. "Jenny, don't get him so close to the smoking section," he called.

She glanced back at him over her shoulder and nodded. Once he felt like Noah was safely away from the second hand smoked danger, he turned back to Emma. "I'm sorry. What is it?"

"Well, it's...I know we weren't actually planning on this, but—"

"Aw, look, Em. Noah's blowing kisses to all the old men at the bar."

The next thing he knew she had grabbed both of the sides of his face in her hands, forcing him to look at her. "Would you please listen to me!"

"Jesus, what is the matter with you?"

Her green eyes narrowed at him. "I'm pregnant! That's what is the matter!"

His heart jolted to a stop. "Y-You're what?"

Emma's expression momentarily softened. "I just came from the doctor. That stomach flu I thought I had...yeah, that's not what it was. I'm six weeks pregnant."

[404]

"Holy shit…but we were using condoms."

Pink tinged her cheeks. "Not the weekend at the lodge."

He leaned over and lowered his voice. "Yeah, but I pulled out."

Emma cocked her brows. "And you're Mr. Super Potent Sperm, remember?"

Aidan swallowed hard. His mind whirled with out-of-control thoughts. He was going to be a father again. He hadn't even thought of the prospect of having more children until Noah was at least two, if not older. Sure, his sisters Angie and Julia were fourteen months part, but he had never imagined having two so close together. Noah would still be in diapers when the new baby arrived. Jesus, he could barely survive all of Noah's changings…what would it be like with two?

"Aidan?" Emma prompted. When he met her gaze, he could immediately read how she was feeling. She was thrilled at the prospect of another child to love, but she was also fearful of his reaction.

He brought his lips to hers and gave her a deep, reassuring kiss. When he finally pulled away, tears shone in her eyes. "Does that mean you're okay with this?"

His hand went to tenderly touch her abdomen. "I'll admit I'm scared shitless at the prospect of another child, but we've already been through so much. Another baby will just mean more love."

Her bright smile warmed his heart. "Oh, Aidan, you made me the happiest woman in the entire world by giving me a baby. Then you made my life complete by giving me your heart and your love. I can't imagine anything more amazing than another child of yours." She then gave him a lingering kiss.

When she pulled away, he grinned. "Does this mean I can expect your libido to be kick-starting soon like when you were pregnant with Noah?"

She gave him a sly grin and then winked. "Oh yes."

He closed his eyes in exaggerated bliss and brought his hand to his chest. "Be still my heart."

She nudged him playfully as Nikki returned to take their orders. When Emma ordered her usual Rib-eye, Aidan stared at her in surprise. "You're ordering a steak?"

"Sure, why not?" she replied as she handed the menus back to Nikki.

"I thought meat made you sick in your first trimester when you were pregnant with Noah."

[406]

Emma shuddered. "Oh it did. I couldn't even stand the smell of it, remember?" Surprise flashed on her face as the wheels turned in her head. Without missing a beat, a smile spread across her face. "I guess that means this baby is a girl!"

"Oh God," he moaned.

Emma tilted her head to the side and gazed up at him. "What's the matter, Big Papa? You don't think you can handle a girl?"

"I think I'll be fine until she gets to be a teenager, and then I may end up in prison for cutting some little horndog's dick off!"

Emma laughed. "Poor thing. With you as her daddy, she won't get to date until she's thirty."

"And it'll be a good thing because if she's half as beautiful as her mother, she'll have all the boys chasing after her."

Tears sparkled in Emma's eyes at his compliment. "You're so sweet."

"It's the truth."

"But I do remember you saying you would bring some mighty fine genes as well."

"We're a good baby-making pair, aren't we?"

Emma snorted. "In more ways than one."

Aidan laughed. "Who knew you would be so fertile and I would be so potent?"

"That just means after this baby, we'll have to be more careful or consider more options."

Aidan shook his head furiously back and forth. "Don't even think about suggesting a vasectomy!"

Emma rolled her eyes. "I was thinking either birth control pills or something for me. Don't get your balls in a twist that I want to take your manhood or something."

Aidan couldn't help sighing with relief. "That's good to hear."

"But don't think just because I'm going on birth control, I'm finished with baby-making."

He arched his brows at her. "Oh really?"

"Mmm, hmm. I want a big family just like yours."

"Em, I don't think I ever signed on to father five kids."

"Oh but you're *so* good at it," she teased.

He groaned. "There goes you and that mouth again."

"Well, I'll think of cutting myself off at three if you'll shut me up and kiss me."

"I'll be happy to oblige ma'am."

Aidan brought his lips to hers. Just as her warm mouth opened invitingly, a high pitched wail caused them to break apart. They watched as Jenny hustled a red-faced, crying Noah over to them.

"What's the matter, sweetheart?" Emma asked.

"Muh! Muh!" he cried.

Emma shook her head and grinned as she took Noah from Jenny. "I can't believe he can say dada all day, but I get called 'muh'!"

Burying his face in Emma's neck, Noah's cries quieted as Emma hummed to him. Their food arrived then. "Wanna come to Daddy, Little Man, so Mama can eat?"

Noah tightened his arms around Emma's neck at the insinuation. "Come on now. Mama needs to eat for your little brother or sister."

When Aidan reached to take Noah, he screamed and clung to Emma. "Oh Jesus. He's getting to be such a Mama's Boy," Aidan lamented.

[409]

"There's nothing wrong with that. I seem to recall another Fitzgerald boy who was one, and he turned out all right," Emma replied, while rubbing wide circles across Noah's back and kissing the strands of his strawberry blonde hair.

Aidan nodded at her insinuation to him and his mother. She was right. He had been a Mama's Boy and proud of it. "Well, that's true, but did have some screw-ups until he found the love of another good woman," Aidan replied.

"Then we'll just have to hope and pray Noah finds the same one day." Emma smiled at him over Noah's head. "And until then, he can be my Mama's Boy."

Aidan grunted. "Come on, Little Man. You're really a Daddy's Boy, aren't you?" he prompted. Peeking through Emma's auburn hair, Noah grinned at Aidan. The small gesture caused Aidan's chest to clench, and he fought to breathe.

"Are you okay?" Emma asked.

"I'm more than okay." He leaned over to kiss Noah's cheek before kissing her tenderly on the lips. "I'm fucking amazing."

Acknowledgements

Thanks first go to God for the amazing blessings I've received with the publication of *The Proposition* as well as through every facet of my life.

To every reader who picked up **The Proposition** I am forever in your debt. Your support, appreciation, your love of Aidan and Emma, your love of my supporting cast, your messages and emails, fan videos and Pinterest pages —it saved me. Words would be inadequate to express how much I appreciate and love you guys!! Big hugs and kisses—I'm a Southern gal, and we're huggers!!

To my late mother, **Ginger Jackson Ashe**: A posthumous thanks is needed for this amazing woman who gave me life. For twenty-three years, I was the main focus, the main joy, and the source of tremendous and unfailing love until she was taken from us far too soon. In every strong woman I write, in every mother whose entire world is her child, in every woman who deals with the hand life has given her—it is because of my mother. From the time I was a little girl and wrote my first story, she believed in me and my writing, although when she said I would be a Pulitzer Prize winner, I was quick to respond with "Dime Store Romance Novelist!" Her sacrifices and her love sustain me ten years later, and they are a blessing each and every day. I love and miss you, Mama!!

[411]

To my late grandmother, **Virginia Jackson**: I never though I would be writing a posthumous thank you to this amazing woman whose unexpected loss in May 2012 shattered my world. Although a diminutive woman, she was coined Big Mama by my cousin and myself, and it was a name that stuck for so many people. From the time I wrote my first few words, her support was unfailing. No matter how many rejections, no matter how dark the path to publication seemed, her belief that I would be successful and a star(her nepotism, lol) never wavered. Just like my mother, she is every strong woman, every amazing mother, and every sassy and tough talking gal—a true Steel Magnolia of strength, beauty, and courage. I love and miss you, Big Mama.

To the best writer buddies and friends anyone could ever hope for: **Kelli Maine, Michlle Valentine and Emily Snow**. It has been an honor to trudge through the writing trenches with you the last three years. I wouldn't be able to make it a day without you guys and your support. I owe a tremendous debt to your eagle eyes, your plot magic, and your cheerleading. LOVE YOU!!   Thanks to **Kristen Proby** for your support and pimpage.

To **Hannah Wylie**: I'll never, ever forget what you have meant to me and my writing. From that first read through of The Guardians up until The Proposition, your support has been unfailing. You've been a cheerleader as well as one to commiserate in the bad times. Thank you again for being a critique partner and friend.

Cris Soriaga Hadarly: Words seem inadequate to fully verbalize what you have meant to me and my writing. I couldn't have hoped or asked for a better reader turned fangirl turned friend. Your love and support have been bright light in my life, along with that beautiful, infectious smile of yours. I thank God for it. I want the most amazing of 2013's for you, my love!!

Michelle Schultz Eck: I thank God for putting you in my life and putting us in close proximity geographically! For all your help and support on promotion for *The Proposition* as well as your eyes on the prize aka the sequel!! Your honesty and unfailing support has meant so much along with our bond of loss.

Brandi McGee Polatty: Thank you so much for your friendship and support. I feel that you were put into my life for a reason as well as being geographically close!! Thank you for the amazing website. It rocks!!

I wouldn't have had the amazing success with *The Proposition* that I've experienced without the appreciation and support of some fantastic bloggers: **Literati Literature Lovers, Aestas's Book Blog, The Book Avenue Review, SUBCLUB Books, Flirty and Dirty Book Blog, Shh's Mom's Reading, Ana's Attic, Into the Night Reviews, Holly Loves Indie, Lori's Book Blog, Kindlehooked, Natasha is a Book Junkie, Three Chicks and Their Books, Sinfully Sexy Book Reviews, & The Rock Stars of Romance, and Tina's Book Blog.**

Heather Gunter: Thanks for being an amazing reviewer and for being my partner in crime to get my first, and most likely only, tattoo!!

Besides my Naughty Mafia ladies, thanks to my early eyes on the sequel with **Denise Sprung, Marilyn Medina, Michelle Eck, and Lisa Pantano Kane.** Thanks for telling it like it was and letting me know what was working or not working.

Marilyn Medina: my sista from another mista and Golden Girls twinsie, I don't know what I would have done without your support, friendship, and Eagle Eyes. I would have still be grabbing up things and missing ridiculous typos!! You donned your feathered hat and pimped me to the world, and I'll never forget it or you, my love!

Elizabeth Martinelli aka Mama Liz: I don't know where I would be without your love and support. You've stood by me in the darkest times and been a friend and second mother to me. Your support of my writing has been unfailing. I am blessed and grateful to have you in my life.

Paige and Enzo Silva: You've been the best IRL friends a girl could ask for. You stood by me in the good and bad, and I'll never forget your love and support. You've been the best cheerleaders and the best "talk a gal down from the ledge" friends.

To my second parents **Jimmy and Joy Stephens,** along with my adopted sister, **Missy Mulkey**: Words are inadequate to give thanks for what you have meant to me my entire life, especially in the last year. I thank God daily for your love and your support and for giving me parents again when mine were lost.

To **Elizabeth Harper** for her love and pimpage of *The Proposition* when I was just an unknown Indie writer. Thanks as well as to **Mersina** on Goodreads for her fantastic GIF whored out review of The Proposition! I still smile when I look at it!!

To **Raine Miller** for her business savvy and talking me down from the ledge as well as her amazing books! Drinks on me in Vegas!

To the ladies of **The Smutty Book Whore Mafia** for giving me lots of support, but most of all for the laughs, naughty conversations, and "shiny" pictures—as well as growlers or my own personal "howlers"!! You gals rock!!

Other rocking gals that need thanks are the gals in **The Rock the Heart** fan group for all your support, laughter, and naughty talk!